# Don't Cry For Me

# David Jones

## List of Characters

| | |
|---|---|
| Jonathan (Gwynfor) Jones | CEO of Shell |
| Caradoc Jones | brother of Jonathan |
| Princess Alexia | British Princess |
| Gavin | her valet/equerry |
| Prince Arthur | her son |
| Jan Willem van Kempen | former CEO of Shell |
| Hendrik ter Haar | former chair of Shell |
| Catrin Prys-Jones | Argentinian nurse |
| Eluned Prys-Jones | her mother |
| Maria Echevarria/Lady Buck | Argentinian socialite |
| Richard Cobbold | Chief of Staff of UK Armed Forces |
| The Boss, Tenson | Head of British Intelligence (MI5/6) |
| Jake Diamopoulos | US Secretary of State |
| Steve Carter | newspaper magnate |
| King Willem Alexander | King of The Netherlands |
| General Ricardo Suarez | Argentinian army general |

# Chapter 1

'Hello, is that Jonathan Jones? This is Henry Atkins, the consultant at Ty Coch. It's about your brother, Caradoc Jones. His condition has worsened and he's asking for you all the time. I'm afraid we're going to have to section him if there's no change. I think you ought to come up here as soon as possible. Please ring to let me know.'

All his other messages on the answer phone had been straightforward business ones though some of them did demand urgent attention. But this one was the last thing he wanted to hear now.

He would have to go of course. He remembered with shame the fact that he had not found the time to visit his brother, when he had first been diagnosed with PTSD, post-traumatic stress disorder, after his experiences with the Welsh Guards in the Falklands. Indeed, he had been one of those hardened people who had not accepted fully that it was a medical condition. Hadn't many other soldiers who survived the fire on the ship at Bluff Cove coped more adequately with the tragedy, however harrowing the sights they'd seen? Even more difficult to cope with was his recent failure to support Caradoc when he had been arrested and put on trial for grievously wounding a policeman. He had atoned for this to some extent when he had begun to pay the fees at the nursing home. This had been the only alternative to custody.

He drove the difficult 250 miles journey from London to the North Wales holiday resort of Colwyn Bay without a break and driving on autopilot, had been entirely oblivious to his surroundings and other motorists. He had tried to rationalize his ambivalent attitude to his brother. They had never been close and his brother had been far more Welsh than he had been, going to the local Welsh speaking comprehensive and feeling thoroughly at home in the local pubs. He had accepted naturally the renaissance in Welsh culture and language that was totally divorced from his own experience. He had been surprised that his brother had joined the army, yet local unemployment was high and although quite bright, he had been unable to get a satisfactory job locally and he would never have left his own community to seek work elsewhere. Although he had achieved far more than his brother, he was strangely jealous and envious of him. It was perhaps because he knew who he was, even if he didn't know where he was going.

He drove along the street of smart hotels until he came to the three storey red brick house which had been converted from a small B&B into this private nursing home for twenty patients. Yet in its own field it was nationally known, not because it was better than its competitors but because there weren't any. It was known because it was the only place where ex service personnel could go for treatment for PTSD. Once they had left the military, they became the responsibility of the National Health Service and not surprisingly, they were a very low priority. Yet he had qualms about the place. They could not detain or protect their patients; they couldn't even stop them going out drinking and this was a major problem for people already suffering with their mental health.

'I'm very pleased you were able to come Mr. Jones,' said the consultant, who apart from nurses was the sole medical staff member at the place. He had jumped at the chance to run the place even though he was basically at the mercy of the private owner.

'He's really gone downhill badly very quickly. He keeps on saying he's killed his brother. Maybe your physical presence here can jolt him out of this delusion. We've sedated him for the last couple of days, but he's not under sedation now. I'll take you to him.'

He was led into a not unpleasant room where he saw his brother with his hollow sunken eyes and pallid almost translucent appearance. He hugged him powerfully yet was not sure if he'd really been recognized until his brother started ranting on in an almost manic and pathetic manner and in Welsh which he found it increasingly hard to follow.

'Nobody here will listen to me Gwynfor.'

He still called Jonathan by his original Welsh name.

'I keep on telling them about the ship and the fire and the horrible, horrible crime I've committed, but they're not listening. Please Gwynfor, you'll listen to me won't you.'

'Of course, I will, my dear, dear brother, I'll do anything to get you out of this nightmare.'

At this Caradoc changed his demeanour, his voice became quiet and controlled and his pleas almost rational.

'I want you to go and find him. I want you to go and see his grave. I want you to tell him I'm sorry. I heard him scream "paid a saethu" (don't shoot), but it was too late. It was him or me and with my training it was him. Look, take this.'

He took out from his locker a small, badly wrapped package and handed it over, before slumping helplessly in the seat with tears of rage and anger and hurt cascading down his cheeks. They stayed together for ten minutes, but Caradoc did not say another word and he left quietly walking slowly down the corridor. Just before he reached the door a shot rang out. He ran back in, but he was too late. There was nothing to be done except vomit.

# Chapter 2

The province of Chubut in Patagonia, in the south of Argentina was Wales's only colony if one is not to believe the stories of Welsh speaking Indians in the mid-west of the USA, who claim a Welshman called Madog was the first to discover America. Many Welshmen prospered in Argentina and became wealthy ranchers on estancias of thousands of acres and apart from their names they were totally assimilated into the Spanish speaking culture of Argentina. But those in Chubut remained true to their heritage and to this day there are Welsh speakers there. The town of Trelew in particular has Welsh chapels and tearooms serving traditional Welsh dishes to the inhabitants as well as any stray tourists. It was to Trelew that Gwynfor Jones turned to with the crumpled photo in his hand. It was a photo of a very young-looking Argentinian soldier but at the back was the name Gareth Jones and the address in Trelew.

He had flown in with Aerolineas from Buenos Aires to Trelew airport. Before leaving the airport he had seen a memorial painting of a fighter plane commemorating the death of an Argentinian air force pilot from Trelew who had been killed in the Falklands invasion. His name, - Rhodri Thomas.

He'd booked in at a central hotel, Hotel Centenario, one of the very few in Trelew but still only about twenty minutes from the small airport.

As he came down from his room he glanced once again at the young receptionist and nodded slightly as he passed her desk. She was clearly not one of the locals but wherever she was from, her stunning Latin looks and tall, firm body with swept back black hair and lively eyes would have made her stand out in any company.

'Ah. Englishman. You are very welcome here, Sir. But pardon me for asking, 'Why are you here, this is not a place for tourists. You must be a journalist.'

'No, no I'm a businessman. Why do you think that?'

She'd already seen when he'd handed in his passport that he indeed had OIL COMPANY EXECUTIVE as his occupation.

'Journalists are the only foreigners who come here,' she continued in excellent but heavily accented English. 'They all think they can dig up something nasty, maybe about the Malvinas war, but of course they never find anything. Everything is fine here. They're wasting their time.'

Her tone was now quite strong and he almost felt he was somehow being warned off.

'No,' he said defensively. 'I'm visiting someone, perhaps you can help me.'

And he passed over the photo to show the address on the back.

From the feel of it she knew it was a photographic print and very casually she turned from him to look at the map on the wall while at the same time quickly turning over the card to reveal the faded print of the young Argentinian in military uniform.

'Yes, I know where it is. This is a small town. I will show you.' She took a small booklet from a nearby display stand and opened out the map. She circled a street not far away from the hotel, and taking him by the arm she pulled him towards the door. 'Here I'll show you. You go down the street here till you pass the small cafe on your left. Then you take the second right turn after the cafe. It's about 200 metres down that street.'

And she pushed him on his way gently while giving him a look of intimate invitation and promise.

He walked down the road, flustered and aroused. She quickly ran inside, picked up the photo from where she'd placed it carefully under the map and quickly photocopied the image. She ran out after him shouting.

'Excuse me Mr. Jones, Sir, you've left this behind.

He'd only gone about twenty metres and embarrassedly thanked her.

How easy it had all been. I could become quite good at this she thought. What especially pleased her was that she just knew he had no inkling of what had gone on.

He barely noticed the unusual warmth of the photo. Besides his hands were very sweaty and he made nothing of it as he stepped into the cafe. He needed to rest and compose himself for the ordeal ahead. He didn't quite know how he'd cope with what he had to do. His brother Caradoc's anguished final look continued to haunt him when he least expected it. It had been three weeks since the funeral. At this moment it was an overwhelming, almost overpowering image.

----------

The cafe was the Welsh cafe he'd read about in his Welsh Guide book, the only guide book to have very much at all about this godforsaken place. He picked up the menu and felt strangely comforted by the meagre fare on offer. It was in Welsh and Spanish.

| | | |
|---|---|---|
| Cup of tea | Disgled o de | Taza de té |
| Speckled bread cake | Bara Brith | Pastel de pan moteado |
| Bread and butter | Bara menyn | Pan y mantequilla |
| Cheese | Caws | Quesa |

'Hello,' said the crumpled, stooping and weather-beaten old lady dressed in a traditional Welsh woollen nursing shawl, *siol fagu*, with its patterned design and wide fringe, as she stumbled slowly to his table.

'And what would you like to eat then with your cup of tea my dear?' He understood some Spanish but her unusual accent totally defeated him.

So, he answered her in Welsh.

Despite her frail appearance she was suddenly galvanised and she gave him an almighty hug.

*Cariad bach, mae'n dda cwrdd rhywun o Gymru. Beth ydych chi'n gwneud yma?* And she whispered *"Mae'n beryglus siarad a chi. Dyw pethe ddim yn dda o gwbl. Duw an helpo.*

'Dearest loved one, it's good to meet someone from Wales. But what are you doing here? It's dangerous to talk to you. There's bad things happening here. God help us.

'But I'm very old and it doesn't matter what they do to me. They're watching all the time. Somebody here could be spying on us. They take photos of all of us going to Moriah, our chapel, and warn off people from coming here or any other Welsh speaking place. Only the old are not afraid.'

But she clearly was, her voice trembled and a feeling of fear pervaded her person.

*Cer nawr.*

'Go now.

*Cyn bod rhywun yn meddwl fod ni'n rhi glos.*

'Before anyone thinks we're too close.'

She ushered him out and he put all thoughts of a nice cup of tea out of his mind. What was he to make of that? The muddled meanderings of a senile old lady? Or were they really being harassed? If so, it was obviously disturbing but at a low level and not all that dangerous surely.

----------

But now came his hard task. The door of the decrepit two roomed run-down clapperboard house slowly opened and a young woman in elegant city clothes answered. When he introduced himself in Welsh, Catrin Prys-Jones immediately took him in to meet her mother, who sat motionless in the corner chair, almost bent double.

'I work as a nurse in Bahia Blanca. It's about 500 kilometres north, but I come to see her as often as I can. Her sister looks after her when I'm not here.

'She's hardly moved since Gareth was killed, except to go to chapel.'

Like the old lady in the cafe, her Welsh sounded strange, unlike any regional dialect he'd heard in Wales. But amazingly, it was totally understandable.

On hearing her son's name, the old lady spoke up from her corner in a firm and strong voice, slowly but clearly,

'The bastards took Gareth bach away to their army, they took him away, away from here, where he belongs. He was a gentle, lovely boy. He didn't want to fight. Not those poor boys on the boat. They were all Welsh, weren't they?'

'I know. My brother was one of them. On that boat.'

Oh, this was so painful. His hands were moist, his heart pounded and sweat dripped off his forehead. As he handed over the photo a puzzled look momentarily passed over his face. Catrin scraped off the blob of Tippex from her brother's arm and weeping gently she passed it to her mother.

'But how did you get this?' they both cried.

'My, my brother gave it to me. Just be before he killed himself,' he moaned in anguish.

They both looked up incomprehensibly.

'My brother killed your Gareth.'

Yes, indeed. Caradoc Jones had killed a fellow Welshmen, a brother in spirit, if not in fact. And he had known it because the Welsh cry "Don't shoot" had been the Argentinian Gareth Jones' last words.

He took out the package and opened it carefully. In it was a wristwatch and a little black notebook diary.

He turned to the last entry.

June 15th 198

'We've been in Port Stanley 14 hours. It's cold here and we're all wet and tired. There's only a few hundred of us. They say they're coming tonight or tomorrow. The British I mean. The Major says if we hold them for a while, help is coming from our planes and navy. Nobody of course believes it. I'm going to die, we're all going to die in this awful place. I want to come home to you, to a nice, warm place. Mam, I'm scared. I hope to see you. Mam, dearest Mam, and Catrin too. I love you. I love you so much.'

The three of them hugged each other in a wonderfully serene and comforting silence.

It was the old woman, Mam, who struggled free from their embraces.

'Catrin. Take him. Take him there.'

# Chapter 3

Jonathan and Catrin struggled through the bushes until they came across a small rock almost totally obscured by the dense growth. She lifted the rock and in a hollow, there stood an earthenware vase with a few quite fresh daffodils in it. Beneath was a homemade wooden headboard painted white. The inscription all in Welsh, was very simple.

*Gareth Tudor Jones      19 mlwydd oed*
*Unig fab annwyl i Marged a brawd i Catrin*
*Bu farw yn amddiffyn gwladwriaeth nad oedd yn ei chydnabod*
*Duw cofia amdano.*

Gareth Tudor Jones      19 years old
Dearest only son of Margaret and brother to Catrin
Died defending a state he did not recognise
God remember him.

'They buried him in a military cemetery in Puerto Madryn. But Mam and I went there and dug him out. Yes, the two of us we did it.'

She was very excited and proud and relieved that she could tell someone what they had done. She stepped

12

closer to him and held his face firmly. She grew more agitated and began trembling.

'And brought him back home. Mam struggles here every week and I visit every chance I can. But we have to be careful.'

She embraced him powerfully and he grasped her tightly as she began to moan.

'They're not dead, are they? Our brothers.'

'No, they were both victims,' he gasped as he realized what was happening.

'He was more than a brother to me.'

She pulled him to the ground.

'He was my twin,' she screamed.

'Come on, let's be part of them.'

And they were now moving against each other in the madness of loving forgiveness and atonement.

'Let them live in us.'

As they moved slowly apart, she announced solemnly.

'I forgive your brother.'

As they got back on to the road, they heard the whine of a small moped moving away into the distance. They saw the rider's long swept back black hair blowing in the wind but not the camera hung around her neck.

----------

As he wearily but exaltedly entered the hotel, Maria Echevarria was quick to spot him. Had she been waiting?

13

'Mr. Jones, Have you had a good day? You look tired. Perhaps a little drink with me. I'm off duty.'

She looked as if she was on duty. But of another sort. Her tight skirt clung magically to her thighs and her low-cut top was, well, low cut.

'No, I'm ........ oh alright.'

He really needed a drink and some sort of return to normality. He had a bottle of Quilmes beer and she had a glass of Malbec.

It turned out that Maria was quite a clever girl. She was studying computer science at EAN, Escuela Argentina de Negocios in Buenos Aires.

'My uncle owns this chain of hotels. I can work in any of them during my vacation.'

'But why here?'

'I prefer this to a bigger hotel in the city. There really isn't very much to do and I
can study undisturbed a lot of the time,' was her convincing reply.

'But what about you? Did you have a successful day? Did you find the person you were looking for?'

'No. I was trying to trace my great Uncle who emigrated here from Wales. But the people I visited couldn't help me I'm afraid.'

'So, you didn't succeed.'

'No.'

'So, you didn't find anyone you knew.'

'No. No, I didn't.'

'Did you meet any Welsh people with your own name perhaps?'

He really couldn't understand or take this insistence on her part, and rudely excused himself as he was catching the early flight to Buenos Aires next morning.

Besides he couldn't face any longer the provocatively displayed view of her left nipple.

----------

Two nights later at 2 a.m., Catrin Prys-Jones and her ailing mother were taken away in an unmarked dark green Ford Falcon and were never seen again.

# Chapter 4

It had been a difficult year for the Jones' family. Gwynfor's father had died suddenly and Gwenna Jones found it hard to raise three children. Ten-year-old Gwynfor himself was no trouble but her disabled six-year-old daughter needed constant care and attention and she also had two-year-old Caradoc to contend with.

'Come in Vicar,' she said, answering the knock on the door. She knew he was visiting today and had put on her favourite dress but she still looked haggard and exhausted.

The Vicar looked well though he liked the odd tipple. He had plenty of exercise walking every day to visit his parishioners before he retired to his study every night to compose Welsh poetry, his one true love. He was a leading Welsh poet who had won the chair at the National Eisteddfod for composing in the ancient strict metre called *cynghanedd*.

Gwenno's husband had been a Sunday school teacher and Gwynfor was about to join the church choir. She herself was strictly chapel.

After the customary cup of tea and the biscuit, the vicar turned to her and said sympathetically, 'Mrs. Jones fach. How are you? But don't answer that. I can see that it is a struggle for you.'

Mrs. Jones blurted out without restraint. 'Yes, yes, it is. I'm hardly coping. It's a nightmare sometimes.'

'Well, listen here. I think I have some good news for you.

'I have become aware,' he said pompously, 'of a boarding school that takes pupils from disadvantaged backgrounds like yours on free scholarships. It is just the thing for Gwynfor who I know from Mr. Evans, the headmaster, is a very clever little boy.'

'But where is it? He wouldn't have to leave here would he?'

'Well, yes. It is a boarding school.'

'I can't have that. He wouldn't want to go there.'

'Well the boarding is the idea. It would take away your responsibility for him and give you more time to raise the other children well. And it wouldn't cost a penny.'

'But he helps me here. He's a good little boy.'

'Now, now Mrs. Jones. He will quite honestly have a much better education there.'

'What's wrong with our grammar school? They say Gwynfor will get in there.'

'Nothing, nothing at all he replied defensively. Don't get me wrong. But these private schools, they've got connections, contacts. He'll end up getting a top job and a good future and will be able to help you financially, I'm sure.'

----------

Gwynfor Jones was nothing if not confused. He had

been born into a small close-knit Welsh speaking village of under a thousand people in agricultural West Wales where everyone knew everyone and a sense of real community existed. There was the local primary school, where every teacher knew every parent, the church and the chapel, the shop and the pub and the tiny concrete block village hall where he had recited poetry in Welsh in the annual Eisteddfod.

At the age of 11 he had been plucked from this secure home environment and had been transplanted to an English Public School, Christ's Hospital in Horsham, West Sussex.

So here they were.

'Mrs. Jones and Gwynfor,' the latter name totally mispronounced, 'I'm Gerard Tomkins, the Senior Grecian, or head boy to you. I'm here to show you around and introduce you to the school.'

Who was this boy? He was dressed in a very strange way. He was wearing the traditional breeches and yellow socks and the long, down to the ground, dark blue Housey coat. Yes, this exceptional uniform had been worn by the pupils ever since the school was founded in 1536 by King Edward VI.

'So here we are walking down the Avenue,' the Senior Grecian spoke confidently in a posh English accent. The Avenue was an impressive wide road flanked on either side by a long line of Lime trees.

'Each of these buildings on this side is a boarding house. You'll be in this one, Peele A. It's got lots of sporting boys in it. They won the inter house cricket and rugby cups last year.'

They passed three more boarding houses before coming to the quad.

'Our quad is bigger than that of any Oxbridge College,' boasted the Senior Grecian.

The quad was indeed massive with a central path from one side to the other with cloisters on two sides.

'On that side is Big School, the main school hall, and there's the chapel.'

The elaborate chapel was large enough to accommodate all eight hundred pupils who were there every morning and twice on Sundays to constantly thank their founder Edward VI, without whose beneficence none of them would be there.

'All along the walls inside it's got a series of famous paintings of Biblical scenes by Sir Charles Brangwyn.'

Gwynfor suddenly piped in. 'Is that the same Brangwyn who painted the murals in Brangwyn Hall in Swansea?'

But the Senior Grecian totally ignored him and continued, 'And there is the Dining Hall. The pupils are marching into lunch soon, so while we wait here to see that, let me tell you something about the history of the school.

'The school was founded by Edward VI in 1552 to educate the poor boys of the streets of the city of London. It has remained true to that principle for over four hundred years. even though in 1901 it moved from the City of London to here in rural Sussex. This was a very clever move as the school still owns the land in the city of London. They get millions of pounds rent a year on the office properties built on that land. Some say we're "the richest school in England." This money is used to give boys like you from poor backgrounds a free boarding school education.'

Boys like me? So who was he, thought Gwynfor.

Where was he from? Had he forgotten where he came from in a mere seven years?

He knew his stuff, but it wasn't quite what he was meant to convey. The financial details were something the school liked to keep very quiet about for obvious reasons.

Soon all eight hundred boys and girls, yes girls too, assembled together on both sides of The Avenue all dressed in full Housey and suddenly, they were all marching briskly and efficiently behind the magnificent sounds of the school marching band.

'Our band is famous. They are all good musicians themselves and have marched before big international rugby games at Twickenham and also before cricket Test Matches at Lords,' chimed the Senior Grecian before deftly joining the front of the march itself by the side of the band captain. He had an addition to the uniform, a sort of leopard skin cloak and was nonchalantly twirling a long ornate silver pole and now and again hurling it into the air with several twists before catching it again and marching on.

----------

But it was a harsh baptism for Gwynfor. It took him less than three months to see the other side of the place.

He cried himself to sleep in a bleak and draughty dormitory with large, uncurtained windows, on very hard horsehair beds with twenty other boys. Many of these spoke with strange cockney accents which he took a long time to decipher, almost as long as they had taken

20

to understand his very strong Welsh accent. Teachers and pupils alike could not pronounce his name and he soon changed it to Jonathan and began to slowly transform himself too, for reasons of self-preservation.

The years went by, but Jonathan never forgot how he came to be in this alien place, lonely and scared.

He hated the vicar and all that he represented with a secret but powerful passion. His Christian charity had led to Jonathan being bullied mercilessly in a systematic and brutal way. The fact he was developing physically into quite a big and strong young man did not stop the bullying. He still had a reputation as a nerd with his metal framed, thick lensed National Health Service glasses. The aspects of bullying which the staff had been aware of had been tolerated by them as character building, presumably because they had survived it themselves at their own public schools and were unaware of how it had affected them.

He hated just as much the institutionalized bullying of the CCF, the Combined Cadet Force, in which he had been made to carry and polish a rifle and had shooting practice on the very day that 16 schoolchildren had been brutally murdered in Dunblane. Others had been seduced by the free helicopter rides as the British Army recruited its future officers from the public schools of England.

Others had also been bullied and made miserable too but what was worse in Jonathan's case was the school holidays. Most of his fellow pupils could look forward to going home but they were no respite for him. Although he was the upstart Taffy in school, he was, to his Welsh contemporaries at home a boy who went to a posh English public school and had lost his roots and

is background. He was thus totally alienated,
ily way to cope with this was to bury himself
... ... rk and repress his inner rage.

In this way he had become a model student with ten grade A's at O level and four A 's at A level and this had led him to a first class Honours degree in chemistry at Imperial College, London. Here he had been accepted as an able hard-working student who had also blossomed for the first time socially, enjoying his rugby which was the one thing that paradoxically, his Welsh background and English public-school education had both fostered.

# Chapter 5

The non-descript Ford Scorpio sped along the country lane in the early hours, followed by an unmarked police car. The Scorpio was driven by the Prince's own chauffeur and a bodyguard sat in the front passenger seat. The Prince was seated in the back with Lady Princella, a long-term friend of his father. Prince Arthur, now fourteen was dressed in the scarlet hunt colours. These gave him a quite flattering appearance, although he had been irked that four sittings had been needed to get a proper fit as he was actually quite tall and skinny and ungainly in stance. He was however developing into an attractive young man, not bedeviled by any of the anatomical peculiarities which had become such a trademark for his father. But he was dreading today. He dreaded every day that he was involved with the hunt to track down and kill a living creature. It was not something that he ever wanted to do.

Besides he was more nervous and worked up than ever today. He hated it all but no one ever asked him for his opinion. It was all sort of compulsory.

He had hunted before several times and was, luckily for him, a good horseman, but always near the back of the hunt with the ordinary members. Today he was wearing the full hunt colours and would be initiated into the hunt proper. That is provided everything went smoothly. It was a top secret meet and had only been announced by word of mouth to faithful followers. This was essential to avoid drawing the attention of both the paparazzi and the hunt saboteurs. He was honestly equally scared of both with good reason. Hopefully the police would be ready with their road blocks should any news leak out.

Lady Princella turned to him as he left the car.

'Now be a good egg. Today is a special day for you and your father. This is your initiation day into the hunt, a very special thing in our way of life.'

He ignored her and turned to the driver.

'Why does Father always ask her to look after me? He's got plenty of other servants," moaned the young Prince to the driver. But he sort of knew that Lady Princella, who was never unkind to him but still quite distant, was more than a servant to his father and had been even when his mother was around.

He thought of his mother as he felt the comfort of the envelope in his pocket. He had written yet another letter to her that he would post secretly. He kept on doing this, though he never ever got a reply.

He was not officially allowed any contact with her as she was persona non grata with the royal household since the divorce.

They soon arrived in the large secluded car park of the magnificent Gun Inn, the HQ of the local hunt, to see the arrival of the first horsemen. Back in the 1800's coach and horses used to arrive here to deliver mail to the area. Now it was a small but prestigious four-star hotel.

The Master of the Hunt, Colonel Steven Peters, the

third Earl of Egremont, an old friend of the family, came forward to greet them wearing the traditional scarlet coat to the ordinary layman. Traditionalists could see it was no ordinary hunt coat, being square cut in front and carrying five buttons.

'Welcome to the hunt, my dear boy, I mean, Your Highness. This is a special day for you and us.'

His country life since he had retired from his career in the Guards was clearly suiting Colonel Peters as he looked fit and well, except for his plump red cheeks perhaps revealing too publicly his penchant for the whisky bottle.

His white breeches were wide at the waist and emphasized the brown leather riding boots with their mahogany tops.

He turned around and said, 'Meet my three huntsmen for today. They are the only ones invited to wear red and the hunt button.' His three huntsmen, all quite dashing and looking excited, were wearing four buttons, unlike the ordinary members, who were confined to a mere three.

It was time for the Prince to meet his father, Prince Henry, the Duke of Devonshire, who came across to him almost as an afterthought and gave him a brief and perfunctory handshake. He was looking older these days, if not wiser, since his public cuckolding and humiliation at the hands of his former wife. Despite her increasingly bizarre behaviour, she had always managed to maintain public sympathy at his expense and to his great chagrin.

However, the Prince was not at all put out by his father's totally unemotional and detached greeting and was in fact greatly impressed by this aloof public style, in contrast to the embarrassingly gushing behaviour of the mother who had abandoned him. And yet it made him   ache even more for a warm hug from his long departed and now unmentioned mother.

'You're looking well, Colonel Peters,' said the Duke.

'Well I hope to emulate my great grandfather. He died in his saddle at the age of eighty-four,' he guffawed.

Prince Arthur  mounted the mare which had been especially prepared for him, his spurs glinting in the morning sun. To outsiders he looked immaculate in his red costume. He was inwardly raging at this outrageous event. He was supposed to be very proud to be wearing the four buttons of the huntsmen.

He turned and looked around at the assembled horsemen and women. The noise was getting louder as the dogs got more excited. They are not fed on hunt day.

'Where's Caroline?' he asked no one in particular. She was the only one he knew here. Little did he know that Caroline, the Countess of Athlone's daughter, was sobbing miserably in the ladies' toilets of the hotel. She had been banned from hunting that day after the Master's inspection, when she had been publicly admonished for having a cutting whip instead of the correct hunting whip with thong and lash.

The hounds were now yelping impatiently as the huntsmen made their way slowly through the gates, followed by the small number of specially invited ordinary members in their black coats, who were close friends of the Prince's father. Though clearly inferior in the eyes of hunt experts, they still looked splendid mounted on their magnificent hunters. This was after all one of the richest hunts in England and looked pretty much as it had done for the last several hundred years.

The only concession they seemed to have made to the modern world was to stop wearing top hats because no-one had designed one which satisfied the compulsory safety regulations. The huntsmen were now all compelled to wear the normal riding cap which doubled up as a crash helmet.

Although not officially invited today, there were a number of foot and car followers who, although well known to the Master, had been thoroughly vetted and searched by the police during the assembly time.

Also, there were the terrier men, all employed at the local estates with a half dozen very excitable fox terriers.

'Let's head to Winsley Green covert,' shouted the Hunt Master.

This was a copse of trees and undergrowth in an open field. The locals all knew where the foxes were located.

'Loo in,' cried the Master, the traditional call to the hounds to enter a covert, followed by cries from the others and a blast of the horn.

Soon a scent was picked up and a whipper-in shouted "View ahoo" to say that he had spotted the fox. The hounds were quickly on the move followed by the Master, and the joint masters, huntsmen and members all in strict pecking order. It was left to the followers to close any gates and try and keep some semblance of hunt etiquette and care for the countryside. A good chase ensued with several false trails and crossing scents. In each case it was the joint master's responsibility to decide which to follow up.

'He's getting tired, he's gone to earth,' shouted one

of the terrier men.

'Now it's our turn.'

They got their spades and quickly opened up the entrance to the tunnel they had blocked up earlier in the week.

'Just let one in first.'

They let loose one terrier who scuttled down amidst great expectancy. He soon emerged yelping with blood streaming from an eye. The fox is no mean fighter. They quickly pulled him away.

'Let's have two dogs this time.'

They let in two more terriers. This time they were longer underground and when they finally came out covered in blood there was no further noise from the tunnel. They had done their job. The terrier men and several others now began digging to locate the dead fox.

'Damn it. The terriers have got him,' said the Hunt Master.

The huntsmen hid their disappointment. They had hoped the fox would have emerged from the other end of the tunnel for the chase to continue.

'OK let's try Rags Bottom. We saw a fox there last night.'

The Master and the huntsmen in red were all accomplished riders and took the fences and small hedges with no trouble. But several of the members, were more renowned for their wealth and connections than their riding skills.

'Bridlington's taken another fall I see. Serves him right for trying to ride that mare. The arrogant old bastard.'

'Not as bad as old Coxton though. He's not jumping at all. Look he's dismounted and they're opening a gate to let him through.'

This time the hounds had their way and the fox was unable to go to earth. The top dog had failed to nip the fox behind the neck for a clean kill, the ideal way to dispose of the fox according to hunting lore. Several dogs had begun to pull hard at various parts of the fox and were ripping him from limb to limb.

'Pocklington, do your job,' shouted the Master.

He aimed his gun preparing to shoot the fox.

'It's no good, I can't get a clear shot,' he said after a while. 'The hounds are all too close.'

'OK. Stand back then,' said the Master.

The Duke and his son had witnessed all this and a few minutes later, the Duke presented to his son the bush of the fox and amidst much congratulation initiated him in the hunt by crossing his forehead with the freshly dripping blood of the now dead fox.

The Prince turned away straight afterwards and openly vomited. He felt the cruelty they had inflicted on the fox was matched by that inflicted on him. He would never ever choose to do this if he was free. He was now shaking and sobbing.

Some of the huntsmen whispered but loud enough to be heard.

'What a wimp.'

'What a coward.'

'How embarrassing for his father.'

In the distance one of the paparazzi who could ride had turned up. A huntsmen grabbed hold of his camera and threw it to the ground while the other beat him on the head with his hunting whip.

" Who-whoop," went the cry to signify the fox's glorious end.

# Chapter 6

In his final year at Imperial College, in the so-called milk round by leading UK companies, the prospect of a career involving foreign travel offered by Shell Oil had impressed Jonathan Jones. He had likewise impressed them, and he had found himself posted to the company headquarters in The Hague for their high-level training course.

He soon fell in naturally with the other trainees into the readymade and bustling social life for trainees, revolving around the younger ex pat community, mainly the young teachers at the British School. For a drink with a girlfriend, the late-night bars of the Denneweg and Lange Voorhout in the Hague were a pleasant change from the pubs of England, with no one frowning on someone dropping in for an hour to read the papers or a for a quiet game of chess while drinking nothing stronger than a Douwe Egberts filter coffee. But there was a wild side to this social life too.

----------

'Watch out,' one of the Shell boys shouted and he and several of his mates ran ducking and dodging around the bar. Darts were randomly being thrown in all directions by a colleague who was blindfolded. Yes, they were human dartboards. They scurried around laughing, carrying beer glasses in their hands. This was the version of darts they played at the Drop Zone, one of the Irish and British pubs in The Hague frequented by the hard-core ex pat drinkers. And this was where the Shell boys gravitated to as an all-male group.

It was packed out, and there was a raucous atmosphere with everyone drinking to excess to the background of some very loud heavy metal music.

Jonathan was not playing the human darts game. He was standing at the bar watching the bar man and pub owner showing a patron how to chew and eat a beer glass. The small thin Dutch glasses were just right for this apparently.

'You chew and bite on each little piece one at a time until they're small enough to swallow,' he said as if it was the most normal thing in the world.

'He's doing well for an alco,' commented another bar leaning person. 'They say he's an ex British paratrooper.'

'Well he's a psycho alright. I've seen him fight. He's totally vicious and brutal.'

He certainly looked the part. A big burly bearded man with a red and pock marked face.

'Yes, apparently he's done something pretty dark and mysterious in the past and is not able to return to the UK for some reason.'

An evening in this and other similar pubs was a regular night out for the Shell boys but it was Brendan's birthday tonight, so after a couple more hours boozing, the organizer - they always had an organizer – shouted, 'Let's go boys, on to the next treat.'

They were noisy but not physically threatening as they staggered down the street. They soon found themselves entering an unmarked door of a non-descript house with blackened window panes. They were in an upmarket sex club, with quite an expensive entry fee.

'Fifteen beers please,' ordered the organizer at the bar, guessing how many had dropped out on the trek from the Drop Zone.

Soon they were singing and talking with the scantily dressed hostesses. But they were not the normal clientele. The boys continued to booze and banter in a group and generally entertain the girls, who seemed to be enjoying the antics of these unusual visitors. They seemed happy to forget their normal role and just enjoy themselves.

'Come on birthday boy,' said a male manager. 'Let's go with a couple of our girls. They want to see you in your birthday suit.'

Two girls grabbed him by the arms and tried to march him away. But no, he was not having it. He stood his ground and stayed with his mates quite content to drink, laugh and get pissed.

----------

'Come on hurry up they're ahead of us,' shouted the young lad dressed only in his underpants and a red bow tie. His friend, also in underpants and a red bowtie, ran into the carriage from the previous one.

'Get up there.'He immediately went on his knees and his friend clambered on one knee and shoulder and in one swift move he was in the luggage rack. He crawled energetically along this through the carriage over the bags. He hurried along as he could just see his opponent in the blue bowtie ahead of him on the opposite luggage rack.

'What are they doing?'

'It's a race of some sort.'

'That is disgusting. They should be thrown off,' muttered a prim looking young woman.

'Oh, I don't know. Some of them are quite fit,' giggled another.

'Come on! Faster! You crazy guys,' shouted some French teenagers.

'Ooh! This is naughty,' said an elderly woman, smiling broadly.

'Come on Les Bleu. You will need to be faster than that in the match.'

A group of teenage girls started clapping and cheering and there were lots of catcalls, boos and whistling. Those further along the train could hear the noise but there was no way they could anticipate what was about to descend on them.

This relay race of five in each team continued along the full length of the Amsterdam to Paris express train. This was the Shell rugby team on their way to a France v England rugby international at the old Parc de Prince in Paris.

Five Shell boys were umpires or referees positioned strategically along the train to maintain the strict and complicated rules and report any infringements to be punished by forfeits. Needless to say, they were dressed in clown costumes and moved along on fitness bouncy balls. Jonathan was one of the referees.

He had joined the Shell based Te Werve rugby club for the game itself, as he was now over six foot tall - a giant for a Welshman, well-built and pretty fit. His new contact lenses allowed him to embrace in this exhilarating contact sport. For many others the club was merely an opportunity to behave even more outlandishly. It was easy for him to avoid this sort of thing as the others were too drunk to notice he was usually a timekeeper or judge rather than a participant. In other words, he was regarded as one of the lads.

----------

That they got away with this sort of thing was in itself an interesting phenomenon. Unlike football hooligans, they never tried to intimidate or involve other people and were not physically threatening. It was a very in group sort of phenomenon. They completely ignored outsiders almost as if they didn't exist. As long as they did not get involved in trouble with the police, which was in fact, very difficult to do in Holland, the company turned a blind eye on all their exploits and was very tolerant and liberal, especially as the sexual exploits of the Shell crowd were an open secret.

Jonathan was intrigued that these wild party boys were all highly intelligent, university educated men with top degrees. They were all happily right wing without being overly interested in politics, and clearly both chauvinist and male chauvinist in both theory and practice. They would be happy to work hard anywhere the company sent them and pick up the monetary rewards and enjoy a wonderfully pampered lifestyle, without questioning too much the moral and political issues which were always lurking beneath the surface of what they did. This seemed in general to be the sort of person that Shell looked for in its higher-level executives of the future. He was amused that once again he'd surreptitiously slipped through the selection net. He'd been happy to go along with the crowd wherever he found himself without ever feeling he belonged to it. His chameleon like behaviour had initially been essential for his survival but now it was so ingrained and habitual it was actually allowing him to prosper in any environment he found himself in.

As always with each entry of new trainees, they would become lifelong friends as their careers brought them into contact intermittently in different parts of the world. For Jonathan though, it would be truer to say they would be acquaintances rather than friends. That, paradoxically, was one of his greatest strengths. For him The Hague years had been even more significant for he had also met his future wife, Anja, although neither of them was to know that at the time. She was Dutch and worked as a secretary in the Shell HQ. This was how many of the Shell graduate trainees met their wives. And many of the secretaries, although no doubt competent, well qualified and good at their jobs, were daughters or nieces of high-powered Shell employees already halfway up the greasy pole. It couldn't possibly be deliberate, but this systematically bound the new future leaders, Dutch or otherwise, more tightly into the traditions of the Shell family, which was Dutch in its origins and Dutch to the core.

After his training was over, he passed all the assessments and tests with glowing colours and had been flagged already as potential top management material. He was first posted to Brunei for Shell Exploration. Here he had been introduced to the way in which an international company treated its new highflyers. Excellent free accommodation and regular flights back to The Hague allowed him to carry on his courtship. The relationship, which could easily have petered out with distance, flourished.

# Chapter 7

She would show him. She was furious. That morning, in one of their regular rows, her husband, the Duke had complained that she was not a country girl interested in the pursuits of landowners on their estates and that she was only interested in fashion and glamour and being seen.

This was of course true, but she didn't want to recognise the truth about herself, especially in an argument with him.

'Come on. Put your wellies on,' she shouted at her young son, Prince Arthur, who looked on with mild surprise.

'What for Mother?' he asked. 'You never take me out when we're staying here.'

'Come on, let's get ready.'

'But you don't even like it here.'

'Come on, let's go. We're going out rabbit hunting.' She pulled his anorak on him. As a six-year-old he was still struggling with this. He was frail and sensitive, not a tough boy at all, as the Royals were expected to be. And being educated privately with his own personal tutor, he was isolated; he had no social skills at all.

'But it's cold mother. What is rabbit hunting?'

There was no answer.

'But you don't like the cold and what is rabbit hunting?' he protested.

She knew what it was but that was all. She had no idea how to carry it out. She had never been rabbit hunting herself, coming from a town background.

She had seen her husband, the Prince, going fox hunting but only from a comfortably warm 4 x 4. To her they looked utterly ridiculous in their bright red costumes and funny hats all on top of massive, smelly horses. It seemed a totally pointless and boring activity to her. With their strange calls and language. But not cruel. She had no feelings or thoughts for the fox.

Maybe rabbit hunting was something she could handle. But she needed help and this came in the form of her PA, Gavin, who knew everything. She had asked him to come along and prepare things.

He entered the room carrying a case which he proceeded to open in front of them. It contained two 0.22 air rifles, which are suitable for rabbit hunting on a small scale.

'Here we go,' she screamed, and they all climbed into the Range Rover.

It was all very basic. The valet drove along one of the estate roads for about fifteen minutes until they entered the woodlands.

'And here we are,' she said and as they left the car at the edge of the woods, she gave him one of the air guns.

'This is not a cowboy gun,' he said. 'Why have I got this? And you still haven't told me what rabbit hunting is.'

'It's shooting bunnies, you silly boy, it's shooting bunnies.' She was still in a state from the crazy row that morning.

'Bunnies. You mean like Jemima and Edward.' They were his pet rabbits that he adored.

'Well, their poor, country cousins who live outside in the woods.'

'But I don't want to shoot them. You can't shoot them.'

'You need to grow up so you can show your father what you can do and what I have taught you. So, the first thing is to shoot a few rabbits. We may even eat them later,' she added mercilessly.

'What?' He looked at her uncomprehendingly and was beginning to shake. He had seen her in a mood before, many times, but not quite like this. She was what they call hysterical.

Why was she so nasty to him? She was always shouting at him for something or other. Or for no reason at all. Not like his nanny, who was nice and kind, looked after him and cuddled him a lot. She loved him. But she, she, his own mother, was horrible.

After a brisk ten-minute walk, they reached a clearing and sure enough there were plenty of cousin bunnies about. Three or four scampered happily out of the woods only a few metres in front of them.

'Go on, aim and shoot at one of them. Best if you wait until one of them stops.'

He just looked at her imploringly with tears in his eyes.

'See what you can do.'

He just took the gun and nodded meekly. His was not to question why.

Two more rabbits emerged and she shouted loudly.

'Come on son. Shoot.'

Nothing. The rabbits were standing still. And they were looking straight at them. Still nothing.

He was holding the gun and pointing it in the general direction of the rabbits but not really aiming at all. And he was now shaking and sobbing loudly.

'For Christ sake, do it. Just do it. Shoot.'

He turned towards her – she was a few metres away and pulled the trigger wildly. She let out an almighty scream, crumpled to the ground and held her leg.

Gavin ran across, held her tightly and shook her strongly until she stopped screaming. There was a small dark spot halfway up her left leg.

'Look, it's just going to sting a bit and you'll have beautiful circular bruise in a couple of hours. But you're OK. Air gun pellets will kill rabbits but not humans. Pull yourself together woman. You will be alright.'

She just kept on groaning and moaning but she was calmer.

He took the guns away and bundled them both into the Rover. One in the front and one in the back. Both whimpering like little kittens in water. He waited a while to catch his breath and this gave her time to exert her position of power once more.

'Not a word about this. Both of you.' She looked at them sternly. 'Not to anyone. It didn't happen. Right?'

Gavin nodded. The Prince, now huddled into a ball, just looked down, more frightened than one of the rabbits would have been in their car headlights at night.

This was bad. This was bad enough reflected Gavin. But he had seen worse from this family. He would stay silent to keep his job, but he had no sympathy, no affection, no bond for this mad woman. He would faithfully keep her secrets and not sell them for lots of money to a tabloid newspaper as was clearly possible. Well, not yet anyway.

# Chapter 8

They all piled into the telepherique – the cable car. British package holiday makers stood side by side with millionaires from Geneva and local snowboarding yobbos. You couldn't really tell them apart by appearance unless you were a real expert on ski fashion, even more of an expert on skis and ski boots. Today there was an additional group that Jonathan was a part of, selected from a wide range of disciplines to attend an elite conference at this highly desirable location. They were all high flyers, several years into their respective careers and destined to be future leaders in their fields. It was a really international clientele, but it was the Americans that could be heard the loudest, always confident and totally boyish and open in their enthusiasms. Jonathan stood next to the exception, a rather serious and earnest young Greek American by the name of Jake Diamopoulos, who had teamed up with him as he'd heard of Jonathan's ski prowess and wanted to seek his guidance in his quest to be the best at everything.

But everyone's attention was drawn to the loud boasts of the tall, blond and extremely athletic looking Texan, Steve Carter.

'Call that a black run, we have molehills bigger than

that, man,' he laughed when the moguls of the Diamant Noir were pointed out to him

The telepherique carried over 2000 skiers an hour to the Grande Platieres, the highest point in the Grand Massif ski domain. Some resorts had faster transportation speeds with high speed trains in tunnels but there was nothing to beat this, as the view during the ascent was stunning and if you tired of that, there were the skiers themselves. Although the telepherique had only been open half an hour, last night's 30 cm fall of snow had brought out all the powder buffs and there were wonderful serpent like tracks covering the mountain, some of them from terrifyingly steep descents. You could see some of the off piste skiers gingerly walking up to the entrance of a narrow corniche. Others emerged from the corniche to enter a virgin area with elegant, almost balletic and apparently effortless turns. Beautiful cotton wool powder snow sprayed in the air all around them until they were almost obscured.

Also scattered about were skiers of all levels of competence or incompetence as they made their way down the huge Flaine bowl on a variety of different pistes from the easy motorway blues, to the steeper reds to the Diamant Noir black run itself, which in several places went under the telepherique itself. There were cheers and several "oohs and ahhs" as some spectacular falls were observed.

The view as they emerged from the cable car station was spectacular. The sky was cloudless and a very strong blue colour. Straight ahead across the Desert du Plat, a vast protected valley was the surprisingly smooth summit of Mont Blanc and in a line to its left, one could see Mont Maudit, Mont Blanc de Tacul and The

43

Aiguille du Midi. This has its famous tower at its summit from where one began the perilous descent to the Vallee Blanche Glacier. Further along were a whole chain of the sharply pointed peaks of the Aiguilee Rouge. Sunlight reflected from the crevasses of the huge glaciers. A glorious view indeed.

'Enough of this, we're here to ski. Let's warm up,' shouted Brian Stellard, one of the top instructors of the Ski Club of Great Britain, who'd been specially hired to take Jonathan's group of eight of the most advanced skiers.

Jonathan knew him as a very demanding expert skier who expected the maximum effort at all times. He'd been his instructor when he'd passed his BASI (British Association of Ski Instructors) gold badge, one of the most difficult qualifications in the Alps, both because of the expense involved in paying for all the tuition and the ski experience necessary.

They then made a very fast warm up run down the red Mephisto all the way down the mountain back to the Telepherique. Some warmup. There had been only one brief stop halfway down to check the numbers. Fortunately, conditions on the immaculately groomed pistes were excellent.

After a brief glance at Mont Blanc again, Brian stood in front of the group with a broad smile. All were young, fit, strong, athletic looking and had decent turns even if some of them were lacking in style, and his brief was after all to push them to the limit.

'This time we'll go down the Black Diamond, Diamant Noir. Follow me.

'We'll go for about 200 metres and when I stop I want you all to stop in a line about two meters apart.

44

'Is that clear?'

This first two hundred metres is nice and easy, almost a red but they then had to stop as Bryan had said, as a queue had developed. A queue always develops at this point. This is the couloir at the start of the moguls. They all side stepped cautiously forward to have a look.

There were loud exhalations of breath, some muffled cries and a number of loud expletives. Most people just stood there silently and possibly prayed.

The view from the telepherique had clearly not prepared them for this. They must have some giant moles in Texas. These moguls were all over a metre high and very icy. They were too steep for any of last night's snow to have gathered and the sun had had no time to soften them up. But the narrowness of the entry was the breaking point.

'OK,' said Bryan grimly. 'There is only one way down this. And you won't all be able to manage it. So now is the time to take off your skis and walk back to the telepherique. It's no disgrace. Lots of top skiers have done this at one time or another.

Several took up the offer not knowing whether it would count against them in their appraisal for lacking courage, or whether they would be praised for truly assessing their ability and skill against a tough benchmark.

He turned to the dropouts. 'Ok. Fair choice. Take the red run down from the telepherique.'

He now turned his attention to the remainers.

'First there is the six-foot drop onto the first mogul. See there are only four other moguls in a line. You have to turn on one of these.'

He didn't need to explain why. They could all see the

45

exposed nasty jagged rock face that they would ski into if they didn't manage a turn. Once you have started you just have to turn and keep on turning as there's no possibility of traversing. Most mogul fields are far more forgiving and a traverse, an escape route, does exist.

'Once you have done your first turn you just have to keep on turning. Commit to the turn. That will control your speed.

'After about fifty metres it flattens out a bit and it's possible to stop.'

All this explained the queue. A very strange queue as no one in it minded being passed.

It was Jonathan's turn. He did not hesitate.

How one tackled this determined to a large extent how one tackled life. He retracted his legs and keeping both skis parallel by pressing his ankles together he went turn, turn, turn on every first or second mogul, going almost straight down the fall line. If one didn't do This, one would pick up too much speed and lose control. His style gradually disintegrated and the rhythm went but he managed to keep his skis together till the end, even though the strain in his thighs as his strength went was excruciating. When he started breathing again, it seemed as if it was a purely anaerobic exercise. He looked back up to see what he'd achieved. And of course, to look at the next person coming down. That was always interesting. It was always one at a time down such a perilous slope. Anything else would be asking for trouble.

It was Steve Carter, the Texas molehill champion. But he didn't go far, well, not on his skis anyway. He hesitated on the first vital turn, did not retract his legs enough and coming out of the turn, the fear factor taking over causing him to straighten his legs, his weight went back, lifting the skis off their edges and down he came. His skis came off after the first somersault, one of them going straight down the slope, as the brakes had no chance of gripping on the icy moguls. His other ski took off like a beautifully thrown javelin and stuck into the top of a mogul tip first. Steve himself did all the right things and tried to dig his boot heels into the hard ice as he picked up speed but to no avail. By now his sticks had gone as well, wrenched out of their retaining straps leaving these on Steve's wrists. He shot past his javelin ski and careered down the slope rolling, tumbling, sliding, somersaulting. There was hardly a move in gymnastics that he did not involuntarily perform, coming to a stop only metres from Jonathan.

He was unhurt, but badly shocked and ashen faced. It would be a pretty bad experience when only a small number of colleagues are silent and forgiving witnesses. But in this case a chairlift taking people back up passes only a few metres above the skiers' heads, making it a spectators' dream, and a victim's public humiliation. The chairlift itself starts only a bit below where Jonathan stood and is an escape route for those who do not wish to continue to experience the delights of the run, even though they are only a fifth of the way down. The chairlift is always full.

Most of the skiers on the chairlift have no idea what is involved in tackling the Diamant Noir.

'Hard luck mate,' was the nicest cry from the first group that had observed Steve's spectacular fall.

'A couple more somersaults please.'

The more experienced ones just winced and silently empathized, almost literally feeling his pain.

After commiserating and wiping all the snow off Steve's neck and arms, Jonathan  looked up and said, 'Ok. You need to walk back up to get your ski. Nobody else can stop there on the way down to get it for you.

'Kick your boots into the ice one at a time to make small steps to help your climb.

'Take your time. Be patient.'

The next group of skiers on the chair lift saw him climb breathlessly back up to retrieve his ski. The combination of the hot sun, the altitude and his general state of shock made him sweat profusely but he kept on going, too fast. Patience was not one of his finer qualities. He was only a metre away from his ski when he failed to make a final adequate imprint and down he came again for a third group of chairlift spectators to applaud this unexpected climax to the show.

How can people be so cruel?

Was it dangerous? Was it irresponsible of a qualified ski instructor to take them there? Is there a lesson to be learnt from such an experience? Steve Carter certainly thought so. And he would remember it periodically at crucial times in his ascent up the corporate ladder.

It was a good hour before they were all down relatively safely, though most had fallen more than once.

Bryan called out as they approached a mountain bar.

'Right guys and gals. You all deserve a chocolat chaud. Let's go in here.'

Steve didn't think he was up to further skiing and quietly whispered this to Bryan.

'Fair enough. No disgrace there.'

----------

Bryan was a hard task master and fifteen minutes later they were out again and on their way to the Domaine de Gers, the steepest and most dangerous area at the back of the Flaine bowl.

Here there are a variety of off-piste descents to the bottom of a very long return drag lift. After two or three of these descents even the fittest and strongest are feeling the strain as it becomes harder and harder to maintain the right muscle tension to keep one's weight over the skis. It was exhilarating and punishing at the same time and a real test of character. It was not just a ski run for these people. Confidential appraisal reports about each person's approach and attitude would be going to their respective superiors. Jonathan had clearly fared the best, but his skiing experience was that much greater. Jake Diamopoulos had done very well, his fanatical determination and doggedness making up to a large extent for his lack of skill and technique. But the various skill levels would all be carefully taken into account in the final assessments. Even Steve Carter's decision to quit would be given due credit as it was probably the correct one from an objective point of view.

They did the Gers descent three times taking a different route each time. Even the long drag lift back up, being notoriously steep, is not a place where one can relax and recover.

'Right everyone. Let's end the day by turning right at the bottom and instead of going back up the draglift this will let us join up with Les Cascades, the 16 km long blue run to the village of Sixt.

'We'll stop off there for a drink. And then, because

we're in a neighbouring valley, we can't ski back, so we'll catch taxis back to Flaine.'

'Thank God the pressures off now,' said one of the more tired ones.

They were all pretty exhausted and there were many nodding heads. All clearly feeling the test was over, they set off in a relaxed and slightly unfocussed mood.

'I'll follow you Jonathan,' said Jake, as they began a long traverse. Although it was off piste it was well worn and a narrow path, one ski track wide, had been created by previous skiers. They then began the descent. The steepness made Jonathan take lots of short radius parallels to keep his speed down. He suddenly felt a whooshing sound on his left as Jake shot past him skiing in a straight line in the standard racing egg position. Although he had done the run only once before Jonathan suddenly remembered that there was a very sharp right turn ahead. This was off piste skiing, there were no warning signs to slow down and certainly no strategically placed netting. He immediately and instinctively went into the racing position and the lowered air resistance led to an instant acceleration. Jake was a few metres ahead but with his slightly better stance and his longer skis, he gradually clawed back the gap centimetre by centimetre. As he drew alongside on Jake's left, he lifted his body and using his right shoulder, gave him a vicious shove towards the hillside. His own inner ski rose up clumsily and with all his weight on his outer ski and with massive edging he turned rightwards only centimetres away from the sheer five hundred metre drop onto large bare rocks. Jake had ploughed safely into the bank and had come to a standstill. He was heavily winded and took some minutes to recover. He was about to remonstrate with Jonathan when he took one glance down the slope. The look in his eyes alone revealed the terrifying realization that he had narrowly escaped the premature ending of his life on earth.

'You, you…. you bastard. You just saved my life,' he uttered.

'Yes, yes I did,' Jonathan whispered. And they both hugged each other. In silent relief.

----------

He awoke to the gentle vibration of his bed which the alarm had set off and casually tried out the voice operating systems. First, he asked the curtains to open and heard the dull hum as the electric shutters operated followed by the beautifully decorated sliding panels which acted as curtains. But his mood changed from one of excitement to one of disappointment as the magnificent view of le Grandes Platiere topped by stunning blue sky was missing, replaced by a total white out with virtually zero visibility. There would be no skiing this morning. He looked around at the vast expanse of the apartment with two large south facing balconies. A large bedroom and lounge both had panoramic unimpeded views of the mountains, The furnishings and carpeting were of the latest design and the bathroom had superb state of the art showering and ventilation control. There was multiple channel satellite TV and a private satellite phone and video link to his companies HQ and a broadband optical fibre link for internet access.

He turned over and tapped the screen to his right to bring up the breakfast menu. He chose a cappuccino to be delivered and then tapped out the very healthy breakfast that he would eat downstairs with the others. They had to eat communally to continue the bonding process.

Next he clicked on his internet download and his IA (Intelligent Agent) had really excelled today. First he saw the local snow, visibility and wind conditions from the resorts own web page, followed by a summary of his five most important e-mails and the electronically created recommended replies, only one of which he had to amend. He paused briefly as the wall panel opened to reveal his freshly arrived Capuccino, then looked at the Llanelli Scarlets Rugby club result, an account of the game by his favorite sports reporter and the latest prices of his personal share portfolio. These came with recommendations to buy and sell and the calculated profit. Finally he glanced at the newly downloaded edited version of the talk he, like all the other participants, would deliver the following evening, noted the changes made, and the bookmarked checking of facts and thought his fellow guests would be impressed by the detailed criticisms, rebuttals and comments he would make on all the presentations he had heard in the previous two days.

There were a number of very disappointed people in the small and incredibly luxurious lecture theatre as the lights were dimmed for the presentation. The poor weather conditions meant the morning's off piste ski tour had been cancelled. It was nice to have a conference take place at a ski resort in the French Alps. Even nicer to be the occupant of a two million dollar fifth floor penthouse apartment in a block occupied solely by the conference attendees.

The evening session had been brought forward and the first lecture was titled "Investment in Argentina: Security and Risk."

'The lecturer was a young Ivy League and CIA analyst and the audience was a varied group of military, young businessmen, politicians and academics drawn from the US and by special invitation, the UK. What they all had in common was that they were high achievers in their chosen field and were headed for power sooner or later. To be invited here was a sure sign that they were on the fast track to promotion whether the participants themselves realized it or not. This was Jonathan's second visit to such a gathering and Shell had chosen him to represent them at this confidential elite conference. The first one had been at a wilderness resort in the Canadian Rockies with a grade 6 river for white water rafting.

What appealed to him was the very high-powered nature of the participants, the sheer intellectual power and rigour of the discussions and the no holds barred atmosphere. Also the "empathise with the enemy approach" was quite challenging and one's own interests and behaviour as a country or company were often shown in a bad light.

'Don't forget that before WW2 foreigners controlled over 60% of all industrial investment, with a third of all profits exported as dividends. The British dominated, controlling two thirds of all foreign investment. They and the US owned all public utilities and dominated the economy through their control of the meat packing, shipping, banking and insurance industries. Gasworks, electricity companies and the telephone system were all owned by British and American companies. This was effectively a British colony to quote from the Duke of Windsor, a frequent visitor to the estancias and polo fields attested.

"I don't mind which part of the Empire we give up as long as it's not Argentina."

'It was against this background that General Peron came to power and although vilified by the West for supporting Hitler and being anti-democratic, he basically removed Argentina's status as a colony. The demand for grain and meat was high after the war and Peron used this revenue to nationalize the foreign dominated industries. The railways is a good example. The 27,000 miles of railway tracks were run down and owned by nine UK companies. Britain owed Argentina £190 million for meat bought during the war. Peron wiped 150 million pounds off this debt as compensation and nationalized the railways. He also ended the reviled "standard " system of payment, which was the norm in most industries. In this system workers had to work up to a certain standard. When they reached this, they received progressively less for any more effort, and as they worked harder the standard level was raised. This was ended at a stroke and Peron became a hero of the working classes. This prewar background to the foreign domination of Argentina shows that the hatred against foreign oppression was fully justified and explains the fanaticism with which the Argentinians hated the British during the Falklands War. The Malvinas were a symbol to them of all that they had suffered on the mainland.

# Chapter 9

He wore his sleek £2000 Armani suit with ease and his smile was broad and permanent as he shook hands for the 180th time and had still not tired of it. Anja, looking very elegant in a specially designed Versace off the shoulder creation, was at his side and even more at ease than he was. She had come from a titled family of high achievers and was quite used to meeting and greeting the wealthy and grand of Dutch society. This was the unique get together of all the senior Shell executives around the world. They had all flown into Schiphol airport just to attend this one dinner in The Hague, the HQ of the company, when they would all be introduced to the new managing director. This ceremony was part of the tradition and mystique of one of the sisters as the major oil companies are known. The magnificent Kurhaus Hotel on the seafront at Scheveningen had been closed to the public and hired in its entirety for the dinner. Even the Casino was tonight only available to the Shell personnel. Although totally renovated and not very old, the Kurhaus looked resplendent with its ornate decorated ceiling and massive chandeliers. It had a touch of the classical about it but was also a state of the art modern conference venue.

gratulations Jonathan. You have achieved an feat, you are the first non-Dutch MD of this famous company. And you have achieved this totally on merit. You have proved yourself in a wide range of posts around the world. We are sure you will carry out your functions in a highly professional and competent way to maintain our standing as a company of integrity and good name throughout the industry.'

These were kind and flattering words indeed from the chairman of the group. Also, possibly a bit over the top as far as company ethics were concerned, coming from the man who had been MD while Shell pursued its blatantly anti-environmental policy in the Nigerian delta which had resulted in the execution of several prominent protestors.

Although he was extremely ambitious, Jonathan had never thought he would be standing here tonight, as the company, despite being titled Anglo-Dutch Shell was 60/40 Dutch owned and had always appointed a Dutch MD to maintain its control. The Dutch had been very successful in disguising the fact that they were the dominant partner and most British people still assumed it was a 50/50 split or a wholly British company. He was especially pleased as he believed it was the triumph of meritocracy that he had got the top post. Even a company steeped in tradition had come to accept that merit must prevail and as the chairman had said, he really was the best man for the job.

Anja's father, a director of Philips stood alongside his brother, the financial director of Heineken and their cousin, the chairman of De Telegraaf (the TIMES of Holland). This was a special moment for them as they had managed to convince the Masonic Lodge of

Amsterdam, the leading lodge in the country, to back their man, even though he was not Dutch. Once they had done this, by appealing mainly to members' personal financial interests, the Lodge had evidently, through its many contacts, got the message home, and were as usual quietly content with their hidden power. They were not to know that they were not the only ones who had canvassed the Masonic Lodge.

----------

The two old men looked fit and bronzed even though they both had excessive midriff bulges. They sat around the poolside on beautiful handmade Indonesian wicker chairs around a table on which was a most exquisite lacquered Ma Jong set with original Chinese carvings. It looked as if it should be permanently stored under lock and key but here it was in daily use. The pool was surrounded on three sides by the villa itself which produced excellent protection from the Mistral wind. The southerly view from the open side was truly breathtaking, across the beautiful wooded countryside and extending to the Bay of Cannes and the wider Mediterranean in the distance.

They were part of a colony of Dutch ex pats, but it was a very exclusive "onze sorte mensen" *"our sort of people"* colony of rich retired businessmen, who also had entries in the book of Dutch gentry, the Netherlands Patriciaat.

The villas they lived in for six months of the year were dotted around the village of Cabris, perched dramatically on a hillside a few kilometres to the west of the famous perfume town of Grasse.

Both men were well over 70 and they were very pleased with life and with themselves. They had good reason to be. Jan Willem van Kempen, tall and severe with black pince nez spectacles, was the revered ex-CEO of Shell, and a major shareholder in all the leading Dutch blue chip companies. Hendrik ter Haar, also tall but more genial and friendly, had made his name in banking, opening the first branches of ABN, in Singapore, Hong Kong and Bombay, eventually becoming MD of this prestigious Dutch bank and Chairman of the board of Shell. They were a very discreet and unobtrusive pair who made little impact in the local area. Their worldwide influence could only be guessed at, but never fully known because they revelled in their secret intrigue and influence. They loved the subtleties and bluffs and double bluffs of business almost as much as the very same nuances and intrigue in their beloved Ma Jong. Every morning they would read the Dutch papers, the Algemene Dagblad and De Telegraaf but not the one-day old ones. Theirs was especially flown in for this exclusive community. Then they met at each other's villas with their wives, Annemie and Marjolein, two very attractive women in their early forties. They were sisters, also from a Patriaat family who had made its name in the Dutch East Indies before it had become Indonesia and had thrown them out. The men always played Ma Jong and talked about world affairs. Although they had retired some years ago, the men could not let go. Their whole lives had been active and dominated by their work. They were not as energetic as they used to be – yet the daily game of tennis was a keen affair which seemed to be fought to the death or probably would be one of these days. But their brains were still razor sharp and roamed over many topics and world events but always in the end came back to the company, Anglo Dutch Shell, which they regarded as their own.

Annemie bought out the traditional koffie and Genever on a tray at exactly eleven o' clock. They could have had servants, but they valued their privacy and independence immensely and though very well off, did everything themselves, including the cooking and washing up. Their conversation today was dominated by one thing. The succession. Who would be the new MD of Shell?

'Look. The first thing is always to make sure it's a Dutchman!' said Jan Willem.

'You don't have to worry about that, it's accepted as a matter of course. It's our company after all,' Hendrik interrupted.

'I'm not so sure these days.'

'What do you mean, klootzak?'

'I don't mean it's not our company. I mean the Brits have been pushing for years to break the tradition and have one of theirs as No 1. The word is that this time round they are especially determined.'

'Yes, we have to be careful. It's only a tradition. We can't rely on our 60/40 ownership forever. It's not written down anywhere, so there's no legal basis for it. It should be in the constitution.'

'Anyway, what will be the big thing he'll have to deal with?'

'Or she', shouted Annemie from the airbed on the pool and they all laughed heartily at such a ridiculous thought.

'The bloody Arabs are always the unknown factor. How long can the Saudis last? You'd have thought they'd have been deposed long ago. One of these days they'll execute one too many of the fundamentalist mullahs and the whole thing will go sky high. If the democrats miraculously take over, we'll probably be OK but if the mullahs are in power who knows what might happen. The oil is a secondary factor with them.'

'Let's suppose that happens. What do we do then? Can we bring in new wells much earlier than planned to stop prices going up?'

'Prices will rise anyway because of the instability and uncertainty, and it only brings us short term benefits as it causes inflation and our own costs rise. No, we need to consider new wells and new discoveries anyway.'

'Ah. That's where I've got something to tell you. Hans van Meulen, who works in Exploration, has told me that there's a major find in the seas around Antarctica; they were first led to it by the geological formations revealed by the radar satellites. They're keeping it under wraps and don't know what to do with it because of the Antarctic Treaty.'

'Bugger the treaty. If there's oil there we'll have to go for it.'

'But the treaty forbids all mining and oil exploitation and it's been ratified by the entire world community.'

'Yes! Very foolishly! By shortsighted governments. As I said. Bugger the treaty.'

'The Shell Brits would never agree to that with the sort of Government they've got, if we tried anything.'

There was a long pause as they pondered on this.

Then Jan Willem said very slowly and deliberately.

'They could if they were in a position of real power....
if one of them was No. 1!'

'God Verdomme. You've got it. They'd owe us a
really big favour if we granted that.'

'But we still need a Brit who's willing to break the
Treaty even if he is the big boss.'

'Well let's find out which of their candidates is most
likely to do that and go for him.'

'Find one we can blackmail you mean.'

'Hendrik. You old devil.'

And with that they rose to get ready for a light lunch
at their regular haunt, le Renard, a gezellig bar a short
walk away.

----------

The following evening, they were at their favourite
restaurant, La Coupole, on the outskirts of Grasse and
they sat at their regular table with the best view from a
sheltered position. Hendrik ordered his usual Beef
Wellington, an English/American dish made especially
for him, even though this was a Michelin French
restaurant of many years standing. Jan Willem was more
highly regarded by the chef. He chose Bouillabaisse and
this arrived on a massive silver platter, beautifully laid
out and decorated.

But his mind was not on the meal at all tonight. He
seemed very excited if not agitated. He took out a
handful of scruffy sheets from his pocket and quietly
exclaimed, 'I've just got these faxes from Carel.'

Carel van t'Hek was the head of the Dutch secret

service, the AIVD, The General Intelligence and Security Service, located in the town of Zoetermeer about twenty minutes by car from The Hague. He had also been sax player in Jan Willems' Dixie jazz band in Leiden Universiteit many years ago.

'He sent me these encrypted e-mails all day, but I couldn't decode them. I want writing on paper I said and he relented.'

'Never mind about that. What has he got for us?'

'There's only one man in it. Two other front runners are squeaky clean and totally loyal to the English establishment. Where do we find them? It's someone called Jonathan Jones.'

He passed him the list of names.

'But he's top notch - the best of the bunch anyway. Very clever, a good analyst and very decisive. Very strong character. He'd be my choice anyway. But he can't be blackmailed surely?'

'That's the trump card. We won't need to. His background makes him anti- establishment, anti-English, anti-British. You name it he's the one.'

'What makes you so sure? I've met him. He's very suave and confident and typically public school. Scout's Honour and all that.'

'It's all on the surface. Listen. He's from a Welsh Nationalist background. Welsh speaking family. He's even changed his name to disguise it for goodness sake. His birth certificate says Gwynfor Jones. He was sent to an English public school. Hated every minute of it. Sodomised there and forced to play soldiers with real guns in the school army - what they call the Combined Cadet Force.

'Sounds powerful enough to put me off authority and

the establishment all right.'

'There's more. He's kept very quiet about this, but when he was in college, he was a member of the United Nations Student Association, very left wing in those days but in a highly analytical, intellectual way. But clearly anti British.'

He held up his arm to stop Hendrik interrupting.

'Now here comes the strong stuff. Do you remember those British ships during the Falklands War being bombed by Argentinian planes and burning helplessly? They were trying to unload troops without any air support of their own. It was one of Thatcher's biggest blunders. All the casualties were members of a Welsh regiment. Jones' brother was on one of the ships. He survived but had been in a mental hospital ever since. And two years ago, he killed himself while his brother, our man, was visiting!'

'Jesus! He must hate the British ruling classes and their jingoism after that.'

'That ties in neatly with what we need,' said Jan Willem, completely ignoring the emotional impact of what he'd just revealed.

'First of all, for appointing Jones as number 1 we call in the Shell Brits' favour to support the breaking of the Antarctic Treaty.

'Second. To get the oil out of Antarctica we need the Falklands for another Sullom Voe. It's still a British colony, thank God, so they'll have that for us.

'Third, and it all stand or falls on this, we also need a town in Argentina as another Aberdeen. And Jones will supply that for us to get his own back on Britain.'

To non-oil men, Sullom Voe was the oil terminal in the Shetland islands closest to North Sea rigs to which the oil was pumped ashore. And Aberdeen on the East coast of Scotland became the boom town for the "oilies," the workers from all over the world, the supply ships, the rig yards and all the services.

'So Hendrik. Get up to Amsterdam to talk to your mates in the funny aprons and I'll get all my networks working to make this historic and magnanimous change.'

'Come on, you know I'll wear anything in the right company. By the way, why do you think Karel stuck his neck out to give you all this? Its dynamite in the wrong hands.'

'Ha! I think he's sent it to us so we use our influence to put a stop to Jones' possible appointment.'

After two bottles of Saint Emilion Marquis de Rothberg and several glasses of the 25 year old Armagnac Delord, it was time to go.

As they walked to their taxis his wife Annemie called out to Jan Willem, 'I'm going back with Hendrik tonight.'

'Okay, fine," said Jan Willem. 'Tot morgen,' as Marjolein passed her arm through his. They often did this after a good evening out but not even their very best friends had any inkling whatsoever. They were very discreet.

# Chapter 10

The taxi from Trelew airport passed the Hotel Centenario, which looked as quiet and deserted as ever. He was going straight to Catrin's house as he had a strong foreboding that something was wrong. Six months had passed and there had been no reply to any of his letters after Catrin had asked him to write. The taxi turned into their street and he was about to tell it where to stop when he suddenly realised it wasn't there. The green clapperboard house. There was no mistake. It was gone. Completely vanished. The ground had been cleared and flattened and there was a neat gap between the two neighbouring clapperboards. He left the taxi driver and in a state of utter bewilderment went and knocked on the next-door neighbour. She had seen him coming and had quietly drawn the curtains. He knocked several times, but she did not answer.

The middle-aged lady in the house opposite was more forthcoming, just. She simply opened her door slightly and said quietly with a look of resignation and fear, 'They have joined the disappeared ones.' Before he could react, she promptly closed the door again. His bewilderment had turned to panic, anger, outrage, sheer disbelief and fear.

He decided to visit the grave. This was preposterous. He was now standing on the exact spot where Gareth Jones had been buried but it was now a 4m by 4 m clearing in the woods, totally artificially made and brazenly announcing that something happened here - a deliberate warning to all that this was dangerous territory. Do not meddle. Do not make a fuss. Don't even talk about it.

The only thing left to do was to visit the hotel. Maybe there will be somebody brave enough to tell him a bit more of the circumstances of their disappearance. He asked the man at reception about Maria.

'Yes of course I remember her. She was only here one summer. She was nothing but trouble. With no warning, she used to leave the desk and rush off on her moped with that camera of hers.'

Then in a whisper.

'They say she was one of them - secret service - sent to watch the Welsh here. I'll never forgive myself after what happened. I should never have employed her in my hotel.'

'But what has happened to Catrin Prys-Jones and her mother?'

'Disappeared.' He put his finger to his lips.

'You said your hotel. But wasn't it a chain owned by her uncle?'

'No,' he replied puzzled. 'The hotel has been in our family for 40 years.'

# Chapter 11

As they came out together through the hotel door, they were greeted by a large lens a few feet from them. Flashes went off rapidly as they both stood transfixed. None of the Chief of Staff's training came into operation. A large microphone was thrust in front of him.

'How long has this affair been going on, Chief of Staff?'

'Will you resign?'

'Does your wife know?'

The barrage of questions continued without any wait for an answer. They had clearly been found out, and yes, his whole career was over. He would be in utter disgrace with all his colleagues and his children would be devastated.

His wife may well be secretly pleased he thought angrily.

He turned to Lady Buck and was amazed to see a broad smile across her face as she posed for more photos. She held his arm for the next one and before he could draw away, she planted a firm kiss on his lips to more flashing lights and yelps of delight from the cameramen and reporters. It dawned on him that they had not somehow been found out, rather it was he who had been set up and by his infatuation with Bucky. But why had she done this? His mind in turmoil, he just stood there like a lonely little boy as she stepped into a waiting car with a photographer and reporter and blew him a lingering kiss as they drove away rapidly, horn blazing in triumph. The journalists all followed and he stood alone for an eternal five minutes before quietly catching a cab to his club, the Special Services club in Knightsbridge.

He rented a room for the night as he did when he was sometimes working late, and had a meal delivered to it. Apart from the loyal George at reception, he did not speak to anyone. Today he'd had the afternoon off and had promised to play squash with his son who was home from Wellington boarding school.

But Bucky had phoned and asked him round to the hotel. He'd immediately agreed, such was the naked desire she had so effectively aroused in him with her seductive phone call charm. Normally they would only meet up for a couple of hours in the afternoons when he was on the way back from meetings and he would then return to the Admiralty for a few hours more work before going home. Sometimes when his wife was away, they had spent all night at the hotel.

Nothing had been left to chance in her calculations when they had left the hotel. The press would no doubt discuss the security implications of his affair, but they would have nothing to go on and would have no idea of the precise nature of what had happened.

He knew it was all over, but he was totally paralyzed and had no idea what he should do. He could have gone to the Admiralty and begun to try to explain it all. He could even have gone home and tried to explain it all there. He thought he had been a brave man in his rise to power but he was an abject and pathetic coward now. He just waited forlornly. He did not have to wait long. The daily papers were delivered to his room the next morning. Of course, it had been The Sun newspaper that had set him up, but all the papers had seen its first edition and had quickly changed their main headlines so that his denouement was on the top front page of every single newspaper. A headline and a photo were printed in all.

'Chief of Staff Disgraced,' led the Sun.

'Flanks exposed by Defence Chief,' crowed the Mirror.

'Chief of Staff affair exposed,' was the more sedate headline of the Telegraph and the Independent proclaimed, 'Chief of Staff compromised in sex scandal.'

None of the papers went into any depth as they'd all copied the Sun. The main thrust of many was to criticize the Sun for paying Lady Buck and setting it all up. For that was clearly what had happened. She had contacted them and told them she'd be emerging from the hotel with the Chief of Staff at a certain time. Estimates of the amount of money she'd received varied for £10,000 to £25,0000 and now the Fleet Street pack had been set loose to find out more about this juicy scandal. It could run for ages. One small paragraph at the end of The Times was a jolt for him.

'The Chief of Staff is expected to hand in his resignation today and to face a full security interrogation immediately instead of the usual departmental investigation normal for lower ranks.' This kind of tip off could only have come from the intelligence service itself.

He was about to read more when there was a quiet knock at the door. James, The Butler of many years standing, was there with a letter.

It ordered him to be at his desk at 10 a.m.

*Dear C of S,*

*Could you please be present at your office at the Admiralty by 10 am prompt when we would most keen to discuss recent events with you.*

*Yours sincerely,*

*Charles Carradine*

*Cabinet Secretary*

They had not taken long to locate him or to organize his investigation. He cursed the fact of his weakness, as he did love his job, and the career he'd built up deliberately and assiduously. Why couldn't he have just visited prostitutes as he knew some of his colleagues did. After all, there was an approved list who had been vetted by security and were paid a retainer by them to only see high ranks discreetly. This was acceptable as there was no risk of a set up and complete anonymity on your part. Instead he had succumbed very easily to Bucky's charms. He was devastated that she seems to have led him along the whole time. And for grubby newspaper money too. He truly thought she'd loved him.

Thank God there had been no security implications. Of that he was certain. It was purely a romantic affair, or more accurately, a sexual adventure. She had not shown any interest whatsoever in his work, she was only interested in when he was free to see her. Thinking about her seriously for the first time, he had thought she was of limited intelligence and only cared for clothes and probably men in general, though she'd been very skillful in making him think it was one particular man she cared for. Or had she really fallen for him as he'd fallen for her on that first meeting only three months ago? He left the letter on the desk and slowly put his coat on.

----------

The very same morning Jonathan Jones was sitting at his desk in his London office in The Shell Centre, a prominent and famous building on the South Bank of the River Thames. This is the building that is illuminated on New Year's Eve to mark the coming of the new year in the UK. He alternated between this and his main office in The Hague quite often.

The view of central London was stunning from his top floor corner office as he sat there drinking coffee, and ostensibly going through the papers as usual, to see if any issues arose regarding the company. It was in fact his one indulgence and concession to normal life. In his position, he could easily have delegated someone else to do this. His first startled glance at one of the many similar photos caused him to cry out in surprise. This woman coming out of a hotel with the Chief of Staff was Maria, clearly older but it was her, the jet-black hair, that face and those eyes. They instantly reminded him of the young Maria, even in a newspaper photograph. It brought back to him in an amazingly vivid and terrifyingly strong image the hurt, the pain of their loss. There she was, the only link he had with the disappearance and murder of Catrin and her mother, a link he had been trying to locate on and off for years. Now, suddenly she was in everyone's living room that very morning. How would he find her?

The story in most of the papers was that she was hiding at a safe house with the Sun reporters as she related her story to them for serialization in the coming weeks. One thing he could do was to go to the hotel to see what they knew of her.

He cancelled all his appointments and put everything on hold, much to the surprise of his secretary. He was quickly out of his cab at the hotel only to be utterly amazed at the pack of newshounds baying outside. He'd only been used to intellectual and serious conversations with the business and industrial correspondents. They all knew him, but he would not be recognized by any of these scandal mongers. It was very easy indeed to pick up information, you just collected some of the photocopied sheets which the hotel manager was distributing nonchalantly. It was his brainwave to cope with the mad rush.

Jonathan quickly saw that it was a list of the hotel guest register for the last ten weeks and with one name highlighted nine times. They'd signed themselves in as Mr. and Mrs. A. Soames and were booked in for one night every time, though the newspapers had clearly said they used it only for an afternoon dalliance. Being a fanatic for detail he read through the whole list. And he noticed another name M. Echevarria. This was the name Maria had used in Trelew! She had booked in for one night only, on her own between the seventh and eighth assignations with the Chief of Staff. Why had she done that? It did not make sense unless she was meeting someone else here as well. He was on to something the reporters did not know about. To them she was only known as Lady Buck.

The journalists had by now all disappeared having been satisfied by the manager, but he went to the desk and asked if he could have more details of the bookings. The receptionist was very helpful and gave him printouts of the accounts for the Soames' room. The Soames bills showed some drinks ordered and the room rate itself. But what stood out was the one phone call, an international call, that had been  made on the date of the eighth assignation.  He jotted down the number and excitedly checked phone codes to see that it was a call to Argentina.

He then asked for the Maria Echevarria bill for her one-night stay which the receptionist duly gave him without thinking why. She was clearly enjoying the excitement which the affair had brought to her normally quiet work. Maria Echevarria too had made one phone call and to the same number. So Maria Echeverria was Lady Buck.

But why did she rent a room at the hotel on that date? To make a phone call? He could understand it if she had come on her own before the first assignation, to check out if the hotel was suitable for their meetings. But why come at that time, just before the second phone call to the same number when they'd been together. Popping into a telephone booth at the hotel it did not take him long to find out the call had been to Buenos Aires itself. There was a Shell regional meeting there in ten days' time. Though not due to attend, he could find some reason to go. Better to turn up on the doorstep than try and phone the number himself he thought.

# Chapter 12

Lady Maria Buck swept back her long black hair and her eyes twinkled with the pleasure of her task.

Maria always liked the sex, even with the older men, which of course, made her job easier. As in all other things she liked to be on top, in total control of the situation. The soluble viagra which she added to his whisky and soda, had done its work once again. Richard was only slightly overweight and his greying sideburns added to his air of authority and control. He was a proud and upstanding man and today again he had indeed been proud and upstanding to the end and she'd been able to exhaust him so effectively, he was now snoring loudly. Like all confident and successful men, he had never doubted his prowess down below and though he had never been so big with his wife, even in the rampant early days of their marriage, he had not suspected outside assistance. If he had to explain it to himself, he would put it down to the excitement of the illicit nature of the affair and even possibly the sense of danger. But he did not care to explain. He was totally smitten since the beautiful Maria had come into his life. He loved her sexual teasing and her adoring looks, coupled with her smooth, lithe body. She had really made him feel young again, when perhaps there had been signs he was beginning to lose some of his vigour.

But this time was different. She had also added a sleeping tablet that should work for six hours or more. She wanted there to be no mistakes. She was only a few minutes later than planned when she left the bed and fetched her handbag. She took out the flat, plastic container and from it she carefully unwrapped the pair of gloves that she had used  previously to find the combination on the lock of his attaché case.  The gloves had been subjected to a double-blind test which had proved their efficacy. Although they looked like an ordinary pair of kitchen gloves, these were very special. She had taken a set of Richard's fingerprints on a previous visit. The gloves were produced with copies of his fingerprints imprinted on the fingers. In the lab tests, prints were taken from these and several other similarly produced gloves, and from all the random sets, Richard had been identified positively. It was essential that after the event nothing should arouse suspicion. Wiping the combination lock clean of all fingerprints, his and hers, would have raised the alarm. This way only his prints would be found on the case as normal.

She put on the gloves carefully and carried his attaché case containing his laptop to the table. It was the one thing he always carried with him at all times. Even in the midst of his mad affair, he was, he believed, totally aware of the security implications and always aware of the importance of its contents.

She opened it swiftly using the correct combination on the attaché case lock that she had discovered previously. She pushed back the bedside cabinet and unplugged the phone cable from its socket. She unrolled the cable from the serial com port of the laptop and plugged it into the phone socket in the wall.

Five hours and 49 minutes later it was all over. She had downloaded the entire contents of his 40MB hard disc. Having carefully put the laptop back in its security attaché case and locked it, she replaced the gloves in her handbag and began casually putting on her makeup. It had been a faultless repeat of her previous practice transmission session a few days ago using her own laptop at almost the same time. She had been alone and the data from her hard disc had been harmless but the process was the same. The big difference this time was the presence of Richard and his laptop.

The hotel had been chosen for its discreet nature and quiet location for an affair of this sort as one could expect. Although these considerations were obviously important, they had not been the main factor. Rather unusually and not normally the thing that would trouble a guest, it was the fact that outside calls could be made direct from a room without going through a switchboard PBX and that it was a high-speed ISDN line that had been the deciding factors.

Richard had slept soundly during the whole process, but he was now stirring, and glancing at his watch he jumped off the bed and dressed quickly and for the first time had to rush, so that his absence from his next appointment would not be questioned. He had previously been scrupulous in his timing and demeanour. Quickly kissing her somewhat unfeelingly for the first time, he left alone. Little did he know that he would shortly to be the disgraced former Chief of Staff of the British Armed Forces.

----------

*The Sun will shine in the morning.*

Lady B had picked up this message from www.argentina.gob.ar - the official website of the Argentinian Government, on her PC in the attic of her Kensington apartment. For obvious reasons, Lady B, society hostess and social climber with the most exquisite taste and fashion, did not want anyone to know she was computer literate or, more importantly, the reason for that expertise.

It was the message that told her the download had been totally successful and also that the final stage of the operation could begin - the exposure of the Chief of Staff by the Sun newspaper. This would be seen to be a purely vindictive act by her to obtain money, but it was actually the opportunity for the Argentinians to remove one of the main hawks from the centre of power. The Chief of Staff had always pressed for a strong defence of The Falklands should they be attacked again. And there would surely be some valuable intel on the hard disc.

The message had also been observed by the British Security Services. Such random, standalone sentences always aroused their curiosity. It was a tried and tested method for secret services to send coded messages to their agents in the field. Such an innocuous sentence may have had great importance to an agent.

It may not have a meaning as such, it may simply be confirming an event or signaling the start of an action. But the British Secret Services always took them as potential cryptic messages to be solved.

So, it was handed over to Sean O' Connell, a Maths teacher at Winchester public school, a former GCHQ whizz kid who had moved on to calmer waters. But it was not his mathematical prowess that was needed here. It was for his experience as a crossword solver; not the ordinary TIMES crossword sort which he could polish off in 10 minutes every day. Rather, at a higher level, he was one of the few people in the country who could solve The Listener puzzle, not once or twice but every week for a whole year to win the coveted gold wristwatch. He was being consulted to give any possible leads but even the Listener puzzle had a context, however convoluted and ingenious. This was a matter of thinking out lots of ideas, the more obscure the better.

Even O'Connell would be challenged to make the connection between the message, the exposure by the Sun newspaper of the Chief of Staff and the establishment of Lady Buck as an Argentinian spy.

----------

At about 8.15 p.m. Buenos Aires time, the screen download message began and Pietro Echevarria sprang up instantly from his chair. This was it. Only three minutes late.

'Brillante,' he said out loud.

He looked at the download speed 3k bits/sec, 4kbits/sec, 4kbit/sec, the correct speed for a 128k modem on a good clean line.

He watched anxiously as the modem light flashed green almost continuously and was optimistic it would be an uncorrupted transmission. It actually took five hours 49 minutes. He now set up his system drive to copy the downloaded hard disc contents from his computer. With the zip backup in his pocket he drove rapidly across the city to Avenue 25 de Mayo, the headquarters of SIDE, The Secretariat of Intelligence. The hard disc contents would be decoded directly next day.

----------

The grand apartment was on La Isla, in Recoleta, an exclusive leafy Parisian style neighbourhood of Buenos Aires.

'Yes. My daughter works in London. I am very proud of her, but she is so busy. She is doing very well, a fashion model. Here's a picture of her from Hello magazine.'

John Littlewood, the Third Secretary, a junior graded rank, had been sent by the Head of Chancery at the British Embassy, which was just around the corner, to find out who Lady Buck had been phoning from London. It turned out it was Lady Buck's own mother. He knew that in some small way he was involved in the security service investigation into the woman who had got the British Chief of Staff onto the front pages of newspapers round the world and ignominiously turfed out of his job. This seemed to be a dead-end inquiry but even a negative result was important thought Littlewood.

----------

A few days later Jonathan rang on the Echevarria family bell at the same exclusive apartment block in Recoleta. He had no idea what he'd find here but this was where Maria had phoned both times. It was the only number she phoned. The door was opened by a grand old lady, tall and elegant with coiffured hair, who was clearly a member of Argentinian high society and was dressed for a social function of some distinction.

When he mentioned Maria's name she beamed and welcomed him in. He was shown to a beautiful carved rosewood armchair in a lovely Micado French style drawing room.

"Maria was a very good friend of mine in Trelew, Patagonia, many years ago," he lied and that was all that was required to start Mrs. Echevarria off on an oft related story of pride in her beautiful daughter and her achievements. How she had done well at University and had then gone to England and become a fashion model. Jonathan was shown the usual magazine photographs. Maria had indeed become much more refined and sophisticated compared to the tartish look of her Trelew days. She was still as stunning and attractive.

'I go on and on don't I,' she said in her heavily accented English. 'But I'm so proud of my daughter, not like my son, that good for nothing. He has warned me about speaking to journalists, you are a journalist, aren't you? But I don't care, I have nothing to hide.'

She had assumed he was a journalist and obviously was not her first visitor recently.

'You have a son then. What does he do?'

'Oh. I don't know, he lives in San Telmo barrio, but I hardly ever see him. When he does come home, he sleeps all day and plays games on his computer all night, the *boludo*. He'll never grow up.'

"'It's good that Maria keeps in contact then.'

'Oh! She's far too busy to write, but I don't expect her to.'

'But she phones you though.'

A slight hint of sadness came into her voice as she said again, 'No. She's far too busy.'

Strange. This was clearly the address given on the International Directory Inquiries CD ROM when he had typed in the phone number of the two calls Maria had made from the Corinthia Hotel.

'Can you remember when your son was here last?'

'He was here last week and the week before but only for one day each time.'

'Do you remember the exact days?'

'Let me think' ... as she reached for her social diary. 'Oh yes. it was a Tuesday each time. That's my Bridge day at the Club de Bridge el Recoleta and he was here each time when I came in at about ten o' clock. Tues 17th and 24th.'

'Do you mind if I look at your son's computer?'

She looked puzzled at this sudden, strange request but shrugged her shoulders and said, 'Alright, I'll show you up to his room.'

Unlike previous Shell No. 1's Jonathan Jones knew a lot about computers from his many training days. He could see that this bedroom contained a state of the art set up, way beyond the needs of a computer game.

# Chapter 13

Her photographs of the laptop case obtained after her first tryst with Richard Cobbold had established the case to be a Phoenix high security case. The combination lock was a 3 number type of the highest specifications, with a beautifully made working mechanism. There was no way even an expert lock picker could open it by the traditional method of listening to the clicking in of a correct number into place. Even using a stethoscope, one could not pick such a lock.

Basically, therefore one needs to try out every combination in turn or know the combination. Mathematically with a 3-digit number there are 1000 different possible combinations.

Taking 10 seconds for each attempt it would take 2hr 46 minutes to go through all the combinations, an undesirable scenario. It was thought better to try out specific combinations based on some personal knowledge about him. One would have to guess the combination but from some likely possibilities. He would not have it written down anywhere so it would be a 3-figure combination you would remember for some special reason. With a lower level of security it could have been something simple like his birthday, his wife's birthday, dates of birth of anyone in his family, or any other close relation or three times his age and so on. But for this it would have to be something a bit more unguessable? Nevertheless, she was given the list of possible numbers based on their knowledge of him to try out.

He almost always went to sleep after the main action so this allowed her the time to try out the combinations. From experience she had about 15 minutes each time.

She started off with all the obvious combinations in the unlikely event of the security people not having been through this seriously enough. Then she graduated to more complicated combinations and each time she patiently tried them out using the special fingerprint gloves. This was the only method of finding the combination that was considered as it was thought essential that neither he nor his bosses should have any idea that his case had been touched.

On the seventh session she struck lucky and the case opened. It turned out to be the three numbers on the number plate of the car he had owned as a student at Balliol College, Oxford. They had found a photo of him on the internet standing in front of the car in a copy of Floreat Domus, the college magazine of those days. She only felt relief that this tiresome exercise was at last over whereas in Buenos Aires there was great elation as they were now ready for the climax of the sting. She had identified the laptop and specs so it only needed one practice download session on an identical laptop and then the final once and for all download on his own laptop now that the case could be opened and she had access to it.

If this had not been successfully done then the whole mission would have to be rethought or aborted.

# Chapter 14

Jonathan Jones, Shell's new CEO put the 17-page executive summary to one side. In the past he would have read the entire report of 230 pages but now he had managed to conquer his micromanagement. He was content with reading the summary but had also added on an impromptu chat with one of the report's main authors.

Shell was one of the world's leading companies in producing detailed scenarios about the future of oil, then the future of energy and finally, becoming holistic in the light of global warming, merely the future.

But this particular report, hard copy only with an electronic original on a memory stick locked in Jonathan's own safe, was even more strategic and focused. It looked specifically at Saudi Arabia and its role in the planet's future. Also, it did not look at specific oil or energy aspects alone, it was much more political, looking at the stability and governance of the Kingdom. Needless to say it was also highly confidential and had only five hard copies and a signed reading list of ten people, the report authors, the CEO and Chairman of Shell and a chosen few from the Shell Board.

Unofficially, it was accessible through various means to the head of the Dutch sector services.

He was sitting back in a plush leather armchair in his personal office. Opposite him was the report's lead author, an experienced and highly respected analyst who had written several books about global geopolitics.

'So Jim, I've read the executive summary and I must say I'm still none the wiser. You seem to be hedging your bets yet again.'

He was quite blunt in his appraisal of this report which had taken 18 months of hard work and research from half a dozen leading analysts and consultants.

'Well, it is in the nature of these things that predictions are avoided and we are totally evidence based in our conclusions.'

'OK. Fine. But now give me what we could call the big, big picture going back to the very beginning, the sort of thing that's too nebulous to include in a report of this sort. For the future of our company and the West in general, we need to know what is going to happen there.'

'Well it is a highly sophisticated dictatorship by one family and has been for almost a hundred years. A monarchy ruthless and self-confident, indeed arrogant and it uses its power to maintain itself at all costs.

There are seven thousand Princes as members of the Royal family, but the two hundred descendants of the King himself have the most power. All the government ministries and the thirteen regional governorships are headed by them. The latter must not be underestimated in importance. It's a centralised state but control of the entire country relies a lot on these regional governors and how effective they are.'

Jonathan held his hand up to intervene.

'So it's a modern bureaucracy running a feudal system. What about the religious aspect? To the outside world this seems to be bizarre as the country is technologically advancing at quite a pace.'

'Well the country is run politically by the Saudi king and his family but in reality there is another aspect.

'And that of course is religion. The Ulama, the religious rulers, called the Council of Religious Scholars are composed of 21 members who advise the king on religion. 'They are scholars, learned men, whose role is to guard, interpret and propagate Sunni Islam. He meets those members living in the capital, Riyadh, once a week.

In a wider sense, the Ulama consists of about 7-10,000 people who make up all the Ulama families.

'The Ulama and the monarchy have a past going back for three hundred years to support each other politically and in terms of religion. The monarchy is in charge of politics and the Ulama are in charge of religion. This is why Wahhabism, the most conservative branch of Islam is dominant and others are forbidden.'

'So who has the ultimate power?' asked Jonathan incisively.

'Theoretically the Ulama, as they issue a fatwa to approve the appointment of a new king based on whether they believe he will give absolute obedience to Islamic law. It is upon this that his absolute power rests.'

'But in practice?' he interrupted again.

'Historically it has varied, depending on how secure the Royal family believe their position to be. But they have rarely seriously clashed. For example, the Ulama has issued fatwas saying demonstrations are against

Sharia law and petitions and other such protest are banned. Similarly, the monarchy fully supports the religious authorities in ensuring Wahhabism is the only Islamic tradition. This ideology promotes hatred of all unbelievers, Jews and Christians, and disparages Sufi and Shia Islam. This is particularly the case in education where all boys attend madrasas, which are essentially religious schools, the syllabus being reading, learning verses and being instructed in the Quran. Even at university level, two thirds of students study Islamic education degrees and extensive Islamic religious studies are compulsory for all students, even those studying science and engineering.

'The constitution of Saudi Arabia is literally the Holy Quran and the Sunna – the traditions of the prophet Muhammad. This is the key to the power of the Ulama. It means Sharia law is the law of the land and the rule of law, as they see it, is ultimate obedience to the Quran. The Ulama issues fatwas, the Imans, - preachers, communicate them and the Committee for the Promotion of Virtue and the Prevention of Vice carry them out.'

'What does that latter body actually do?'

'Putting it crudely, they organise the executions, beheadings, amputations and so on that form part of the punishment for illegal acts and offences. You can see it in action after Friday prayers in Deera, sometimes called Justice Square and most often called Chop Chop square, in Riyadh.'

'Nice! So how does it all survive?'

'Oil dear boy, oil. Discovered first by American companies in 1938, Saudi Arabia still has about a quarter of all known oil reserves in the world. Money. From oil exports.

'And arms sales. We buy the oil, produce many things, among them military arms and sell those back to the Saudis so they can defend themselves and maintain and increasingly extend their power. Arms sales topped 8 billion dollars in 2017 with 50% from the US.

'Behind all this is the corruption. Corruption requires two parties, those paying and those asking for payment. Both are required for it to function. Some of it is known; the British company BAE paid over £6 billion in bribes to secure a contract worth £43 billion. Most is under the surface. It is a way of life and is not regarded as immoral. It is the normal way of doing things and underpins and supports the government in power.

'We, that is Shell and other western companies and governments are fully complicit in this system. We depend on it for our profits, maybe for our survival.'

'Is it sustainable? At least until the oil runs out?' Jonathan asked.

Jim began another mini lecture.

'Let's look at population.

'The population is 32 million but there is a large contingent of foreigners, 2 million from other Arab countries, 5 million from India, Pakistan and Bangladesh and 1.5 million south East Asian, such as Indonesians and Nepalese and so on.

'So there are significant groups who would support change, if it was the right sort.

'And despite Western myths to the contrary, they have between 500,000 and 1.5 million Syrian refugees.'

'How does that come about? First I've heard of that.'

'Saudi Arabia and some other countries are not signatories to the Convention relating to the Status of Refugees, so the UNHCR does not count them in the total of refugees.

'Nonetheless the society is racist in the extreme.

'Top of the pile, the Royal Family, the richest in the world, then Saudi Arabs, then the other Arabs, then the 100,00 Westerners, then the Indians followed by the South East Asians. This racist treatment extends to citizenship, rights, jobs, benefits and wages.'

'So, are you now finally ready to tell me what you think will happen?' Jonathan asked hopefully.

'Do you want my honest opinion?'

'Of course.'

'The monarchy has enemies. Osama bin Laden was from a rich Saudi family and

most of al Qaida is Saudi inspired. Fifteen of the nineteen of the 911 terrorists were Saudi citizens, yet America and the UK invaded Iraq and Afghanistan in its war on terror. Are the Saudis for or against terrorism? They have taken some measures against some of its own citizens in Saudi but Wahhabism flourishes and is the main ideology inspiring the Fundamentalists. It is the fundamentalist Islamic tradition.

'It has other enemies too. The Shia minority in the east of the country and all of Shia Islam globally. Liberal critics within, some open and many underground and still, don't forget, tribalism remains strong.'

'So what direction are they really taking? What are they trying to do?'

'They are still enjoying themselves in the rest of the world. Horse racing and so on and laundering some of their money with property and companies in some of the world's capitals. You can see this in Belgravia and Mayfair and Knightsbridge in London. Add to this some totally hypocritical behaviour as regards morals and religion.

'Seriously, within the country they are militarily very strong and are modernising and spending their wealth on education and so on but still with the main aim of maintaining their power.'

'So, with all this going on, are they secure?'

'Who is "they?" "They" ultimately is the King and his three sons. If they were taken out there would be chaos.'

'What could result. What do you really think?'

'There could be only two outcomes.

'The liberals who generally support the monarchy because there is modernisation and some liberalisation going on, could come to power in some sort of new democratic structure.'

'Is that likely? Are they genuinely liberalising? Women driving and so on are small measures.'

Jim laughed.

'Even that is a joke. It is now legal for them to drive, but if you read the small print it is only allowed if the male guardian of each woman agrees. Sharia law rules ok! The grossest example of this is the fact that the evidence of one man in court is still equivalent to that of two women.'

'So, liberals taking over is unlikely. I can guess the other outcome.'

'Yes, the religious fanatics would take over. As they have done in their main enemy's country - Iran.'

'Is that a good example?'

'Well, yes, in some ways. They, Iran, have a ł sophisticated structure and strong systems to run the country in a modern way whilst maintaining the power of the religious state.

'The Saudi Royal Family in power do have the military on their side. That's the key I guess in any situation.

'So the Ulama could come to power if they looked at how the Iranian Mullahs did it.'

'Yes, I do believe they could.'

'So where do we go from here?'

'You mean the West or Shell?'

'Both.'

'Well the western governments will maintain their support of Saudi Arabia but Shell, as a multinational, can think of a plan B if there is a big change coming.'

----------

As one of the authors of the top-secret Shell report on Saudi Arabia, Matias Fernandez from Argentina had full access to one of the few hard copies in circulation. But even he had to sign out for it in the highly secure archive in the basement of Shell HQ in Haagse Hout, The Hague.

He was a leading analyst for Shell and had worked for the company ever since he joined the graduate scheme after leaving college. He had attended Imperial College, London and had a degree in Chemical Engineering followed by a Ph.D. on a thesis entitled "New structures for deep sea extraction of oil." His thesis had not just been a research project, it had proved lucrative for the company who had taken out a patent on his novel automatic oil tap.

Like all Shell highfliers, his induction, lasting many years of training is designed to make him loyal to Shell more than to any national sentiment he may have. They are a multinational company responsible to their shareholders alone and reward their ruling elite very well.

But it doesn't always work. In his case, his parents back in Buenos Aires had instilled in him a strong belief in his nation. He had rejected this for many years but now was adopting it once more. As the world became a more precarious place, a love for one's country was something to be proud of.

This was why he spent an hour and a half at a neighbourhood photocopying shop personally photocopying the 230 pages of the report with the benign title, "Saudi Arabia: The Future." He later posted it from a local post office to a Post Box address in Olivos, a suburb of Buenos Aires where it was picked up two weeks later by someone who worked in the Ministry of Foreign Affairs and Worship.

# Chapter 15

Jan Willem and Hendrik sat down after breakfast around the pool. Croissants and pain au chocolat were the normal breakfast for Dutch expats in the area but it was the full English for them.

'We're both on statins so it's ok isn't it?' laughed Jan Willem.

'Listen, I've got some interesting and exciting news for you,' said Hendrik.

'Aha! That must mean something from Jacob, our man in The Hague, replied Jan Willem.

Jacob van Marken was the present chairman of Shell. He had been mentored and supported by Jan Willem and Hendrik throughout his Shell career. And his family name was also in the Blue book of Dutch gentry, "Nederland's Patriciaat."

'Yes. You're right of course.' And Hendrik returned to his breakfast

'Don't keep up the tension. Just tell me.'

'He's confirmed we've discovered oil in the Southern Ocean. And it's a big find, a very big find.'

We, meant Shell of course.

'Well that's good news but has he told us more than we knew before about its location?'

'Yes. But that is the problem. It's offshore below the

60° latitude boundary to the Antarctic Treaty. So it's subject to the treaty. The good thing is, it's only just inside the area covered by the treaty, so if it were developed, the oil could be taken to somewhere like The Falklands instead of to a base in the Antarctic peninsula.

'Yes, it would need to be  in The Falklands. In Antarctica you have average annual wind speeds of 60 km/hr going as high as 250 to 300 km/hr sometimes. I've looked into this. And the temperatures on the Mcmurdo research station, in one of the mildest locations in The Antarctic, vary between 0 and -25C. So, it's almost impossible to work in those conditions.'

'Coming back to The Antarctic treaty. That came into force in 1998 didn't it?'

'Yes, a moratorium on all oil drilling and exploration for  50 years, so 'till 2048 and then it would all be up for grabs again.'

'But it's not that simple. The UN convention on the Law of the Sea in 1982 allowed countries to extend their continental shelves from 200 to 350 nautical miles. Technically that include the continental shelf of the dependencies of countries too and The Falklands is a dependency of Britain.'

Hendrik really knew his stuff. He had been retired for over ten years but his detailed knowledge of international politics and law was second to none. Except Jan Willem of course.

'Yes. I know that too, but the exact location of the discovery makes it outside that area too.'

'Damn. So back to the moratorium. It's highly unlikely that the signatories would lift it. Besides 2048. That's way too late for us. We'll somehow have to break the treaty.

'The UK and The Netherlands have both signed the treaty and the current left-wing UK government with its so-called ethical foreign policy would not countenance breaking the treaty.

'So we need our own government to break it and support Shell. It is our company after all 60/40.'

'Politically impossible,' said Hendrik. He was always the more cautious but also the more creative.

'But maybe we can overcome it another way?' was his cryptic final remark before they refilled their Douwe Egberts filter coffee.

----------

Later that afternoon, Hendrik was on the phone to his source, Jacob van Marken, the Shell chairman of the board.

'We were really interested in the new find. I'd like to hear more about it, the technical side. Can you send one of your exploration whiz kids down to see us?

That Friday night Hans van der Linden landed at Nice airport from Amsterdam and was soon looking at the menu at La Coupole. Jan Willem and Hendrik and their wives were there. He was also looking at Jan Willem's twenty-year-old daughter, Ria, there for a break from her university studies. She was as beautiful as her mother had been.

Hans was Shell to the core. Tall and fit, with long blond hair and wearing the uniform - red chinos, an open neck shirt and a very long honey coloured Burberry coat. A high-flying graduate trainee and top hockey player, he had been in the Dutch senior hockey squad whilst at Leiden university and been president of the Minerva society, the Dutch equivalent of the Bullingdon drinking society at Oxford University. But he was also very intelligent.

Whilst the women got all the latest gossip sorted, the men probed Hans about all the latest developments in exploration techniques. It turned out that two of the seven main methods of undersea drilling were novel Shell innovations. One involved a floating platform drilling at an angle to the vertical so that the area being investigated was displaced from the location of the floating drilling platform. The horizontal displacement achieved was impressive and was likely to be improved upon.

The other innovation was the Eleuthera technique. This is a production platform on the sea bed itself, once the discovery had been verified, with pipelines running from it along the seabed to deliver the oil at a distant terminal, either a large production rig at sea, or even better, a shore based facility.

Hendrik got very excited at hearing about these and his mind was whirring but he kept his emotions and his thoughts to himself. He would share them with Jan Willem later.

Hans was surprised that after the Friday night meal at the Michelin starred restaurant the two men did not quiz him much more or even show much interest in him at all. On the Saturday he spent the day swimming and sunbathing with lovely daughter Ria around the pool at the villa. They spent the night together too and Sunday morning was a lazy one in bed for both of them before he left in the early afternoon for his flight back to

Amsterdam and he was ready for work on Monday morning.

He had enjoyed his break in more ways than one and knew that this had been a career enhancing experience. He was learning more and more how things worked in this most modern and traditional multinational company.

----------

Hendrik's leisure reading around the pool was not the latest thriller. He was reading the top secret Shell report on Saudi Arabia, that they had been sent by the Shell chairman, their man in The Hague. Hendrik would be one of the very few to read it all – all 230 pages of it. He had also noted that one of the report authors was an Argentinian, Matias Fernandez, who worked as an intelligence analyst for Shell.

He wondered if a private meeting with him could lead to something. This could not be something that he would arrange through Shell though. He found his contact details easily enough on the Shell webpages and had simply phoned him up. He wanted to sound him out about how Argentina looked at the oil business and future prospects.

He took a short visit up to The Hague and went entirely off the beaten track. He did not meet any of his previous colleagues and many acquaintances in the traditional waterholes and private clubs. He was sitting in the open air under a beach umbrella in one of the temporary restaurants set up on the beach at Scheveningen, the resort and old fishing village on the coast from The Hague. Each restaurant had a special corny theme. This one was an Inca camp with many Machu Picchu type statues set out tastelessly between the tables. He and Matias, his Argentinian friend for the night, had ordered and were eating a large pot of mussels and chips accompanied by a bottle of cheap, white wine. Not his normal standard but he found it quite a change,

Matias had wondered what this strange unexpected invitation was all about, but he had accepted without hesitation as his curiosity was well and truly aroused.

Hendrik had introduced himself as a writer who specialises in South American economics, a very obscure and niche subject in The Netherlands. Matias was not convinced and wondered if he was an investigative journalist who wanted to know more about Shell or was even from the secret services. If the latter, he would have to be on his guard as he himself had sent several secret Shell documents to his friends back in Buenos Aires. He was a spy himself.

'So, tell me about the Argentinian oil industry?' asked Hendrik

'It's a joke,' replied Matias. 'The major oil company Yacimientos Petroliferos Fiscales (YPF), is government owned and I think it's the only oil company in the world that has made a loss - 5 billion dollars, one tenth of the national debt. Badly managed and riddled with corruption, it is typical of Argentinian companies. It even wasted money on nuclear power leaving oil and gas reserves untapped.'

'How do you feel about that as an Argentinian?'

'Well it doesn't make me very happy, obviously. In fact, I am very annoyed. My country has so much potential,' replied Matias, who was now becoming quite animated.

'What if I was to tell you that is has more than potential. It actually has a lot of oil on its territory.'

'What do you mean?'

'Well the oil that your company has discovered is Argentinian.'

Matias looked puzzled. No, bemused. He was intelligent but this man was speaking in riddles.

'Don't you know about the oil discoveries?' he asked Matias.

Hendrik knew the answer to this. The Antarctic oil discovery was so sensitive it would be top secret within the company. He had read the annual exploration report which should contain details of all explorations and finds and there was no mention of The Antarctic one.

And before he could answer Hendrik said, 'They have discovered oil in The Antarctic. And the area it is in is claimed by the UK, Argentina and Chile. There are three overlapping claims.'

'So Argentina has a legitimate and equal claim on this oil?'

'Yes, I guess that is true.'

'Why are you telling me this?'

He must be a secret agent, a member of the Dutch state intelligence service, or maybe another one altogether, thought Matias.

Hendrik looked him straight in the eyes but remained silent. The bait had been cast.

# Chapter 16

'The Prime Minister will see you now, Sir.'

The head of British Intelligence, the new organization created from the merger of MI5 and MI6, commonly known as "The Boss", sat down quietly and took out his file on the case. He knew this PM was very much hands-on and would need to know all the details of the investigation up to date rather than a bald summary. He was relieved to find they were alone as he would have had to remind the PM as he had done once already that releasing confidential information to spin doctors to put the government in a good light was just not on.

'Well PM, we do not believe that, thank goodness, there are any security implications although it is of course deeply embarrassing to your government that this has happened.

'He has been a fool of the first order but he hasn't been negligent. There is no reason to believe there has been a breach of security. Unlike the Profumo affair in the past, it seems to have been a purely sexual affair lasting nine sessions. In his file he looked at the nine dates at the hotel in the name of Soames, the false name under which Cobbold had signed in at the hotel. These were the only nine recorded instances of them meeting.

He emphatically denies passing on any information or even discussing anything at all connected with his work. It seems that they were too busy physically involved to do anything else. They never had dinner together or anything and to be honest, she seems to be a bit dumb but very attentive, a carpetbagger as you can see from the way she exposed him to the newspapers. She does not seem to have deliberately targeted him but after she was introduced to him, she seems to have been relentless in her pursuit. Her history is one of repeated cuckolding to obtain money. There's nothing more to it than that.'

'But all this is opinion. What techniques and investigations have you fellows made to check all this out?'

'Well,' he quickly interjected.

'We gave him a full investigation under the truth drug sodium amytal, and he steadfastly stuck to his original story. Then we gave him a full medical and this revealed he'd been taking Viagra, the old codger. But we naturally did not embarrass him by confronting him with this. He is after all, a founder member of the Special Forces Club. He's also been taking sleeping tablets but again there is nothing especially alarming about that. He has done an excellent job and has been a top-notch professional admired by all his peers. He's just been an utter bloody fool. This sex thing again. Thank goodness it was just that though. She's Argentinian and he's got an awful lot of information in his head and on his laptop. The IT security check on his laptop referred particularly to manual protection. He kept his laptop with him at all times and in a combination lock attaché case. Only his prints on it. It had definitely not been tampered with. The only

101

suspicious thing was the telephone call from that hotel room made on the last session. That set alarm bells ringing; a call to Buenos Aires but it turned out to be her talking to her mother.'

The PM thanked him and walked him to the door. He was relieved to hear all this from the safe pair of hands at the head of national security. Although always a bit wary of these old school tie spoofs, he had no real grounds to question the professionalism of this investigation.

----------

Pietro Echevarria, Maria's brother, arrived at SIDES HQ in the imposing ten storey main building located in Ave. 25 de Mayo 11, just across the road from the Casa Rosada, the presidential palace, with a secret underground passage linking them.

When he entered the Secretary of Intelligence's own office on the fifth floor, there was a mad flurry of excitement and the six men present spontaneously cheered. Although very young looking, they were the leading English-speaking analysts of the Argentinian Secret Service, SIDE and only they and the Secretary and Undersecretary of Intelligence, known as "Señor Cinco" (Mr. Five) and "Señor Ocho" (Mr. Eight), knew of the imminent arrival of this top-secret package. Their offices were on the fifth and eighth floors respectively.

Six copies of the hard disc contents were immediately made and two of the men set about to make two separate translations. The other four began reading the original. Luckily, security was weak. Because the secure attaché case in which Cobbold kept his laptop had a secret combination, the actual contents themselves were not encoded. Later, the Brits totally encoded all such content.

The first reading would be done quickly as they were not immediately concerned with the details, although later there would be detailed analysis of the whole text. now they just wanted to know if there was a big thing there of use to them.

The point was that in the vast amount of information most of it would of necessity be irrelevant to one country such as Argentina as it contained minutes of all meetings attended by Cobbold since he had reached his present position and the many memos which he had sent.

Much of it could be very useful directly to third parties later or indirectly in Argentinian dealings with those third parties but what was really of interest to them was the UK's position on Las Malvinas, the only point of direct conflict between the two countries.

Tied in with all this and known even at the time of the Falklands War was the possible mineral discoveries around the islands, mainly oil, and the strategic importance of ownership of the Falklands if any serious finds would be made in Antarctica. Lord Shackleton's two reports on the possible implications of this were important landmarks for successive UK governments even if the media had not grasped their full implications and the public were not aware of them at all.

After eleven hours of concentrated reading of the hard disc contents without a break, one of the Argentinian analysts made a decisive find. It concerned a meeting held between the UK Prime Minister's inner cabinet and the chief of staff and head of British Intelligence.

Minute 37 a
*The head of British Intelligence reported a finding from their operative working within Shell Exploration in the South Atlantic as reporting a discovery of major oil reserves in the Antarctic. Here were also coordinates showing the location of the oil.*

The analysts were amazed that the British government security forces had an agent within a British company. The UK government was quite willing to let the public perceive of Shell as a British company, but the reality was it was Dutch owned and the Dutch government would hear of any important strategic news rather than the UK government. Hence the agent. Shell itself had pointedly decided not to reveal this find as it was in the Antarctic Treaty Area.

Minute 37 b *The PM asked why the find had not been announced by Shell.*
Minute 37 c *The Foreign Secretary explained briefly the terms of the Antarctic Treaty banning development of oil and the international implications of breaking it. The UK would become an international pariah.*

The analysts were clearly highly politically aware and immediately consulted their maps and true to their instincts it did turn out that the location of the oil find was within the Antarctic Treaty area and was disputed territory between the UK and Argentina.

37 d *The Chief of Staff said that if Middle East oil would be unforthcoming, a situation which would be almost certain sooner or later, because of deep seated political instability in the region, then this Antarctic oil would be of strategic importance   not only to the UK but to the whole of the Western Alliance.  Its importance would be such that a breach of the treaty could be considered. Besides it was actually closer to Europe in miles than the  large tanker oil route from the Middle East round the Cape to Europe is now.*

37 e *The Energy Secretary pointed out that in order for this oil find to become useful it would have to be developed and that would take years. The treaty would have to be breached many years before the world community would accept the political necessity for it.*

*He also added that because of difficult working conditions in the Antarctic the oil would have to be brought ashore in the Falklands where a large Sullom Voe type terminal would have to be built. Also, as the nearest mainland is Argentina a base there would be essential for successful development of the oil fields.*

They all looked at each other in amazement when they reached this point.

37 f *The PM*

*The PM declared that this was totally unacceptable and that there was no possibility that the government could sanction the development of this oil.  We cannot break this treaty and betray our international obligations.*

*There was strong agreement all-round the table.*


'Wow! That is quite a find,' shouted Senor Cinco excitedly.

'Keep reading you guys. Let's see if there is even more stuff like that!'

It quickly became apparent that there had been a series of important meetings between the Chief of Staff and the PM inner Cabinet on this very topic.

After the Falklands War after a period of complete lack of contact, there had been soundings and even attempted negotiations between the UK and Argentinian governments. But as the principle that the wishes of the islanders would be paramount had been adhered to by successive British governments, no progress whatsoever had been made as the islanders had steadfastly refused to countenance any change in their circumstances. Greater links with the Argentinian mainland would be anathema to them and had been firmly rejected.

This new Labour government seemed to be trapped in the duty of supporting this, even militarily if necessary. After the war, even the more jingoistic of Brits recognized that sending a task force again at vast expense to the British taxpayer to save 1800 islanders was out of the question so this had led to the building of the long runway at Port Stanley to allow fighter aircraft to be stationed there and be the main defence of the islands. This in itself was a costly exercise and logistically challenging.

The bombshell that hit the analysts was the conclusion of all these meetings. There it was. In black and white.

*After a thorough and comprehensive analysis of the situation, we have reluctantly agreed that should the*

*Falkland Islands be invaded again by the Argentinians, no military action will be taken to defend or recapture the islands.*

# Chapter 17

'Henrietta is that you? Are you there?' squealed the Princess on the phone. She held the phone in one hand and a half full glass of wine in the other and she swayed about in mid conversation. It was early evening.

'Darling, I'm not feeling great. The bad spell has come around again. Come around and join me. I'm getting sozzled here. At home, on my own.'

She was in her mews flat in Knightsbridge. This is where she now lived when in London. Worth millions but still slumming it for her after her marriage had collapsed.

Henrietta turned up half an hour later already a bit the worse for wear herself as she had been in the pub with some friends since the end of work and hadn't eaten anything.

She saw straight away that the Princess was in a bad way. She looked horrific, her hair dishevelled, yesterday's make up splodged all over her face and the overdone mascara seemed to suggest two black eyes from a fight. She was in her night dress. It didn't look as if she had got dressed all day and the remains of a couple of bottles of wine littered the floor. The whole place was a tip from top to bottom. Once a week a cleaner would restore it to some semblance of order, knowing it would be a chore that never ended.

They both met up like this about once a month. And invariably the Princess was in a state. It was a strange friendship. They didn't mix in the same circles at all. Henrietta was a social worker while the Princess lived in deb land. Henrietta was of diminutive height, wore plus size clothing and she was plain, quite unlike the Princess. She was beautiful; she still had a lovely figure and when made up to go out, looked stunning.

But they had been friends from school, very close friends and shared secrets of a profound and disturbing nature.

Henrietta went and hugged her.

'Let's sit down together.' And they both sobbed away.

The Princess literally kicked away the cat and they both slumped on the sofa. The cat scampered away without a whimper, quite used to this behaviour.

These sessions were a mixture of confessional and therapy. Although their darkest secret had been shared long ago, every meeting seemed to reveal additional details that were shocking in turn. Always getting pissed together in lonely and desperate situations, they had both revealed the abuse they had suffered as young girls. Henrietta had been abused by her uncle and the Princess by her father.

Neither had revealed these appalling acts to anyone except each other. It was a very strange bond between them, their lives and their behaviour, although no-one would guess it. They were both very strong and powerful women in public. Their reputations as promiscuous and easy going when it came to men had to be seen in this light. They were exerting their own power and decisions about how they behaved.

Behind the scenes in the secrecy of their own homes and only with each other, they were vulnerable and emotionally exposed. But they always managed to put on a remarkable front when in public.

'I'm a total failure,' groaned the Princess. 'How can I ever get over this?'

'Come on you haven't done too badly. In fact, you've done remarkably well. Getting married to a Duke, third in line to the throne, is not something that many girls can even dream of.'

This indeed was the case. Coming from a semi aristocratic background had helped but her meeting and her marriage to the Prince had been the stuff of fairy-tales in the world's newspapers.

'It was not love, it had never been love, although we produced an offspring, the little brat.

'I married for the glamour and prestige and to be famous. He married to satisfy the norms in his family. But they say he prefers men. Though I didn't see it. He just seemed lacking in any physical passion. He had no sex drive.

'It was not going to last. It could never last,' declaimed the Princess. 'It was an experience I wish I'd never had.'

'But you do have a son of your own,' said Henrietta insensitively. This should have been a comfort to her as the Princess was also estranged from her mother for some as yet to be revealed reason.

'He's useless, he's a wimp, he's just a weed,' said the Princess shockingly.

Henrietta knew how the Princess felt about her son but could never figure out quite why she showed so much anger and venom.

'He's just like his father, a complete weakling. So timid, so… so boring.'

Henrietta knew that the prince adored his Nanny who gave him all the attention and love while the princess just socialised. She had probably never bonded with him at all and had no maternal instincts. But she put all the blame for this on her son. She had never physically abused him, a pattern common among those who have been abused themselves. But she had sacked the Nanny, another form of abuse nonetheless.

There was a pause. They didn't refill their glasses. There were several half-drunk bottles lying about and they merely grabbed a bottle each and slugged down a few more mouthfuls.

This was the stage when they always repeated their never to be answered questions regarding how they had been treated?

'How can men behave like that? How can they do such a thing and get away with it. Why didn't we say something? Why could we not say something? Why is it such a secret that cannot be revealed?' shouted the Princess.

'It's shame, shame, shame. We feel guilty ourselves for allowing it,' she continued stridently.

'The fact we have shared it with each other is a big step for us maybe?' said Henrietta quietly.

'I haven't shared everything, even with you,' said the Princess, even though they had both at different times in the past actually gone into horrific details about what had been done to them.

'There are still things gnawing away at me, destroying me,' she said almost in a whisper.

Henrietta looked at her directly and said quietly, 'Go on.'

The Princess now paused and taking a deep breath, began to talk about her father's death. He had died of a heart attack was all Henrietta and the wider world knew.

'One evening, with only him and me there. He was at it. He was doing his thing with me as usual when he suddenly went all blue and fell over. I knew it was something bad. I just ran out and came back hours later.

'The ambulance had been and gone and the family doctor was there with mother.
She had found father lying there when she came back from her crochet class.

'The family doctor, a so-called lifelong friend, had covered it all up, literally and there was no sign of any untoward behaviour. It was simply a sudden coronary by his account.'

Henrietta just listened and stared. It was not hard to imagine how this would scar someone permanently. And destroy their life, bit by bit, one day at a time, but every day, without a break.

'Mother knew. She saw the evidence that night. But yes, mother knew about it all, all along, and just kept quiet. That's why I don't see her anymore. Nobody can understand my behaviour in cutting her off. If only they knew.'

She was shaking and sweating and had begun to shiver.

'I hated him for what he was doing. Pure hate replacing the pure love of an innocent child. But I also hate myself for what I did, I left him to die. I left him there. I, I killed him. Yes, that's what I did.'

There was nothing Henrietta could say or do. She just held her tightly and they both fell back in pure exhaustion and simply slept through the night.

# Chapter 18

The King's personal security personnel, about twenty in number, were hand chosen to be loyal. So it was quite dramatic when all twenty were suddenly replaced during his visit to Egypt. His immediate advisors also insisted on the Egyptian president's own security guards, allocated to the King, be dismissed and replaced by a completely new group. Were these extreme measures brought on by paranoia at a possible attempt to depose the King or were they based on real fears that this could occur? And who would dare to depose him? Reluctantly, he agreed that it could only be his own son, that he had appointed Crown Prince.

He had appointed him because he was strong and decisive unlike his two brothers. But he had expected him to follow his conservative and careful approach to world issues whilst modernising the country.

His Majesty was watching Saudi TV news in his suite on the top two floors at the hotel with a few of his new closest advisors.

'Today Crown Prince Khalid bin Muqrin bin Majid al Saud, acting King in his father's absence, has dismissed his defence minister and appointed himself to take over.'

The Crown Prince was shown making the announcement and saying this would allow for a more decisive approach to the war against the Shia led revolt in the Yemen.

The King, old and frail but still a massive presence stood up and although trembling and somewhat unsteady on his feet, uttered the strongest of Arabic curses and shouted loudly,

'What is he playing at? Who does he think he is?'

His advisors were surprised but impressed at his wrath as it seemed to them all that recently his powers had been waning.

There were ominous looks as he instructed them.

'Make sure that he is not in the welcoming group at the airport when I return home as is traditional. And make sure my first appointment when I get back is with him.'

----------

'Welcome home, Father,' uttered the Crown Prince, and lent forward to kiss him but the old man stepped back decisively.

They were both alone.

'Welcome home indeed. Just because I'm old and a bit slower moving about than I used to be it doesn't mean I don't hear and see what is going on.

'You have the impertinence to make new appointments when I'm away.'

'But honourable father. You appointed me as deputy King in your absence and I was only …'

'I won't do that again; you can be sure.

'And what is going on when I hear that some of our fellow countrymen who disagree with us are disappearing mysteriously in foreign countries.

'Is that your doing?' he snapped.

'I know nothing about it, father.'

'What about cutting up a body inside a Saudi Embassy? You know nothing about that?' he shouted.

'Nothing. Father.'

'None of this is helping our country's image in the world, an image that I have worked on patiently over the years. It can be lost so easily. You need to be wise not just clever. I'm beginning to think you are too headstrong and a fool.

'And what is more, we have vast military strength, but it is not always a good idea to use it. And besides a hundred-million-pound fighter aircraft is not always the best weapon against a Shia militant on the ground, who can get to know the local people.

'We have gone too far. No. You have gone too far.' He paused at this stage and having exhausted himself with his shouts began to whisper,

'But we have to protect our backs as well as what is in front of us. Our strength over the years has been the support of the Ulama, the Scholars of Islam. It is they who keep us in power because the people's ultimate loyalty is to their religion not to their monarch. Don't ever forget that.'

The Crown Prince was actually wisely not saying anything, but he was devastated by the strength of his father's reaction. He really had thought his father was a doddering old fool and that he could get away with things to pursue his own ambitions.

----------

The Kaaba, in Mecca, the birthplace of Muhammad, is the holiest shrine in the religion of Islam. It is the cubical granite building about eleven metres square and 13 metres high in the centre of the courtyard of the Sacred Mosque, Al -Masjid Al -Haram and is believed to have been built by Abraham and his son Ismail. It is in the direction of this shrine that all Muslims wherever they are in in the world must face for prayer. It is normally visited daily by thousands of pilgrims. It is the lifetime aim and expectation for all Muslims to visit the holy shrine and pay homage to the Prophet, the founder of their religion. It is the Hajj. Whole Jumbo jet loads of Indonesians and other distant Muslims visit – no non-Muslims are allowed even in the city of Mecca itself – to pay their ultimate respect to the Prophet Muhammad. Here, every year, millions of pilgrims walk around the Kaaba seven times in an anticlockwise direction, the first four times quite fast and the last three more slowly as they get closer to the Kaaba itself. So it is not easy to maintain an orderly, devout and devotional atmosphere as they all try and touch The Black Stone on the Eastern corner, possibly a meteorite.

But it was a quiet and contemplative day when the King and his sons, the Royal Princes visited. The Saudi Royal family derive their authority from their role as "Custodians of the Kaaba." It was one of the only two occasions in the year when the Kaaba is opened by the key holder, the senior member of the al-Shaybi tribe, for the ritual cleaning of the sacred Kaaba. The king and his sons use brooms perfumed with rose water to clean the walls. It is an act of deep worship.

But it seemed that something was amiss. Yes, the Crown Prince was missing. The heir to the throne was not present.

----------

The weekly Ulama meeting, the meeting of the 21 Ulams of the Council of Senior Scholars was taking place in the same austere regular meeting room attached to the Al Rajhi Grand Mosque in Riyadh. But this was not a typical meeting. There was only one agenda item.

The leading Ulama were also furious with the Crown Prince. But it was not about his possible involvement in the dismemberment of his enemies. No, Sharia Law did not shy away from such punishments.

It was all about his absence from his role in the holy cleaning of the Kaaba.

'This is outrageous behaviour and unheard of in our history,' began the Grand Mufti, the head of the Council.

'Our holy Prophet Muhammad was grievously insulted by this act.'

'But our monarchy is protected by our Prophet and are our protectors too and we must not forget that,' riposted one of the more pragmatic.

This aroused much ire among the elder Ulama. Several made strong comments about their role. The Crown Prince's action had galvanised them more than ever.

'This is an unholy alliance that we find ourselves in. We need to assert the power of the Prophet more openly.'

'We all know that the monarchy, the thousands of Princes and their families are not always the most devout in their behaviour. Indeed, some of them openly flaunt their libertarian behaviour when abroad if some of what we hear is true.'

'Yes, we need to take an example from elsewhere of how we could act. Our Iranian enemies, the Shia of Iran, have managed to overthrow their despotic rulers and rule with absolute power.'

'Yes, and it works. They have a sophisticated structure where civilians and technocrats control the economy and help the country develop but are at all times under their total control. And they are their own masters in foreign policy.'

There were some nods and mutterings and many thoughtful faces.

All was not well in the 300-year relationship between the Ulama and the House of Saud in the so-called Kingdom of Saudi Arabia.

# Chapter 19

It is interesting that polo, invented in Persia over one and a half thousand years ago and featuring as a ball, the head of your enemy, had become the main sport of royalty and their hangers on in England.

It was to Cowdray Park Estate, a massive 16,500 acres near Midhurst in the beautiful South Downs that they all gathered for the annual British Open polo championships final of the King Power Gold Cup, the premier event in the polo calendar. Polo has been played here on the estate of Cowdray Park country house for over a hundred years and over 450 matches are played here each season.

Sponsored by Veuve Clicquot and other exclusive brands, it is the place to be seen by high society. And the place de la place, the exclusive Ambersham clubhouse with its fine dining and central view of the field. The restaurant itself is sedate and upper class, respectable and well regarded, with its fine dining presided over by a Michelin chef. But much to his chagrin, the food was probably wasted on most of the patrons during polo days.

Lesser orders have other dining and drinking areas whilst ordinary spectators can just bring their own picnics and sit on the grass. But the private rooms of the

Ambersham clubhouse, never seen by the general public or even regular restaurant diners, were something else. This was the place where the Hooray Henries and their female equivalents, especially their female equivalents, the Hooray Henriettas maybe, could unwind, let their hair down and generally behave in a sometimes outrageous manner.

The Princess and her five friends, nicknamed The Famous Six, sat at their own private table. They had finished eating some time ago, expensive dishes left half eaten, but the drinking was still going strong, as the eager waiters topped up their wine glasses at quite a pace. They were all debs from rich families and three had been to school with the Princess.

Lavinia, a largish girl and very funny was standing, struggling with her dress, it kept on slipping off the shoulder. To be fair they were all very scantily dressed, displaying their best and worst assets with abandon. Their desire to be seen and ogled at was much stronger than the expensive finishing school training in deportment and etiquette that their parents had paid for.

'Showing a nipple!' shouted the Princess.

'Yes, nipple in view,' confirmed one or two others. 'Penalty. Carafe of red, on the head,' they all shouted.

'Come on Lav. Down it Lav.

Carafe of red

On the head.

Carafe of red

On the head.'

Lavinia gallantly grabbed a carafe and began swigging. She kept going while swaying alarmingly but also carefully, not spilling a drop.

'Lav. Lav. Lav,' was the screaming, almost incoherent chant as she finished the carafe and banged it down on the table to an almighty cheer.

'Showing two ankles,' shouted Lavinia back. It was her turn to challenge someone in this, their most popular game. She looked around the group and pointed. They all laughed as the Princess was the victim. Their de facto leader and founder of the club.

The Princess dramatically put her legs on the table and they were totally exposed to her upper thighs. A strategically positioned waiter would and probably did, see her panties.

'Can you see my ankles everyone?' she screamed.

'Yes. Down the wine, Down the wine.'

She was soon standing and gobbling up the wine as if it were the last drop of water from a desert oasis.

'Big T, Big T, Big T,' they chanted inharmoniously. This was her nickname from school.

Things continued in this vein for a while, but they were running out of steam.

After they had all done their various forfeits, they calmed down a bit. They couldn't keep up this pace. So, they now turned to their favourite topic. Men.

'Who do you fancy today Princess?'

'Alfy, the head waiter is a big lad.'

'What about that actor guy? Daniel something. From those spy films. I saw him here earlier.'

'Or that fat guy? The boss of the champagne firm. The sponsors.'

'You could be their new cover girl and get free booze for life.'

'And invite us to all those parties!'

'No be fair. The man's got to be a looker.'

'You're right. I'll go for one of the pony boys,' agreed the Princess.

'Do you mean the stable boys?'

'No, no, of course not. I've had them all.' It was almost true. 'I mean one of the polo players.'

'Brit or foreign?'

'Definitely a dago,' she responded.

'Aha. A bit of Argy Bargy eh?'

'Yes, let's go out and see the polo before it ends altogether.'

----------

They were not the greatest of fans. It was the riders themselves that they would be looking at.

The waiters, mostly foreign and used to better behaviour at their previous restaurants and taking pride in their careers as waiters, were amused and bemused. They had been treated badly and hadn't liked the banter directed at them and yet as the girls left, most of them had been given telephone numbers to ring.

The girls made their way to the Ladies to do up their makeup and tighten their
various straps. This was performance time, in public and they had to show a bit of decorum. They all stepped out into the sunlight led naturally by the Princess who was now transformed.

She had not often been seen in public since her rancorous and very public divorce from the Duke. That and the estrangement from her son was the main gossip in the world's press for some time. In England she aroused admiration and opprobrium in equal measure as shown by the mixture of polite booing and cheering that greeted here today. But in the rest of the world, she could do no wrong.

As always in public, she looked stunning. Today she was wearing a navy Carolina Herrera dress and she looked around at length basking in her fame and indeed, notoriety.

She looked on as the match unfolded to loud cries of "Bravo" in Spanish and more subdued, genteel shouts of "Tidy" in English. It was the final of the whole event. The horses looked strong and powerful but seemed to be constantly at odds with their natural instincts to merely run fast in a straight line. Many were converted racehorses who weren't quite going to make it in topflight horse racing. They were forced by their masterly jockeys to stop and start, to twist and turn to suit the correct shot that was required. There was also a lot of physical contact, sometimes with the sticks of the opposing team, sometimes with other horses and now and again with the ground, as falls were sometimes unavoidable.

After the regulation six 7-minute chukkas, the final was won by the favourites, the "King Power" team consisting of two Argentinians and two Brits. The Falklands War and the continuing enmity between the UK and Argentinian governments seemed far away somehow. Indeed, the dashing young Argentinian, Colonel Ricardo Suarez, had been the star of the show.

Tall, sinewy and tanned, with longish black hair, he displayed his dazzling cut shots and his speed and total control of his pony. He had run around his team time and time again to hit the ball between the sticks justifying his handicap of 9 out of 10. Only a handful of players had a handicap of 10, most were Argentinians and he would soon be one of them.

As he dismounted from his pony and walked to the players enclosure to the resounding cheers of the crowd, the Princess broke all protocol and decorum and ran towards him and gave him a big embrace.

Colonel Suarez just smiled broadly and hugged back in a sensuous way. Another lay lay ahead.

This blatant exhibitionism on her part was in full view of all the crowds and was a perfect front page in waiting for the overexcited photographers clicking away furiously.

But one person in particular, on seeing this was, almost physically sick. All types could attend and be spectators outside the paid enclosures. And indeed, someone was watching her from the public area. A small, timid looking man. Bizarrely he was dressed in a dark hoodie with barely half his face visible. He clearly didn't want to be identified and noticed. It was her own son, the Prince. Now twenty years old. He was in fact stalking her. He often found out her engagements and began to attend them, always at a distance, and always in secret.

As ever, he kept a low profile watching from the side-lines. He was totally alone, no friends, and no bodyguard or equerry. His equerry was the one who was aware of his lone travels but allowed them out of kindness for the state he was in, almost as a therapeutic exercise. But he would have been appalled if he knew why he was AWOL. The Prince didn't wish to meet his mother, or confront her. That would be too daring for him. Just following her at a distance, all alone, was brave enough. Why was he doing this? What was his motive? Maybe he just wanted to know what she was up to. Perhaps hoping for signs of a less self-centred, less egotistical behaviour. Or more basic and more buried was the simple fact that he just wanted to see her. He ached to be closer to her, to be part of her life and be loved by her. Yet he also hated her as much as ever. A mother in name only, who had always treated him horribly and abandoned him as a young boy. She was always one for the big public gestures and had embarrassed him on many occasions.

Today, watching from the side-lines, he saw her hug that Argentinian bastard and he cringed. She never ceased to disappoint him with her vulgar and sickening behaviour.

----------

The Princess and the jockey. The beautiful woman and the handsome polo player, the frantic lover and the stud. The whore and the stallion. In his hotel room all that night, they did indeed have hour after hour of unashamedly physical abandon involving almost choreographed, simultaneous, multiple orgasms.

But it was more than that, much more than that. Soon after, she met up with him in Buenos Aires for the start of an intense affair of the sort that neither had previously experienced.

He wasn't just a military officer and a star polo player. He was destined for higher office in the military, supported by his family from a rich landed background

126

and a tradition of right-wing militancy. But they were actually more political than military and he was the cleverest of them all, having qualified with flying colours through his military training and an MBA at Harvard Business School. He was blessed with a multitude of talents as well as his good looks, chief among these was perhaps his way with words. He seemed to have a sixth sense about people and could persuade them, each and every one, in a different way with his charm, his emotional appeal, his intellectual power and rational air, whichever was appropriate at the time.

Another great catch for her, for the second time around, and a clever career move for him if they got together. Argentinian politics was famed for its husband as president and powerful wife syndrome. Or were they genuinely in love?

# Chapter 20

'Look, here they come,' said Suarez' mother. She was standing outside the estancia garden with her husband, the Princess and all the other guests at the Asado, a traditional barbecue.

They looked to the left but could only see a cloud of dust. Then they heard the noise of the horses' hooves and shouts from the riders.

Two horses appeared at full gallop, one in front by a few meters. The Princess could see Suarez was its jockey, although he was hard to recognize dressed as he was in full gaucho clothing. There was the chiripa, a rectangular woollen garment girding the waist, a colourful woollen poncho and the amazing long accordion pleated trousers tied at the ankles, called bombachas, above the large leather gaucho boots.

There were cries of delight and shouts of bravo as they both sped past. They were approaching a metal archway with two rods hanging from it. As they entered the archway, Suarez leading by a neck, they both stood out of their saddles at full speed and reached up a hand to pluck a small marker still hanging from above.

Everyone shouted and applauded at the daring and difficult maneuver that Suarez successfully completed. His rival rider had just failed. This was the climax of several such tricks that the horsemen had performed that afternoon.

'You see. My son. He has beaten the best gaucho rider in the estancia. He is so good at everything.'

The Princess never ceased to be amazed as her lover, Suarez, revealed yet another talent and activity that he excelled at. She was already completely besotted by her handsome superman.

Suarez had shown his skills and beaten a lifelong gaucho at his own specialty. His training in polo had helped but his immense courage and determination were the main factors. She had already seen him expertly lasso a cow from atop his galloping horse and throw the bolas, three iron balls held together by a leather strap, around the legs of another cow, as the gauchos did of old.

His love of the gaucho traditions had been inspired by his reading of the epic gaucho poem *El gaucho Martin Fierro* by Jose Fernandez, that had turned the gauchos into national heroes. These mixed race Argentinian cowboys had been independent herders of cattle since the mid-18th century. Travelling over the vast pampas grasslands of Argentina, they loved their horses more that their women and never settled anywhere very long.

'So, are you proud to be associated with the gaucho traditions?' asked the Princess as she turned to her hosts.

Suarez's father smiled patronizingly as he turned to the Princess although he was by no means averse to her association with his son, quite the opposite in fact. He saw her as a powerful ally and force in promoting and supporting his son to greater things.

'Well we are landowners; we came here escaping from the landed aristocracy in Europe to create our one here. We needed labour and the gauchos were co-opted to work on our land.'

'But what's it like to live out here?' she asked, wondering if she could adapt to it.

He replied, this time quite scathingly as if she had offended him.

'We don't spend much time here. We have managers to run things. Life here is too simple and primitive. We prefer to live in the city with all its sophisticated distractions. We still have our polo though,' he added.

'That is something from the country that we still treasure.'

The Suarez family owned this vast estancia of 30,000 acres, larger than the largest farms in Europe, but they were not farmers.

Despite their distaste for country life they retired to begin the Asado. This traditional barbecue was yet another gaucho invention. Their diet was of necessity beef and Yerba mate, a form of tea drunk from a cup, a hollowed-out gourd through a built-in carved pipe or straw. Both the Asado and the mate had been adopted by city dwellers.

Suarez, still wearing his gaucho clothes caked in dust and sweat got out his gaucho knife, the facon, and cut off a dozen ribs, asado de tira, before breaking them off with his bare hands and handing a few to her.

His mother looked aghast.

'Why Ricardo. You should have showered and changed. You look a sight.'

The Princess half agreed but was still aroused by his manly appearance.

'I am a gaucho today,' he laughed and tore at some more charred and succulent ribs.

This was half in jest as he picked up a glass of the finest Malbec. He had a refined taste too, which added to his magnetic appeal to the fairer sex.

He gently pulled the Princess to one side. 'Here let me show you how the gauchos make an Asado. They first make a pit and fill it with the wood of the quebracho tree. It gives off very little smoke. The pit is surrounded by these metal crosses and we hang from them a whole carcass of a cow, split open to get the heat from the fire.'

'How do you marinate it?' she asked.

He smiled. 'We don't do that; the only preparation is salt added before and during the cooking. This is the gaucho way; beef is his diet. Every bit of the cow is used.

'Here we have morcillas, what you call black pudding, then chinchulines or cow chitterlings which are the inner intestine of a cow and mollejas, your sweetbreads, which is the pancreas.

'We eat it with pan felipe, a sort of baguette bread and salads. These are made by the women. The men do the meat.

'We eat these first as the finest meat cooks for two hours or more.'

But she did see huge pots of sauces.

'What are these?'

'Aha. This is chimichurri, a sauce made from chopped parsley, dried oregano, garlic, salt, black pepper, onion and paprika with olive oil. And here is another sauce called salsa criolla.'

She pulled him away before he could list all its ingredients also. She didn't want him to be a gourmet chef as well. It was all too much.

He still added, 'the sauces are only used with the offal. Never on the steaks.'

They moved away to sit with the others on vast open-air tables laden with dish after dish of meat.

----------

The Asado seemed endless as more and more meat was brought to the tables. In some Buenos Aires' restaurants, each table has a red and a green flag and it is only when the red flag is raised to indicate surrender that the waiters stop serving more meat.

As a respite a guitar and drums began to play and a lone gaucho began to dance, his rugged weather-worn face contrasting to his lithe frame. It was the famous *Malambo*, a highly rhythmic tap dance while wearing heavy gaucho boots. Danced by men only as way of strutting their wares, much like a male peacock.

He danced from the waist down, keeping to a very small floor area with the upper body kept stationary. The dance is the performance of a series of foot movements called *mudanzas*. Each one intricate and difficult with the dancer in charge and the music subtly keeping up as the dance enfolds.

The dance finished to much applause and cheering.

But Suarez was now on his feet and with a dramatic flourish he set the guitarist and drummer to perform at an even faster pace.

Here was the king peacock in action. To much loud handclapping, he performed the northern version of the Malabo, faster, more accurate and with longer and heavier foot strikes. He was the master, with everyone in the palms of his hands.

The Princess and his parents and the whole gathering could only look on in awe as he danced with great skill but also with obvious love and emotion for the dance itself. He and the band were as one as he signalled subtly to them to change from one cycle to the next.

There was huge applause and cheers as he took his bows in dramatic and obvious pleasure. He was mesmeric. Wisely, no one followed him and they returned to yet more meat.

----------

Later, much later, that evening Suarez and the Princess were walking alone under the southern stars.

'There is the constellation Centaurus. Do you see the Omega Centauri, the brightest globular cluster we can see from Earth?'

He quoted from Jose Fernadez's epic poem *Martin Fierro*.

'The stars are the guide the gaucho has in the pampas.'

'You too are a star,' she gushed. She could not contain her intense feelings.

'No, I am a gaucho at heart,' he said. 'I really believe they express the true spirit of our country, what it means to be Argentinian. Not to be corrupted by European influence and culture. The people are not all rich like us, they are more like gauchos, who respect the land and the power it has over us all. Some years the crop is good, some years it is bad. Like life itself. Like the gauchos the people are sincere, loyal and honest and proud. They value hard work and solidarity.

He did indeed seem to be genuine in his love of the people and on their side unlike his parents and their class.

'I want to stop the corruption of our true values into greed and materialism and bring back pride to our nation.'

Quietly he continued. 'I do believe that I am the man to do that. But not alone. You are a wonderful and exceptional woman and you are beautiful too. But more than that I can see that you too want to do good and to be a force for justice.'

Then with great expression and intensity, his eyes blazing, 'You are my Evita.'

'Together we can support each other and do that.' He stopped and looked at her intently, boring into her eyes. 'Will you do that? Will you help me lead our country in a new and deserving path to greater glory?'

'Of course. I do believe you are the one.' And she hugged him powerfully before they kissed passionately under the stars.

It was an unusual wedding proposal, if that is what it was.

# Chapter 21

For a country with its strong emphasis on family, taking the Princess to meet his parents for an Asado at the family ranch, very early in their courtship had signified the seriousness of Suarez' intent.

In this case it was very serious. A mere six months after the Asado, they were married.

Weddings in Argentina are in two distinct parts. The official wedding ceremony is quite straightforward and short and usually held in a registry office but in some high society cases, in a church. It is followed, sometimes the day after, by the wedding reception itself, a massive event, a celebration like no other in the lives of guests and bride and groom alike.

Only close family members were present at this official wedding. Suarez' parents and two brothers, one surviving grandfather and two close friends. But despite the numbers it was a classy event.

The bride looked glorious in a beautiful veiled white dress but was nevertheless wearing the traditional blue petticoat as she was led into the church by her brother to the sound of the wonderful and famous old organ brought especially from Paris. The church was the magnificent Basilica del Santisimo Sacramento in the Retiro area, built by Mercedes Castellano de

Anchorena, the owner of the grand Palacio san Martin. She is said to have insisted that God should have a home to match hers.

The interior is full of wonderful ornate carvings, statues and artwork; the exterior also splendid in its design with its towers topped by rounded turrets

The bride and groom stood in front of the altar, flanked by her brother and Suarez' mother. There is no best man in Argentinian Catholic weddings. The groom was immaculate in his military uniform and his previously long hair was now a very respectable military crop. He looked at her with great tenderness and love, or so it seemed to her and everyone else. He was fairy tale handsome and he knew it.

Vows were exchanged and rings, already exchanged at the engagement as is customary, were switched from right to left hand. This was all purely a formality as the big event was the wedding reception itself, eagerly awaited by the specially invited guests.

----------

The polo club main ballroom, yes, a polo club had a ballroom, was decorated with some colourful bunting but the predominant colour was that of Argentina, the national pride intruded into everything. This was the venue for the post wedding reception of Suarez and the Princess. It was the perfect venue as it was a symbol of the wealth and power of the ruling elite. Membership of the polo club was strictly by invitation only and only the most highly regarded members of the social hierarchy stood a chance, bearing in mind the military and political traditions of the families involved. To some it was the highpoint of their lives to be invited to join.

Similarly, having a wedding reception here was not something you could book and pay for, however rich you were. It had to be proposed and seconded by committee members and voted upon in a very serious manner. But allowing the Suarez family to have it as their venue had not been an issue, so highly regarded were they in the upper echelons of Argentinian Society.

Apart from having been allowed to celebrate the wedding reception here, the event itself was no different from any other wedding reception in its bare essentials. Argentinian society has no airs and graces when it comes to celebrating. The food was of course Asado, a barbecue as insisted upon by Suarez and after they had satisfied their hunger several times, it was all about the partying, which lasted all night. With much dancing and merrymaking. Yes, the cost of booze, only the very best vintage wine was imbibed, and the catering had been excessive and the bands were very well rewarded but essentially it was a big drinking party, starting at about midnight and going on all night until dawn where they then sat down for a big hearty breakfast.

Being invited here was the social achievement of the year and there had been much discussion of who and who had not been invited and why? There were official photographers at the official wedding ceremony, but this party was out of bounds to any media or other intrusion. Security guards were at every door and the gates to the street were locked and well-guarded. The loud sounds of the band echoing across the streets of Buenos Aires were the only signs that something special was taking place. Such secrecy and security gave all the guests a sense of freedom so that they could unwind thoroughly and even behave in slightly undignified fashion knowing that although there would be gossip, it would be confined to their inner circle who all had a vested interest in being together in defence of their privileges and station in life.

Most of the guests were members of the Buenos Aires's high society, other rich absentee landowners and influential members of the right-wing upper classes. The women were dressed in elaborate ball gowns of varying styles, but all had the common denominator of high cost. Many of the older men, although dressed in suits today, had a military bearing, clearly retired officers, some with a dark past. But some of the guests were friends of the groom, with many of his school and military colleagues present.

Noticeable was the complete lack of any friends or family of the bride apart from her brother, who was needed to walk her down the aisle. In her typically selfish fashion, she had not even considered inviting her boozing friends, The Famous Six, or any others and especially no family. They all served their purposes in different ways and attending this wedding was not one of them. They would all be picked up and casually dropped according to her whims and needs. It would be going too far that she was a totally changed woman, a newly reformed character. But she was now totally focused on her new found ambition and determination to make something positive of her life.

Taking a break from the ballroom with nonstop singing and dancing, blaring out on a high-end sound system, half a dozen of the older officers had congregated in the garden. They all had glasses in their hands that had been refilled many times that night. They had gone past the merry stage of inebriation and were now well into the introspective, self-pitying stage.

'Good to see that we are all still here,' said General Enrico Gonzales, a veteran of the Falklands War. I could have been killed in the Malvinas war many years ago.

One of his colleagues remarked. 'I don't recall you ever being in action. You were fely in the control centre a few miles from here.'

'I played an important part,' he remonstrated.

'An even more important one in helping foster out to military families the orphan babies from the disappeared ones,' taunted General Pietro Roger.

Gonzales and Roger had always been rivals and their feud seemed to be as strong as ever.

'Hey, stop using that language. Some things are better not talked of, even now, many years later,' intervened a possibly more sober colleague.

But they ignored him totally.

'I, at least, was there on those islands.'

'Yes, with your badly trained, badly equipped and badly fed conscripts from the countryside.'

'Come on, no quarrelling. Besides, we're all on the same side, we all want the same things for our country.'

'Yes, these civilian politicians are always corrupt and can't run things properly. It always means we have to come in to clear up the mess.'

'The country desperately needs us,' said the mediator with great conviction.

'Doesn't look like our present military are up for it though. We maybe need to have some conversations with one or two of them.'

'Yes, strong words are needed.'

'I think young Suarez today seems to be the one to achieve something. He is very popular and dashing.'

'More important than that, he is very clever and a good military strategist by all accounts.'

They got more and more excited.

'Yes, he has a lot of things going for him.'

'He is a born leader. Very charismatic. You can see it.'

'Yes, yes. He is the one.'

'And his new wife is going to be a strong asset. She seems a very powerful lady in waiting.'

'Yes, I am reminded of the Perons. Maybe there is hope there.

'Yes, you're so right. They may be the new Perons, but this time on our side.'

'Let's hope we're around to see it.'

----------

Some of the younger men, though Suarez was not among them, had also gathered together to take a break. They were covered in sweat from their exertions on the dance floor and their jackets and ties had been discarded long ago.

'Wow! This nonstop dancing is as exhausting as some of our military fitness training,' joked an up and coming army officer and a close friend of Suarez.

'Yes, we need this break to recharge our batteries,' said a more serious and solemn colleague.

'Oh, just enjoy yourself and don't think of work right now.'

'There is no escape from work. It is more than work. It is our mission. I think about it all the time.'

They looked around the group to see if they were all on the same page. Yes, there were no outsiders present.

Trying to be quiet, his attempted whisper still came out loudly. 'We must be careful how we talk. We need to keep this to ourselves, maybe for quite a few years.'

'Hush. Hush. Yes, Suarez would be furious if he knew we had started talking like this in semipublic.'

'Yes, he's our strong man, our obvious leader.'

'He hasn't been acknowledged as such yet,' said Oscar Gonzales, a school colleague of Suarez who had surprisingly joined the navy when his family were solid army people from generations back.

'Maybe we should do so, so we have a more formal existence. So far it is only a shared wish, a shared understanding.'

'Yes, we should do it. Make him our leader and officially commit to the action we all desire.'

'We must succeed where our fathers failed. We must learn from all their mistakes
and worse. They did many bad things to achieve their aims.'

'Suarez will lead us to a better way of doing things. We all have a deep understanding of this.'

'We need a target we can focus on.'

'Maybe a deadline too, so we don't waver.'

'Yes, do we all agree?'

They all looked around and none demurred.

But was there a hint of disappointment or disagreement from Oscar Gonzales. He had been a secret rival to Suarez throughout their lives with Suarez always coming out on top, never even realising that his friend was bitterly envious of his effortless success at everything he did.

# Chapter 22

Not long after the wedding, the campaign had begun. No-one knew it was a campaign, not even her PA, but it was in full swing.

The Princess was her sparkling self and looked radiant with her carefully coiffured hair and her figure-hugging trouser suit even though it was only six a.m.

She was seated in the back seat of a large Nissan 4 x 4 and they were travelling from their hotel in Puerto Madryn, Patagonia, along a gravel road on a 95 kilometre journey to Peninsula Valdez, a world heritage site. The landscape was arid, barren and flat with some branches and bushes sticking out here and there. Their angulation showed the direction of the strong prevailing wind that was also a feature of the area.

Her PA, Gavin, sitting in the front passenger seat, had been with her for many years, in fact ever since her marriage to the Duke. He was an old friend from England, former husband of one of her best friends. Suddenly he turned around to her and shouted,

'Damn we have someone following, paparazzi, I think. Yes, I can see some telephoto lenses. Speed up driver.'

But there was no way they could out speed their followers on this type of road, they were going at the maximum speed for any comfort already.

'No, its fine,' she said nonchalantly. 'I told them to come along, told them where we were going and what time.'

'What? I only told the main Buenos Aires and local papers of your visit and said it was private.'

'Don't worry. It will be fun.'

After a couple of hours they arrived at the tiny village of Puerto Pyramides, which was where you boarded the boats for whale watching.

They had heard that the Southern Right whales were there in large numbers, close to the 1,000 per season record, and there would be no problem seeing them at close quarters.

There was local TV crew already there, quite a few reporters from the Nationals and the local papers and even a few hundred spectators, a very large crowd for such an isolated, low population area.

On the boat, exclusively for them, the helmsman set out and said, 'We will be able to get very close today, the weather conditions are good and you will have a great view.

She went up to him quietly and said 'Please don't go very close, stay well away from them.'

'But Princess, I am an expert sailor and have done it many times.'

'Please listen to me, listen,' she said firmly. 'I will double your fee. Not too close.'

He was puzzled but the money was the main factor, so he obeyed.

The paparazzi and the journos had hired two or three other boats and were following closely, maneuvering for the best position for photos of the Princess and the whales together.

But whatever they did the photos were dominated by her in the foreground with the whales just tiny spots in the background despite being over 14 metres long and weighing around 40 tonnes. Exactly as she had intended. No beautiful shots of these mighty mammals for them but many of a dazzling Princess with her winning smile. Yes, they were frustrated but they took the best shots they could. But she wasn't going to be outdone by the most spectacular animals on the planet.

On landing she walked up to the spectators who were crowding round. They were waving Welsh, Italian and Argentinian flags. No UK ones for obvious reasons despite the object of their affection being an English Princess. There had been no security and control from the handful of police who had belatedly arrived.

'Can I have selfie?'

'Of course.'

Request after request, all met with patience and good humour. She was such an actress.

She spent the next forty minutes smiling and talking to the most photogenic spectators, young children and mature adults alike.

They then sped off back along the dusty potholed road with Punta Delgado, the breeding grounds of the giant elephant seals as their next destination. There is a colony of about 20,000 Southern elephant seals, here to mate, give birth and molt.

She had told her PA to let all the reporters and photographers know where they were off to.

After a light private launch at a nearby closed restaurant – she needed some time to herself, mainly to redo her makeup and hair - she was off again.

She walked along the wooden walkways among the sand dunes toward the beach where hundreds of these giant seals were basking. They were packed close together leaving hardly any beach in view. Their vast bulk making it hard to move out of water, they slid along slowly on their bellies when bothered to move at all.

The males make up only a small proportion and have harems of over a hundred females each and they mate up to fifteen times a day. They are truly enormous, 4000 kilograms and six meters long, with strange trunk like noses that they use to generate a fearful noise intended to keep rivals at bay.

She went very close to them this time. They were so huge and ugly and noisy there was no way they could diminish from her image in any photo.

Cameras flashed continuously and she again spent more time talking and being photographed by the spectators than she did looking at the strangely splendid elephant seals, a force of nature not to be missed. But she didn't really show more interest in these than in the whales. For an ambassador for the WWF she was distinctly cool. She had invited herself to be the Argentinian Ambassador for the WWF and they had been flattered and had eagerly accepted her offer.

The journos and photographers were packing up and getting ready for the next visit which they all knew would be the famous penguin colony at Punta Tombo, where hundreds of thousands of penguins were based. This was the most popular tourist destination and people could walk freely among all the penguins and get the most amazing photos.

The Princess turned to her PA and said, 'Best to tell them were not going to the penguins. No need to upset them when we don't turn up. Just tell them we're going back to Puerto whatever it's called.'

Again, he obeyed orders. He had known the penguins were not on the itinerary and had assumed she didn't want to make it a long and tiring day with all the long, slow travel between venues.

The guide turned to her and said,

'Normally tours stop off whenever I spot a local animal such as the long haired armadillo who are very rare and native to the area.' But she ignored him completely and just told the driver to head off back without any stops. She just didn't seem interested.

So, the driver was surprised that when they returned to Puerto Madryn town, she immediately went on a walkabout and spent the next two hours talking to and being photographed by many of the locals who had by now heard she was in the area. Again, the photographers and TV crews had a field day.

She was even interviewed by one of them and feigning surprise, she carefully recited but in a very professional and natural way her prepared statement. All in Spanish. Her Spanish A level and a few hours of practice just about allowed her to get away with it.

'I have enjoyed visiting this wonderful place as the WWF Ambassador and I will do all I can to preserve and conserve all the diversity of nature we find here. From the wonderful whales and elephant seals to all the land animals in the Peninsula Valdes. But I will also ensure that none of that is at the expense of your jobs

147

and your welfare as the historic people of Patagonia. I know you are proud of your Welsh and Italian heritage as well as being loyal Argentinian citizens. Thank you all very much.'

A masterly speech written for a promising up and coming politician which is exactly what she was. Her speech writer was Steve Carter, the son of Richard Carter, the ageing newspaper magnate, who liked to support or even select future leaders in the countries he did business in.

There were many cheers and she spent another ten minutes saying goodbye to all and sundry with much handshaking and quite a few hugs.

Today had been a typical day for her. In public she acted like a member of royalty, visiting various well-known places and attending deserving causes such as hospitals and schools. This had raised her profile and her popularity in the country to a high level and she attracted crowds wherever she went. Although she acted and felt like royalty, taking advantage of everything she had learnt during her marriage to the Duke, she still managed to convey the patently false impression that she was a commoner, one of them, an outsider from the rich and powerful.

Her public performance today was her visible part in promoting the team. More and more people were becoming aware of the rise of this exciting and charismatic couple.

But in private, she had a role too. She often contributed ideas and possible actions to advance her husband's ambitions and was a strong moral force behind him, encouraging him at all times in believing he had a duty, indeed a mission to save his country.

Together they were a remarkable pair and were single-minded in their preparation for power.

----------

'Why didn't you want to see the penguins?' asked her PA over dinner.

'Oh, come on. You must have caught on by now. Everyone just loves penguins. Penguins are far too cute and cuddly to be in my photos.'

Despite a highly successful day, Gavin her PA was on edge. In fact, he was permanently on edge as life with the Princess was not straightforward. He could feel in his pocket the envelope that he had received about a week ago. It wasn't the first one. He had three or four more in his case back at the hotel. They were from her estranged son and somehow always found their way to him. He couldn't ever find the right time to give them to her. There never was a right time, but he felt it was his duty to do so. So today maybe was a better chance than most.

He handed it to her over the dinner table in silence.

She looked at it, and at him with a withering look and tore it open. There were three or four pages but before even finishing the first one she stopped abruptly.

'He's pathetic. Just pathetic,' and threw the letter back at him across the table.

Yes. On the surface all seemed well. But her own family situation left a lot to be desired.

After she retired, he picked up the letter and began to read. This could be something for his memoirs of his life with the Princess down the line when he retired. He already had a lot of material. He had first had this plan from the rabbits incident many years ago. Or for much more money it could be tabloid material right now. His face became redder as he turned the page.

Oh my God, this is bad, he said to himself.

His face turned purple and his hands shook.

And louder for the whole room to hear, even though he was on his own.

'This is terrible. My God. This is dynamite. I guess I have to tell someone. They need to know about this. Poor boy.'

# Chapter 23

Today the Argentinian parliament had voted by a large majority to default on its 82 billion dollars in sovereign bonds, the highest in the world, in the worst economic crisis in its history. And it is a sorry history. Argentina has defaulted on its internal debts five times and its external debts seven times in its 200-year history.

To roars of approval the president declared.

'We must take the bull by the horns.' And promptly he defaulted on money owed to internal and foreign lenders, among them the World Bank and the International Monetary Fund.

There were loud cries of 'Argentina. Argentina. Argentina.' The president nodded his head in acknowledgement.

Such irresponsible international behaviour led to further economic problems and rampant inflation, the main feature of Argentinian society. Successive civilian presidents all vowed to curb and indeed eliminate corruption but all failed due to insincerity in some cases - they themselves were corrupt - and less commonly due to inability and incompetence.

The military were despairing of such irresponsible behaviour, they did in fact crave respect from the outside world and had ideas of their own of how to eliminate corruption and run the economy.

It seemed to be how things were fated to happen in Argentina. Since 1930 and The Falklands War in 1982, Argentina had 24 presidents and only 13 were civilian and all had been overthrown by the military. But things had sometimes become complicated. Peron, although initially a trade union leader, almost always wore a military uniform when in power and in his early years, 50% of expenditure was on the military. Likewise, the 1976 military government appointed a civilian as economics minister albeit an Old Etonian, a Harvard graduate and from a rich landowning family.

Since the Falklands War there had been a break in this sorry tradition of incompetent government alternating with military coups.

But still the military felt the time would come again to intervene to save the nation. This next time it would be different, there would be no dirty war against their opposition; they hoped to gain power and respect from the people and thanks for their patriotic action. But how to achieve this?

Suarez among them bided his time, still playing polo occasionally at his beloved Esperanza polo club, more often than not imagining different scenarios and strategies that could one day satisfy his overwhelming ache, it was almost a physical pain, for power.

Supporting him in his polo playing was only one of the outward manifestations of the Princess' activities. She was tireless in her courting of the people, constantly on the go and gathering support for her husband.

----------

It was May 29th, Army Day in Argentina, a national holiday for all.

The Banda Militar was at its splendid best as it marched through the imposing entrance arch of the Colegio Militar de la Nacion, The National Military College, founded in 1869 and now based at El Palomar in Buenos Aires.

All eyes were on the marching as the band was followed by the various Regiments of Cadets - all on this passing out parade - having completed their training at this prodigious location.

First past came the infantry with their traditional Mayer rifles and all amazingly goose-stepping along, the only regiment allowed to do this step.

Next came the Armos regimental cadets with their M4 rifles and all marching the high step in perfect symmetry.

Bizarrely on foot, there followed the cavalry. The cavalry troops all carried lances and marched in the trot march as if trying to emulate their missing horses.

The Argentinian army knew how to put on a show and led the world in ceremonies.

They all marched passed the dais on which were assembled the top military brass of the day, all wearing their full regalia. They all saluted the current Chief of General Staff.

It wasn't enough for this to be the passing out parade for the new recruits, it was also the inauguration of a general to the high command.

The soon to be General, Roberto Suarez looked magnificent with his full insignia, in his red trimmed shoulder boards with the gold braid suns. But today he also wore the golden wreath leaves of a general on his coat lapels.

As the band went silent, the Chief of General Staff began his address.

'My fellow Argentinians, my fellow officers in the Army of our Nation, I welcome you to this inauguration.

'You newly qualified cadets are an excellent example to us all in our dear Argentina. You are now professional. You are all technically trained to a high level, our new Officer company, paid career men dedicated solely to military matters, having passed through our academies of advanced training, having been selected to do so on objective criteria for promotion based on ability.'

This was rich coming from the very same person who had authored the notorious Full Stop Law that limited the prosecutions of over 600 officers implicated in the Dirty War that had been the overriding feature of the last military Junta.

This sounded progressive and egalitarian, democratic and liberal but in truth it was still members of certain grand families with a military tradition who had marched past. But there was now an element of selection within this privileged group.

No, it was militarism that was on show not military professionalism. These highly political animals dreamt of military coups, thought in terms of ruling the country, not serving it.

He turned to Suarez.

'Before you we have a prime example of this professional army. General Suarez began like you, not that long ago and has advanced quickly due to his high standards, his dedication and his remarkable ability.

'He has already served for two years as head of one of the three regional divisions
within Argentina and today I am promoting him to be head of the FDR, the Fuerza de Despliegue Rapido, the Rapid Deployment Force which serves as out first line of defence.

'We can be reassured that our country will be in safe hands in the future with such an outstanding soldier here today.'

Watching with great pride and passion was the Princess, his wife and consort.

Despite her obvious defects, she was a  determined and ambitious woman with the sticking power to play the long term game.  She was wily and clever with her own political instincts and antennas. She knew she would not be able to make an impact in the UK after her fall from grace. She would only ever feature in the gossip columns. In Argentina there were much bigger possibilities in a country that had adored strong women in the past. She hadn't seen Evita Peron, wife of General Peron the former Argentinian leader speaking from the balcony of the Casa Rosada, the pink walled palace and seat of government in Buenos Aires. Evita was adored, no idolized by the people.  But the Princess had seen Madonna singing from the very same balcony in the film of Evita, possibly an even more powerful and dramatic image.

Together they would make a powerful team and both Princess and General had been quick to realize that.

# Chapter 24

The 58-meter-long yacht, "The Lady Halla," built at a cost of over ten million pounds would be every ordinary mortal's dream, its appearance at any port guaranteed to bring gawking onlookers and gossip column journos flocking. Not so to Richard Carter, media tycoon extraordinaire and legend. To him it was just a private and more important, a more secure place to stay than hotels with all the attention that would generate. He'd only been persuaded to buy it by his son who thought he was now in charge of the day to day running of the empire as CEO. Dad had retired to the title of President and was now only doing 100,000 miles year travelling to all the outposts as opposed to the 250,000 plus he was used to doing before he had begun to slow down since his triple bypass op. He was after all 83 years of age and quite frankly he didn't look well. He walked slowly with a stoop and was looking thin and gaunt. His physical appearance didn't bother him too much. He'd never actually looked well even in his prime, but his phenomenal energy was legendary. Even now his brain was totally alert and his mind, from the moment he awoke each morning was full of ideas for

156

acquisitions, and new developments. He was still as excited as he'd ever been at the prospect of meeting new people and outdoing them, sometimes when they went away certain they had got the better of him.

He lay back on his leather chair flicking through the images on the giant screen in the yacht's very untidy conference room, which also served as the lounge and comms room. He didn't see the point of tidiness when convenience and speed were the key to efficiency. The images were of the headlines from the online editions of his main newspapers, downloaded from the secure network which he ran from his own satellite COSAT, characteristically called Carter's Own SATellite. His comms system could not be bettered by the President of the USA. In fact, it was identical as his own comms company produced the White House version. His version had been tweaked up to do exactly what he wanted. He was still the first person to see the first editions of all his major papers as they were downloaded straight from the editor's office  wherever he was the instant the editor was happy to go to print. Thus, he was able to instantly intervene and suggest another headline or leading article or change the slant if he felt it necessary. And he still often did. What was most remarkable about this was that long ago he had adapted himself to working an 18 hour day, being awake for Europe and the States if he was in the States, being awake for Europe and Asia if he was in Europe and likewise for Asia and the States. He was completely aware at all times when his newspapers were about to come on the streets or online wherever he was  in the world, and it was actually becoming easier as there was no set deadline for online publications. They were continuously updated as news broke.

'Hi Dad, can I come in,' said Steve Carter.

Steve was being trained by his dad to take over, but progress was slow. He had been given the title of CEO and been put in charge of mixing the cocktails and some general basic inquiries, but his dad was still top dog in every way.

'That Argie general who wants to see you, I've checked him out as you suggested and you were right as usual, there is a smell about this one. It could be pretty big.'

'Well what have you got on him then?'

'His father was a Falkland's veteran who's in a group who have pledged to recover them. His son coming today is very bright and has been to all their top academies as well as having degrees in economics and an MBA from Harvard. But he's no academic, he'd done very well in the infighting on the way to the top and he's clearly in line to be their top military man in a few years.'

'All good stuff son but what's his drug? Give me the dirt, man.'

'Well that's just it, there doesn't seem to be any. He's a ladies man with lots of conquests, but that's quite normal in the macho culture he's in. No gambling, no drugs, no vices at all apparently. He plays polo and tennis to quite a high level.'

'OK I'll see him as soon as possible. Cancel any appointments that clash.'

'He's coming in half an hour instead of the Union leader Alfonso. I've already told him to piss off.'

'Good man.'

The Lady Halla had the number 1 berth at Punte del Este, the Uruguayan resort frequented by the

Argentinean rich who came from across the River Plate in their own yachts. But General Suarez arrived in a nondescript taxi dressed in a smart white summer suit and hat. He was also wearing sunglasses and apart from seeing he was tall and fit; it would have been difficult for anyone to identify him.

He was welcomed aboard by Carter's son Steve, who led him into the bar aft of the ship. He left the two together knowing that this conversation was not for him.

'General Suarez, welcome. Have a scotch, and take a seat.'

'Thank you, Mr. Carter,'

'Ah, call me Richard and tell me, to what do I owe the pleasure.'

'Well, Mr. Carter, Richard. You are a very successful and clever man, and I admire what you have achieved, especially in our country, which now has an excellent television network and newspapers of a high international standard. We welcome that and would like it to continue even when problems occur in the country which have to be corrected .... dramatically.'

He paused for effect and then just when Richard was about to intervene, he held up his hand and continued.

'Yes, I know what you are thinking, after such a long time of democratic government, longer than at any other time in our country. But there are still grave problems with our economy and inflation and recent events have made many people of pride very unhappy.'

He was obviously referring to the South Atlantic Islands treaty recently signed between Britain and Argentina.

'What do you want me to do?' asked Carter quietly. He knew when to be obsequious and to play his hand cautiously.

'Well, I don't expect you to support us but perhaps you will be tolerant and show some understanding for our position.'

'But General, you know that all my editors and TV newsmen are independent minded and will judge the situation accordingly.'

'But Mr. Carter, I also know that you have the greatest skill in choosing editors who share your philosophy and wider interests. Your action in China to ensure the expansion of your interests there was most impressive, indeed, statesmanlike.'

He was referring to the fact that Carter had removed the BBC World Service channel from the satellite transmitting into China.

Richard Carter smiled sweetly at this and waited patiently for the bottom-line statement and especially how it would be delivered by this urbane and sophisticated military man.

'If your editors really have been well chosen by you, I am sure you will be able to continue to contribute to our media debate and that all your interests in our country will continue to prosper.'

Carter was beginning to become quite perturbed at the possible world-wide consequences of what he thought the General was planning and said questioningly.

'But General, do you really feel that your people are ready for a change along the lines you propose, and how would the world community view it?'

'I understand your concerns and I think you will find that our people will be more than pleased and that the world community will also welcome the wider changes.'

Carter was now extremely ill at ease as he was totally at a loss as to what was being suggested, a position he rarely found himself in. He could not foresee any circumstances when world opinion would be happy with what he thought was coming. He decided to become more challenging.

'I really don't see how you can be so confident of this. You know that ....'

'Richard, you have to trust us. Or your businesses here and in other countries allied to us would also find themselves in a downturn,' and with this even more enigmatic threat he got up quickly, bowed politely, made his way out, up the gangplank and walked briskly across the road to hail a taxi.

Steve entered to see his Dad in a strangely agitated state.

'Steve, there's something big going on, something very big. And for the first time ever in my life as a journo, I don't think it's a good idea for us to find out what it is.'

----------

The doors of the Esperenza Polo Club Dining Room in Buenos Aires were closed and the curtains were drawn. It was about 11pm and other guests had gone home. It was a strictly private meeting. About 15 men sat around a large table dressed casually as they had been watching polo during the day and some had indeed been playing. It had been a match between Esperanza and Militares, the  military academy team, so all had a legitimate reason for being here, though to some the polo had merely been a pretext to attend this meeting. They were in fact all high up members of the Argentinean military. In fact, two of the service chiefs were here. Only the head of the Navy was not present.

General Suarez, their unofficial leader began quietly.

'Gentlemen, thank you for coming. We have been meeting regularly in different places patiently reviewing the situation and biding our time, perhaps too patiently for some of you. But we have never, never forgotten why we meet and now, we believe the time has come. The South Atlantic Islands treaty signed last week by our President and the British Prime Minister was the last straw. We waited patiently throughout the years of Menem, who although he said we would not use force, never stopped proclaiming that we would recover our Malvinas. His successors have finally done what we have always feared. They have given away our Malvinas. We were all very young men, when we were humiliated and disgraced by Thatcher. Such a strong leader, in contrast to our leaders, who had led us to this incompetent invasion without proper planning. We will plan properly and we will succeed.

'But first I want to ask if anyone does not feel the time is right. We have to be united in everything we do.'

'General Vitorio, the Commander in Chief of Armoured Units, the tank divisions, was the one to speak up.

'What has the time come for exactly? Are you proposing a coup? Because I don't think the time is right for that at all. People have become used to democracy. They are not discontent enough to support us. We would have great trouble being accepted. And yet we must take power if we are to regain Les Malvinas. Only then would we be forgiven.'

'I agree,' chimed the Chief of the general staff of the Airforce, 'We can't announce what we plan to do when we get power and yet we will never be accepted if the people don't know our plan. We would not be able to run the economy with the world and our own people against us.'

There were several nods of agreement to this. There did not seem to be a solution to this impasse.

They all turned to General Sanchez again, he was the man with the ideas and the air of easy authority which surpassed all theirs.

'Come Suarez, tell us why you think the time is finally right?' called Vittorio. He would need a lot of convincing and his support was vital as in any coup; armoured cars were the essential symbol of authority.

General Suarez stood up this time and slowly addressed his fellow conspirators, not defensively in view of the obvious opposition and doubt but with great boldness as he unveiled his sensational ideas.

'It does indeed appear to you to be a Catch 22 situation, but if we use our imagination and look for a daring solution, we could achieve all our aims for the glory of our country.

'My plan has four parts, three short term and one long term, but the key to its success is that the three short-term parts take place simultaneously.

'First of all,' and here he held up a document, 'I have been given this by a high official in the intelligence services. It provides incontrovertible proof that the British will not use force to regain Las Malvinas should they be invaded. We presumed this to be the case last time. Now we know it is true. That is a major advantage.'

He spoke carefully for half an hour outlining his plans to a more and more startled audience.

His audacity was outrageously convincing. With an almost evangelical zeal they all agreed to meet two night later to hammer out more details.

# Chapter 25

Steve Carter, Jonathan Jones, CEO of Shell International, his chair of the board, Jacob van Marken and General Suarez were on board Steve's father's yacht, "The Lady Halla." It was moored in its regular mooring in the Yacht Club marina of the Uruguayan port of Punta del Este, a playground for rich Uruguayans and Argentinians. It was the most exclusive and secluded mooring. Steve's father had been super rich and cherished his privacy. Nothing but the best for him. But even he, supposedly indestructible, had died and now Steve was at last his own boss.

Steve was the host and had sailed the boat in from Rio. Jonathan and van Marken had flown in. They were not sure how General Suarez had travelled from Argentina, but he arrived by local taxi, dressed unobtrusively in civilian clothes.

Steve had retired to his cabin. The other three were all seated round a table on the front deck with some papers in front of them.

This was an unusual location for a meeting to negotiate and hopefully sign an oil deal agreement between two parties. But it had to be, as one of the parties, in this case, General Suarez had no legal authority as yet to sign such a deal. He had not yet taken over his country from a civilian government as head of a military coup. Likewise, the two most senior Shell personnel were here without any knowledge of anyone at Shell, least of all the board. But Jonathan and the Chair of the Board were confident of their power to act and their ability to persuade others to come on board at a later date.

After the preliminary introductions were over and they were all sipping a Fernet con coca o amaro, Jonathan began.

'So, my dear General, we hope all your plans are progressing.

'We don't need to go into what we know about them or how you know about our oil discovery.'

They all smiled in a conspiratorial way. Such were the machinations and goings on in the murky world of political and economic power.

'What we need to do is agree that from Shell's point of view, first of all, we are the sole partners with Argentina in the development of this oil.'

The General nodded. 'Yes, we accept that totally, you discovered it and you are the ones with the technical expertise to exploit its development.'

'And for our part,' the General continued, 'we will allow you to use our territory, both on the mainland and our offshore islands for use as bases for landing the oil and for the construction and servicing of all the technical side of things, machinery, rigs, pipelines and so on. In fact, we insist on this as it will bring much needed jobs to our countrymen.'

'We welcome that offer, General. That will make our task economical and efficient.

'Now, as for the oil itself. There is a delicate matter of its exact location.

'It is south of 60° latitude which means it is subject to The Antarctic Treaty signed by Argentina amongst many others. It forbids the development of oil and other minerals and it extends to 2048. Clearly, we can't wait that long to develop it.

'Shell have a plan that we could use for extraction. The oil is only slightly south of the 60° latitude, in other words only just within the Treaty boundary. We have developed new technical capabilities to extract the oil undersea within the Treaty area where the oil is located and bring it up to the surface outside the Treaty area.

'This plan may work temporarily but it is impossible to hide this method indefinitely. Therefore, as a backstop we would require you to break the Antarctic Treaty if necessary. This would be an unpopular move but if we are to recover the oil, it is something that may need to be done, General.'

Suarez pondered for quite a while and then declared, 'If that is necessary to develop the oil, then so be it.'

'You would break the Treaty?'

'Yes.'

Without looking at each other, Jonathan and van Marken breathed a huge sigh of relief.

'Now the percentages. We propose a simple 50/50 split.'

'Agreed,' replied the General, this time with only the barest of hesitations.

So that is how big deals are done. Decisiveness based on previous reflection of what is going to be proposed.

'Excellent,' said the Chairman of Shell and he was leaning over to shake the General's hand when Jonathan interceded.

'There is one other thing.'

'And what can that be?' said the Chairman in ignorance. He thought he was party to all that was planned.

Jonathan took out a newspaper photo of Maria and the UK Chief of Staff of the armed forces.

'Do you know this woman?'

The General shook his head.

He knew her very well both physically and as the Argentinian Mati Hari, one of their leading spies.

She had been good at talent spotting and had quickly got the up and coming General into bed. It could certainly be a good career move. But then he had met the Princess. So, Maria did not become Evita.

Jonathan continued, 'She was involved in obtaining important information from the British….'

'Yes, I do in fact know this,' interrupted the General. It was pointless to deny this further. 'But what has this got to do with our discussion?'

The General had also been shown the contents of the hard disc, but he was certainly not going to reveal that.

The General was not going to say that it was Maria's hard disc that had revealed that the Brits were not going to defend the Falklands - maybe the most important secret knowledge in all his plans. This is what had inspired him up come up with the invasion plan.

'It does not concern that relationship with the British Chief of Staff directly but other things she has been involved with, especially early on in her career.'

The General and the Chairman both leaned forward and listened intently. Where was this going?

'I have evidence that early on she was involved in the disappearance of women from Patagonia. Any of Welsh background were not trusted, rounded up and probably killed.'

The General cried out, 'This has nothing to do with our discussions about oil development. It is an internal matter for us.'

The chairman also looked at Jonathan in consternation.

'Jonathan. This is political not business. Just drop it.' He was concerned that what appeared to be a done deal could unravel somehow.

'No Jacob, it is not political or business. It is personal. Intensely personal.

'I know two of the women who were abducted. Very well.'

His voice was quaking - he was getting quite emotional. This was the first time that he felt he was acting morally in any aspect of his life, business and personal. He had always been a chameleon. A coward, even. Always ducking any controversial moral issues and doing what was needed to advance his career, learning how to climb a greasy pole as well as anyone.

'So, what is this leading to?' asked the General.

'I want you to put her on trial for human rights abuses.'

'What!' uttered the General and the Shell chairman, both caught totally off guard by this sudden development.

'I want all the bodies of the disappeared ones from Patagonia to be brought back and buried there. In their homeland. And a memorial erected there to commemorate this.'

'That is ridiculous,' uttered the General.

'That is bizarre,' shouted the chairman.

'You can't let this deal depend on this irrelevant personal quest, no, this, this vendetta,' he added.

'I can and I will. It is our oil, Shell oil not Argentinean.'

Turning directly to the General, he said, 'If you take over our concession you will provoke international outrage. No one will trust you again and you will lose all global support for your coup.'

The chairman looked aghast. He had seen his own chosen CEO, previously a brilliant technical negotiator, going to pieces in front of him. There was no way out of this mess, this blunder, this mental breakdown.

There was silence and the General got up and walked to the side of the deck, looking out to sea.

A few minutes later, he came back towards them and simply said, 'I agree to this action.'

The chairman of Shell looked shell shocked; Jonathan looked triumphant. This was his most important achievement in life, his first truly meaningful one. He had been determined to bring justice to Catrin and her mother, and to honour her brother and his own in some way.

The General was a superb politician. His fast whirring brain cells had led him to see that carrying out this action, though it would annoy his colleagues, would give him strong support within the country, from the people and even stronger support from the wider Western world, where human rights were still important. A General of a military government promoting human rights and justice. That would be a masterstroke.

Never mind that he was betraying those who had helped him on his way to power.

They all shook hands quietly. An hour later they had all signed a one-page agreement that put in black and white all they had agreed to.

# Chapter 26

This journey was never ending. Jonathan was beginning to regret his plan to visit the Shell oil rig in Antarctic waters. Travelling by boat was out of the question but he hadn't really appreciated how far and long the journey would be by plane. He had travelled from Holland to Brice Norton airfield in Oxford, UK, where he had caught the weekly flight to The Falkland's via Ascension Island. His first leg to Ascension Island, four thousand miles, had taken eight hours and there was no inflight entertainment system, so he had been unable to relax viewing the latest movies, the only time he ever watched them. He had entertained himself by reading the latest quarterly Shell accounts; yes, he read the 42-page document that contained all the details of the companies vast and complex dealings. He was reading the first draft for his eyes only. Most of the report was in black but some parts were in red and would be redacted at his say so to be replaced by an alternative version in blue. This was the creative accounting version that would be presented to the shareholders and the markets. He had been two hours at Ascension Island airport, literally a rundown shed while the flight was refuelled. It was not quite the exclusive VIP lounge he was accustomed to on his travels. He had not been amused by the antics of the squaddies at the airport. Still he may have behaved in the same way if he was on his way to a six-month tour on The Falklands. He knew the Shell high fliers from top European universities would have. He was glad to be back in the plane where their raucous behaviour was somehow at a lower key.

They finally landed at Mount Pleasant air force base on the Falklands. But there was no time to rest. He was quickly in a rundown 4 by 4 taxi from Mount Pleasant to his next flight from the small airfield, just outside Port Stanley, the island's capital. It took 90 minutes to cover the 35 miles as much of the gravel road was either semi flooded or potholed. He didn't see much of the town, not that there was much to see. With a population of only 1,820, it was not much more than a large village. He did however see the memorial and monument commemorating the liberation of the islands from the Argies by Margaret Thatcher's band of heroes.

The De Havilland Canada Dash-7 (DHC-7), a 4-engine turbo prop, is a relatively small plane for a journey of six hours and 1900 kilometres. His next port of call, as he continued on his journey to the rig was the British Antarctic Survey scientific research station Rothera, on the Ross ice shelf. He was accompanied on this plane by a roustabout from the rig itself, who was returning from leave. You could tell Mike had the strength of a bear and was as hardened as any man could be, as he'd been working on offshore rigs from their first use about 30 years before. Jonathan didn't identify himself as the Shell CEO, merely a visitor to the rig. In that way he hoped to get a more honest down to earth account of what it was all about working in these hostile conditions.

It turned out that Mike was very knowledgeable compared to the average roustabout but only in his specialised field of interest. In the same way that someone can be a Formula 1 nerd for example, Mike was a nerd on the design and construction of oil rigs.

Jonathan was aware that Shell had been a world leader in the development of oil rigs for offshore drilling with each successive design being bigger and better than before as the sea depths they were required to operate in became deeper and deeper. But he did not have a detailed knowledge of these developments.

'So, Mike, tell me about some of these big rigs you've been working on.'

'You found the right man here,' he replied. 'I know more about rigs than anyone. I'll tell you about the biggest and meanest rigs around.

'From the early nineties with first the Augur platform and then the Mars platform, Shell held the world record for deep sea rigs. Both drilling in almost 3,000 feet.

'But this depth was almost doubled when the first subsea developments took place with the Mensa platform drilling at 5,300 feet. The designs all differ with different means of mooring and floating.

'You know don't you, that on land, these giants are too heavy to stand vertical and would collapse under their own weight. They were built sideways and pulled out to their locations sideways by tugs until they were erected vertically. Although most of the structure was invisible under the sea some of these rigs were taller than the Eiffel Tower.'

'So, what's the biggest ones?'

'Berkut. A fucking giant stuck out in the Russian Far East. 200,000 tons – that's the weight of 500 Boeing 747s to give you an idea. Working in -50 C.

'Had a soft spot for Perdido, drilling in 8,000 feet of water in the Gulf of Mexico. That's one and a half miles depth of water. Towed sideways all the way from Finland.

'Then there's Hibernian, only 40,000 tons weight above water but supported on a solid lump of 600,000 tons of concrete  just sitting on the seabed, called a gravity support rig. She's at sea off northern Canada and been designed to withstand 6 million ton icebergs.'

'So things have changed a lot in your time?'

'Yes and no.

'The biggest change is in the size of the buggers, the sea depths they have drilled in and something that people don't realise. They only hear of the sea depth, but the oil and gas reservoirs can be another 30,000 feet below the sea bed so we drill down maybe 40,000 feet altogether.

'But rigs have always been rigs - all looking the same above water and all being as ugly as fuck. But they've obviously got bigger. Some platforms above water are forty storeys high. And it's got a bit more comfortable as time's gone by.

'You've done this all your life. Are you used to the danger?'

'I've had mates die - drownings, fires, just plain daft accidents - but that would happen in lots of physical outdoor jobs. Things have got better since they separated the living quarters from the main rig where all the dangerous stuff was.'

'So, what about working down here?'

175

'Well you'll see. When I said all rigs are the same, maybe that's not going to be true anymore, as you just can't make them bigger and bigger. We've showed we can cope with oil in the Canadian Arctic and offshore Alaska. But offshore Antarctica is something else altogether. The hardest place on earth to extract oil. Colder, stormier, more isolated, but that's only the start of it. You have glacier ice, sea ice and icebergs. And these days because of global warming there are far more and bigger icebergs breaking off from the glaciers.

'It's led to a new design where the rig is not permanent. The wells are all on the sea bed and everything is pumped up to a ship that can sail away when conditions are bad, ice cover, storms etc.

'Down here is no different as far as everyday life on a rig is concerned. You've got enough people to choose your mates, there's only one pub but it's not far away,' he joked. 'And like all rig routines, you've got so many weeks on and so many weeks off. So you live two lives really especially if you've got a family. The main trouble down here is not the weather, I'm used to that, but it's so fucking far from anywhere decent. We can go to Stanley, but Stanley is a dump. It would be nice if we could go to some towns in Argentina.'

After six hours they were there, at the Rothera research station. Here scientists stayed for long stints in very difficult conditions. The scientists, up to a hundred in summer, do a wide range of research from evolutionary biology to polar magnetic field studies and many other projects in this unique environment.

It was 15° C below zero with a 40 km/hr winds when they arrived at the research station. But it was not raining or snowing, just an average day. He wondered if

176

the Sikorski S92 helicopter flight out to the rig would be on today. He wasn't sure if he preferred to stay here or on the rig itself.

He was told it was a normal flight out to the rig. The turbulence and constant buffeting was somewhat off putting but thankfully, he did not need the sick bag. It had been bad enough with the constant noise from the engines making all conversation impossible. But this may have been a blessing as even he wasn't sure he could take any more detail of the different types of rigs that Mike had been on, fascinating though it was.

----------

As the S92 helicopter approached, he could see not a conventional oil rig, as most people expected. They were preparing to land on a ship, but not any old ship. This was a super tanker sized FPSO, the Futura.

He was welcomed on board by the captain, having almost had his hand crushed by Mike's farewell handshake. Yes, there was a captain as it was a ship of sorts though not like any other he had seen. Besides it stayed in port most of the time except the port was on the open sea and thousands of miles from civilisation.

He was allocated the guest cabin next to the captain's own. It was good three star standard and after a relaxing shower he was having a gin and tonic with the captain and Harry Robertson, the chief production officer, the man who dealt with the oil side of things.

'Yes, it's an FPSO, a Floating Production, Storage and Offloading facility, the state-of-the-art method of oil production in ultra-deep water.

'But I'll let Harry take you on a guided tour. It's more of a factory than a ship if you ask me and he knows more about all that side of things.'

They donned heavy weather gear and they both cycled away and it seemed almost like they were on dry land. Today there was hardly any movement of this giant ship. There were cycle lanes marked out with arrows and even some road signs.

'So it's nine hundred feet long and truly unique. It is modelled on the Shell FPSO "Terr" on duty in the Gulf of Mexico but has been massively strengthened to be an ice breaker and to withstand smallish icebergs. This is our biggest danger. There is very little scientific data on the size and frequency of icebergs. We need to track them and predict their movements. Huge icebergs are continually breaking off from the Antarctic ice shelf and the only thing we know for certain is that this is increasing due to global warming. The sea ice, every winter effectively doubles the area of Antarctica. But it is only 3 to 6 foot thick and we can cope with that with the new ice breaking oil tankers coming on stream.

'Instead of a ship mooring alongside a conventional rig platform and risking collisions with the platform in bad weather, the FPSO is the platform.'

Nearing the bow, they now stopped next to a huge yellow cylinder protruding through the deck floor.

'This is 82 feet in height and 82 feet in diameter but it is not part of the ship. It is the world's largest buoy and sticks through a huge circular hole in the ship from top to bottom. But in bad weather this 3150-ton buoy

178

can lower itself below the ship, allowing the ship to sail away freely to calmer waters. It takes about two hours to disconnect.

'It is the buoy not the ship that is connected permanently to all the pipes and moorings. The buoy itself is moored permanently to the seabed and is connected to all the oil, gas and power lines on the sea bed. The brainwave is that the ship, the FPSO, rotates freely around the buoy as the wind and currents take it. It weather vanes.

'To show the sort of challenges we had to overcome, the original buoy was designed to be a hollow steel structure but simulations and calculations showed this would not work and it ended up being made from synthetic foam.

'What I can't show you is just as remarkable but it is all on the seabed. The construction of the undersea wells was quite an achievement and they are constantly monitored and controlled remotely. They were built and are serviced by remote controlled vehicles. We also use mini submarines. There's also subsea storage of oil and 2 phase pumps to pump oil and gas long distances before they are separated. The pipeline will go from here to the Falklands where a new super-sized Sullom Voe will be situated and also Ushuaia in southern Argentina will become the new Aberdeen. Oil will then be transported in conventional tankers with LPG ships for the gas, which is liquified before transportation.'

Sullom Voe was the facility built on the Orkney islands to process UK North Sea oil and Aberdeen on the west coast of Scotland was where all the infrastructure and oil support businesses and contractors and companies were based.

Harry, with his vast experience and detailed technical knowledge was one of the very few who knew about these plans; he had been consulted as to their feasibility at an early stage.

They cycled on and stopped by a maze of pipes.

'All these pipes here are connected via the buoy to the six subsea wells situated in the sea bed at a depth of about 9,500 feet. Wells on the seabed at that depth are subject to massive pressures of 300 times atmospheric pressure due to the weight of the water above them. So, they have to be strong with thick walls, all adding to the complexity of the installations. And of course, the sea bed is not flat and smooth here.'

He could see a bewildering collection of large diameter pipes.

'This one pumps up oil from one of the subsea wells and that one pumps up gas. Both oil and gas are processed on board and then stored in special tanks on the ship, basically like a conventional oil tanker in that respect.

'The steel pipes are called lazy wave risers and have S shaped bends in them that can compress or expand to cope with the movement of the buoy. The pipes themselves are a challenge as their total length is so large, they have a significant weight in themselves.

'Wow! Any other challenges?' he laughed. It was truly a triumph of modern science and engineering and very costly.

----------

Later that evening the captain held a reception on his behalf and Jonathan had asked for a cross section of staff to be present. This had caused some consternation as, just like the military, there is strict hierarchy of privilege on board ships and some of those present had not been in this reception room before or enjoyed its luxuries. However, the fact that the CEO of Shell had visited this distant location after a very long journey was well appreciated and news of it would generate a genuine morale boost to the company.

But only the captain knew about the sensitivity and the importance of the visit and he and Jonathan sat down for a last private talk before his departure the following morning.

Jonathan cut straight to the point.

'I know you are no ordinary captain and are very well acquainted with the Antarctic Treaty of 1991.'

'Yes, I am. No mineral exploitation below the 60° line. To be reviewed again in 2048.'

'Also, despite your plea of ignorance about the oil side of this venture I am sure you know that this ship Fortuna is moored just outside the 60° line of latitude. All fine so far as the Treaty is concerned.

'But the exploratory drilling used drilling at an angle to the vertical so they penetrated the sea bed well inside the 60° latitude line, discovered reservoirs of oil there as predicted by our preliminary seismic and radar surveys.'

'Yes, I am aware of this but sworn to secrecy. I also know that the six subsea wells producing oil and gas are well within the 60° line.

'In other words, we are technically in breach of the Antarctic Treaty. Well I think the word "technical" is redundant.'

'Indeed. What is more, it may only be a matter of time before this becomes known to the outside world. It is not a small undertaking after all.'

'So, what are the plans if this happens? In particular what do I say as Captain, the man technically responsible for this. And here the word "technically" is necessary as it is Shell itself that is responsible.'

'Well there are two aspects really, one political and one commercial.

'We hope to have in due time, support for our breaking of the Treaty from the national authorities who will have jurisdiction over this territory.' Jonathan was being deliberately cryptic here.

'And we also know from the exploratory drilling and the seismic surveys that the vast bulk of the oil and gas reservoirs are well within the Treaty area.'

'So, in due course, with the appropriate backing, you would want to move Fortuna and the whole production system inside the Treaty area?' the captain asked.

'Yes, that is the intention. So, we await for events to unfold in the not too distant future.'

'And these events, are they random, or do you have some influence over them?'

Jonathan smiled but not entirely enigmatically.

# Chapter 27

The restaurant was huge and garish with its bright white lights and whirling dragon statues. The table was laden with dishes of all sorts - fish parts and other horrific looking bits of birds and ducks and goose feet. All Chinese delicacies no doubt but Pedro Garcia and his colleague Pancho Rivera were missing their beloved Argentinian chiaroscuro steak barbecues.

They had flown to the new Hong Kong International Airport on Chek Lap Kok, an artificial island and taken a short taxi ride to the Auberge hotel, the only hotel on Discovery Bay. They thought they had been brought to a quiet backwater, but it still seemed teeming with people to them. Although nominally part of Hong Kong it was still a 25-minute fast ferry ride to Central Pier, Hong Kong Island.

They were the guests of two Chinese men who were gulping down all the delicacies in what seemed to them a very crude, indelicate manner.

'So, we are all happy,' beamed Tommy Ho. 'It is a good deal?'

'Yes, we are very pleased,' said Pedro. He had taken over as the main speaker from Pancho who was looking a bit green, from trying to cope with both the copious quantities of sea food and the third or was it fourth bottle of strong rice wine.

And so they should be. It was a massive deal.

'I think you will like our little boats.'

He was referring to the five antisubmarine warfare P18 corvettes that the Argentinians had purchased.

The P18 was 1800 tons with a range of 2000 nautical miles at a speed of 18 knots. It was equipped with an AK176 gun, two 30mm cannon, 4 YJ83 anti-ship missiles, FL-3000N surface to air launchers in an 8-cell tube and a helicopter landing platform.

'I am sure they will come in useful,' grinned Tommy again. 'What are you going to call them?'

'The Malvinas Class.'

'Aha. Very good.' And they all laughed loudly. But it was a packed and noisy restaurant so they did not attract anyone's attention.

At this moment Tommy seemed to sober up and become very serious.

'We, the Chinese government support your claim to the islands. It is your Taiwan. We strongly support you.'

It was indeed a massive secret deal. And it was a cashless, untraceable transaction. The five ships were a barter purchase exchanged for $250 million of Argentinian commodities that the expanding Chinese middle classes were clamouring for. This included thousands of tons of prime Argentinian beef from the best pampas ranches. This worked out at a cost of $50 million per ship.

The Chinese had given them a discount compared to the price they had got from Nigeria, Bangladesh and amazingly, the land locked Kazakhstan, for the same class of ships.

As they shook hands, they felt pleased and looked forward to reporting personally to General Suarez, who had sworn them to secrecy, even from their Argentinian secret service bosses.

As for the money laundering, the General would use the huge secret fund granted to him by the president, without parliamentary consent to buy the commodities through intermediaries on the Argentinian market.

Pedro and Pancho seemed to be full time buyers of military equipment these days.

They had been wined and dined in a French chateau as they bought four Super Etandards from France, the very same but much upgraded planes that had fired the Exocets at the British ships in the previous Falklands War.

They had also savoured the best Russian caviar in Ulyanovsk, Lenin's birthplace, 500 miles east of Moscow on the banks of the river Volga, after buying six MiG 29 fighter planes through intermediaries at a private aircraft company. These intermediaries were all ex-Soviet era pilots with strong contacts in the Russian military aircraft industry.

And their next visit would be to an exclusive spa on the Dead Sea to buy some more Skyhawk jets from the Israelis. Argentina had a strong link with Israel having South America's largest Jewish community. Some of these were contributors to Suarez' secret fund. In this way General Suarez had built up quietly over the years, the strength of the Argentinian armed forces.

Suarez and his colleagues were much more sophisticated than their predecessors and had learnt a lot from the mistakes of the Junta. They had also patiently built up the military strength of the country, leveraging their power with the civilian governments with their promise not to intervene in politics. In particular, their close cooperation with the intelligence services and extensive use of INTEL had allowed them to make an accurate risk benefit analysis of their intentions. It is always good to know how your enemies will react and cultivate allies who will support you.

# Chapter 28

Jan Willem's son from his first marriage, Caspar, was visiting them at the villa near Cannes, one of his irregular visits.

He was in his thirties and although not unfit - he was a keen cyclist - he did look strained and overworked.

'Hiya Dad. You're looking well.

'Hiya Annemie.' She was his father's young and attractive second wife and his stepmother.

He kissed her on the cheek three times, barely touching her face, as was the traditional Dutch custom.

There was no heterosexual attraction in Casper's case. He was visiting with his husband of ten years, Jan, a psychiatrist, who also looked overworked. They were not typical of the modern Dutchman, who usually had a good work-life balance.

These visits were surprisingly friendly despite the many differences between Caspar and his father, both socially and politically.

Caspar, although very able, had not followed in the business footpath of his father and grandfather. Quite the opposite. Everything they stood for was anathema to him. As a student he had been a leading environmental activist and had been on the Greenpeace ship Arctic Sunrise that had attempted to board a Russian oil drilling rig in the Arctic Ocean. He and other activists had been detained by the Russians for two months.

Now he was the young, handsome and charismatic leader of the Dutch Green Party, Groenlinks, and had led them to be the third largest political party in the last general election.

They always had intense discussions at these visits. Both he and his father relished the intellectual nature of their duels. It was an excellent example of mutual tolerance and respect that Dutch society was famous for.

As they sat around the pool in the evening after a wonderful barbecue, Caspar began,

'I see that Shell have published their latest scenarios for the future. He was referring to the long document called "Shell Energy Transition Report."

'Have you read it, Dad?'

'Of course.'

Father and son both were some of the very few who had read and digested every word of it.

'I'm amused that you've called the three scenarios, *Mountains, Oceans and Sky*. How clever to make a link with nature in mere titles of economic forecasts, suggesting there is a sympathetic approach to the environment.

He still regraded his father and Shell as inseparable and made out he was the author or contributor.

'Still not as bold as British Petroleum rebranding BP as Beyond Petroleum.

'Do you really think you can hoodwink the public into believing you are environmentalists after all the environmental disasters you oil people are responsible for around the world?'

'Come now, son. Our scenarios are state of the art and are highly regarded globally. It's a serious report about the future based on rational analysis of the situation regarding global warming that we, as a company take very seriously.'

His dad also talked as if he was still working as opposed to being retired for a good ten years.

'Yes, I suppose it does illustrate a change in your approach. In the nineties you and the other oil giants were sponsoring right wing think tanks to attack the early IPCC reports and to deny the science of global warming.'

'Yes, I admit, we have now accepted the scientific consensus and wish to be a serious part of the moves towards reducing the global carbon footprint.

'Our three scenarios talk of three situations that could occur.

'The first *Mountains* would be one in which there would be concerted government action. The second called *Oceans*, would be more uncoordinated private actions by business as governments fail to get their act together. But both scenarios see net zero emissions by the end of the 21$^{st}$ century.' *Sky,* the most optimistic scenario sees both governments and business collaborating strongly to reduce emissions earlier.

'Yes, the first two would both be disasters for the environment and fall well short of the goals of the Paris climate agreement on keeping the global warming below 2°C.'

The Paris agreement was based on the sixth report of the IPCC, founded in 1990 by the UN and the WMO, the World Meteorological Organization.

The Intergovernmental Panel on Climate Change was composed of thousands of scientists specialising in this field who were charged with investigating the science of climate change. The physics is well understood and established. And each successive assessment has produced more and more scientific evidence of anthropogenic – man made – emissions of greenhouse gases that result in the heating up of the atmosphere and the consequent climate change.

'The situation is getting desperate. Greenhouse gas emissions have in fact gone up by 60% since 1990,'

But his father, Jan continued with his case, also based on facts.

'Population will increase from 7 billion to 10 billion and the energy demand of the population is rising as they strive for the higher standards of living that we take for granted.

'I'm thinking here of the 1.1 billion with no electricity, and the 3 billion who currently rely on energy from wood and dung for heating and cooking.'

'But you're seeing that as a way to sell more oil and gas. They're new customers. You say in the report that in all three scenarios, the demand for oil and gas will be higher than today in 2030.'

'Yes, I do. That is what the figures lead us to.'

'Even your third and most optimistic scenario, with governments and business working together would only reduce the carbon content of your energy products by half by 2050.

'You'd still be producing 85% of today's oil, a mere 15% drop but the IPCC report says we need to reduce oil by 78% by the same date to keep warming at 2°C.'

'But to meet rising demands in the growing and developing population new oil and gas production will be essential,' countered dad.

'No. No. No. Where will you get it? Don't you dare develop oil in the Antarctic. We have plundered that place enough already in a very short time. It was only discovered in1820 and fur seals and elephant seals were wiped out by the end of the 19th century and we killed a million whales in the 20th century.'

He was getting very emotional here. He had seen the whaling with his own eyes and tried to stop it physically in the Greenpeace ships. It was still happening despite the International Whaling Commission ban.

'And I bet you haven't heard of the penguin oil factory there where they clubbed penguins when they came ashore to molt and boiled them for penguin oil. 130,000 penguins a year.'

'This is all very well but get back to the point.'

'OK,' he said calming down a bit.

'Yes, I agree with you that there will be a growing demand for energy but it doesn't have to be oil and gas. It's all about the mix.'

'We have been moving from oil to gas in power stations.'

'Gas is still a fossil fuel emitting $CO_2$.'

'But oil is still needed for heavy transport and chemical production.'

'By chemical production you mean plastics of course.'

'But we have been investing in renewables too, as you know.'

'Yes, I do know. But only non-US oil companies. They have a different political climate there as regards global warming with Presidents amongst the main deniers.'

'We oil companies have set up the OGCI, the Organisation for Global Climate Initiative to promote change.'

'Yes, that's what the PR people call green washing.

'Here you are under more pressure but why is it that the big oil companies between you have only spent 1% of investment on clean energy and oil companies own less than 2% of operating solar and wind energy.

'I'll tell you why. It's all a pretence. It's all about the bottom line and this is not in your report.

'You get a 22% return on onshore oil, 7 to 9% on wind energy and 5 to 7% on solar. That's what decides your policy and then leads to three scenarios produced by an oil company that all feature a big future for oil and gas production.'

They could have gone on all night but there was only so much that even zealots can effectively convey.

So, they turned off the outer pool lights and retired to bed.

# Chapter 29

The Teton Mountain Lodge and Spa was a luxury hotel positioned slope side in Teton Village, the main resort area of Jackson Hole. The town itself was about 11 miles away but what mattered to them, as keen skiers, was that they were within close walking distance of the main aerial tram ski lift which takes you up to up to the 3000 metre summit of Rendezvous mountain in 12 minutes. The lodge itself had its own luxury indoor and outside pools and a 22-person rooftop hot tub.

But Jonathan, Jake and Steve were all up to their necks in their own hot tub. Each had a beer in his hand and the rising steam slightly obscured their view of the Jackson Hole ski runs. All three looked tanned and fit but today they were totally exhausted. This was their regular annual get together, just the three of them without their wives and family. They had become close friends ever since they had met in a conference for highfliers many years ago in the ski resort of Flaine in France. Jonathan was the only good skier then but all three were now expert skiers. It was why they had chosen Jackson Hole, famous for its challenging trails. Fifty per cent of them were classified black or double black with such blatant names as The Headwall, Dicks Ditch and Expert Chutes. Jackson Hole in Wyoming is situated in Teton National park. Even the airport car park had moose in it, chewing away at tasty rubber parts of the parked cars.

'Wow. We made it,' shouted Steve, always the most raucous. He still had his flowing blond hair and was still exhibiting a six pack that he had developed many years ago.

'We sure did,' replied Jake, in his own subdued but no less ecstatic tone. He was the least demonstrative and yet most intellectual of the three but was still an all-round American frat boy.

Yes, all three had successfully negotiated the dreaded Colbert's Couloir, the scariest and most dangerous trail not only in Jackson Hole but in the whole of North America. Regarded year after year in polls as the scariest entrance, it is a regular for the ski and boarding professionals who try and outdo each other with outrageous jumps and backflips.

Even Jonathan was serious when he said, 'I'm glad I was wearing a spine protector today.'

He was modest, as he had made the best run of the three without any danger of falling.

They were content to be in their own hot tub rather than mixing with the other guests as these days they were public figures and liable to be recognised and more likely criticised, something they preferred to avoid.

'Do you remember when you skied right into that wall of snow in Flaine, Jake?' teased Jonathan.

'I sure do. You pushed me into it you bastard, but seriously - you saved my life as I was headed for a big drop.'

'We've done well not just as skiers,' said Steve, who was now a media mogul in the States and CEO of Carter

194

Communications, a multimillion-dollar organisation that he had taken over from his father. Most commentators thought this was wholly on merit as he was the third eldest son. He had worked his way up in other media companies beforehand by his own efforts and talents.

And Jonathan too was a CEO, the boss of the mighty oil giant, Anglo Dutch Shell.

But it was the quiet Jake who had scaled the greatest heights. Jake Diamopoulos was the US Secretary of State.

And inevitably their conversation turned to their work, which apart from these rare breaks, dominated their lives. They lived for their work. Even this was a working break. Even though they were sat in an open-air hot tub drinking beer. They liked to touch base and talk about their work, they were literally now world leaders in their respective fields and had power and influence which they revelled in. All who have reached their levels have this abiding passion and ambition to succeed.

'So, what's happening in your world, Jonathan? What's the big news? I want to be the first to put it into our media outlets. I want get the scoop. It's what drives me on day after day.'

Jake too, although he didn't mention it was looking for inside information from the head of a global multinational.

'Well,' said Jonathan pensively, appearing to be reluctant to divulge too much. 'We've discovered a major new oil field.'

'So, what's new? That's what you do,'

'Well its complicated,' he whispered.

'So!'

'The oil is in a protected area, where oil development is banned.'

'That hasn't stopped you guys before.'

'It's also in territory claimed by three different countries.'

'But I'm going too far here,' he mused and paused suddenly.

He did in fact know that one of them would figure out what he was now only hinting at. Although Jake was the politician, Steve the media man was every inch a political animal too.

Jake had not only figured it out but had gone one, maybe two steps further.

And your problem is that you need the support and backing of one of those countries and you've got the wrong country behind you - at the moment.

Steve, no diplomat and not even subtle, burst in at this point.

'So you need the Argies to support your claim and help you develop it.'

Jonathan looked shocked and had a pained look on his face at this moment, but the conversation had developed exactly as he had planned it. Steve would not jeopardize the plan, he merely wanted to be the first to announce it after it had taken place. As for the Americans, they would see it was in their interest to support it. And knowing about it in advance, they would not panic and automatically oppose it when it took place.

Looking uncomfortable, he deftly changed the conversation.

196

'So, Steve, what can you tell us before you tell the whole world?'

With a mischievous look on his face, Steve began.

'Let me tell you a little story that I've just remembered. And I am only telling you. I will certainly not tell the whole world about it. Not yet anyway. I was on my Dad's yacht somewhere in South America, I think and we had a visit from a local. He was in civvies, but he definitely looked like a soldier to me. He hinted that he and his mates were going to take over the country and he wanted my dad to support him after they had done it. He seemed a very clever man, said he had a degree in economics from Harvard. I'm sure he'll be successful.'

Steve smiled, a most disarming smile.

And Jake too, with only a slight hint of a smile on his face, knew he had some interesting things to say and do when he got back to work.

----------

'Is that General Suarez?'

'Yes, it is. Who am I speaking to?'

It was a highly unusual phone call. It had come through on his own private cell phone that he only used with his close family. Only they knew the number and its existence.

'This is Jake Diamopoulos, the US Secretary of State.' He paused to allow Suarez a moment to digest this.

After a lengthy silence, Suarez replied. 'How do I know who you say you are?'

'You will have to trust me. I have some important information for you.'

He dived in at the deep end.

'We, a very small number of us here, but that includes the president, know what you have planned,' and before Suarez could reply, 'and we wish to support you.'

It didn't take long after his return from Jackson Hole to the State Department in Washington for Jake to figure out who the mystery man in South America was.

He and his team had homed in on the promising up and coming guys in the Argentine military and one man stood out. General Ricardo Suarez. He had indeed studied economics at Harvard and had already made it to the top level in the Argentine army.

US interests focussed exclusively on material resources to be developed. It didn't matter who would develop them or how. The might of the US would support them in return for a suitable share of the cake.

'But to gain our support you must ensure that you have learnt from the mistakes of your predecessors in such action,' continued Jake.

'No large-scale arrests, no special measures. Nothing to antagonise the outside world. It is in your interest to do this to get your people's support also.'

Suarez reflected that it would indeed be a huge step to have the support of the US for their coup.

What was going on? Last time the Americans had supported Thatcher. They had shown her satellite photos of the location of the Argentinian navy that helped her sink the Belgrano and win the war. The US

Secretary of State had been made a knight - Sir Caspar Weinberger, for US help and support. Suarez knew all the history, even the non-public bits. He even knew that Kissinger had told the previous Junta to do all their dirty work quickly before human rights campaigners in The States could act.

He composed and asserted himself.

'If you are right about these actions of ours, then what do you want from us? I know the US does not act politically out of the goodness of its heart.'

'You are quite right, General Suarez. We have our interests, you have yours. Sometimes they coincide. In this case they do.

'We will support you if your actions are moderate in exchange for 40% of your share of all the oil.'

Suarez was stunned. He could not believe that they knew about the oil too. They knew about the coup and now the oil. But they didn't know everything. They didn't know about the invasion.

'Yes, I hear what you're saying. I will need to think about it and consult my colleagues. I will come back to you.'

'I don't think so General. You know it's a good deal and besides if you don't agree to it, we will put a stop to all your plans. You must decide now.'

They had figured that getting Suarez alone to decide was more secure and more likely to be successful. Knowledge is power and they knew nearly everything.

He had no choice. But it did still seem mutually advantageous.

'Very well. I accept.'

'You're a wise man, General. We know we can put our trust in you to carry these things out efficiently and to keep your word. Best regards to you and your family.'

# Chapter 30

Christine Henderson had just come in from horse riding on her favourite coastal run. This was a daily occurrence. Still unmarried, she had a very simple life living on The Falkland Islands. She was important on the island being one of its ten elected councillors. In this particular context she was a big fish. She was one of the few who had a broader experience than just island life, even though it had only been for a couple of years.

She had been plucked from the island as a bright and attractive sixteen-year-old and awarded a scholarship to Atlantic College in Wales. The college at the bequest of Lord Mountbatten, a former chair of the college board, had asked the island authorities to select one person for an island only scholarship. So, she had been chosen and had enjoyed a lively two years of drinking and debauchery as well as just scraping a 24 point pass out of 45 score in her International Baccalaureate Diploma programme examinations. Competition for scholarships from other countries led to many students getting high 40's scores. She was an example of politics being more of a factor than ability. Others who could fit into that category were the sons and daughters of Royal families who had also been to Atlantic College. To preserve and gain political influence the college overlooked these few anomalies to its normally very stringent entrance procedures.

But she was now puzzled by a phone text she had just received and opened.

It simply said.

*I think you should take a short holiday off the island. You are going to have some unwelcome visitors. Jake.*

The only Jake she knew was the one she had lost her virginity to at the college and apart from that one event after a raucous party near the end of her time there, it had not been a relationship as such, even though she had become pregnant. They had not really kept in contact and she had told him about the pregnancy before she left college and returned to the islands.

She knew Jake was now a famous and important person. He was Secretary of State in the United States government. This connection led her to decode the message. They were going to be invaded by the Argentinians again. It was something that someone in Jake's position might know.

Jake was giving her a secret warning. He obviously felt some guilt at abandoning her.

The Christine he knew would simply think of her own personal interest and safety. But he had misjudged her. She had matured and become more responsible and less selfish. So now, to her, the world had to know about this.

The Atlantic College connection immediately led her to think of Willy, another former student and close friend of hers. He really was the most important person she knew. A king no less.

She had been in his gang at college, one of the pretty girls amongst those who liked to enjoy themselves and were not very hardworking. Apart from Christmas cards she did not have any contact with him now, but she did have his number. It was always in those Christmas cards.

'Willy, it is me, Christine.'

'Who?' He sounded puzzled.

'From the Whitaker dorm in college?'

'Aha. Yes. Of course. How are you? You went back to the islands after leaving, didn't you?'

'Yes, I was homesick. I could have gone to study at university maybe but basically, I'm an island girl.'

Even now, after all these years, she found this painful and could not tell the truth of what had happened.

'Mummy, why are you crying?' She wiped away the tears, stroked her little boy's hair and returned to her call.

'But Willy, I need to tell you something. You need to tell the world about it. We're going to be invaded by the Argentinians.'

'Oh. Right,' he stammered. He really didn't like political stuff and didn't really want to be involved.

'So please let the world know. So it can be stopped.'

'Yes. Yes. I'll see what I can do.' And he abruptly put the phone down.

He wasn't naïve. The fact that his wife was Argentinian made this an embarrassing piece of knowledge. Should he be loyal to his family and stay quiet or should he do his duty as King and inform his government.

He hated being dragged into politics. It always led to trouble.    Loyalty to friends and family were what motivated his moral compass.

He decided he would just do nothing.

----------

Twenty minutes later the Boss, as the head of British Intelligence was known, was meeting with his PM in the PMs office in the House of Commons, not their normal arrangement, far too public, but speed was essential.

'Prime Minister. GCHQ have just told me that they intercepted a phone text from Washington to Port Stanley in the Falkland Islands.'

He paused for dramatic effect.

'So what's it about?'

'We think the Argentinians are going to invade the Falklands.'

The PM looked blankly at him. No trace of anger or even surprise.

The Boss was also not surprised as this government had already made it plain to the secret services that the Falklands were not going to be defended again.

The PM wasn't even cross that his friends across the pond, by not letting them know, were betraying their closest ally.

The Boss said nothing. His role was not to question his masters however supine, cowardly and unpatriotic they were. But even he was shocked when the PM seemed to dismiss the whole business as if it was a minor matter with no historical or national importance.

'Thank you, that is all' said the PM.

The Boss left quietly closing the door behind him. He reflected that closing the door on this matter was not necessarily a course he could accept. In the car back to his office, he pondered how he could unobtrusively influence matters.

# Chapter 31

It was now past midnight and the Prince had not returned. His equerry, despite his embarrassment phoned up the chief protection officer.

'The Prince is missing,' he blurted.

'What?'

'I can't get hold of him on his phone.'

'What?'

'I'm afraid the Prince is missing. He hasn't returned from a private trip he made today. On his own.'

'Why the fuck didn't you tell me about this trip?'

'Well, well, um, we have um allowed him to go on day trips like this before and there's never been a problem. He always wears the official disguise we all came up with when we don't want him recognised.'

'Why don't I know about these trips?'

'Well we, I, the Prince and I, thought it was better you didn't know as it might get you into trouble.'

'You fucking incompetent idiot.'

As his job was to ensure the Prince's safety, he had no respect for anyone who could compromise that.

Quickly calming down. 'So where did he go?'

'He said he was going to Aldershot to meet some army mates of his from his Afghanistan tour.'

'And has he gone there before?'

'No, he lied.

'And I suppose you don't have contacts for any of these mates?'

'No.'

'So where could he be?'

'I don't know. I just don't know.' And he collapsed into his chair.

----------

A COBRA meeting was instantly convened in "The Cabinet Office Briefing Room A." These are emergency meetings held at a time of some national crisis.

Present were the PM, the Foreign Secretary, the Home Secretary, the head of British Intelligence and by special invitation, the Prince's chief protection officer and the hapless equerry. He  now seemed as if all the life had been drained from him. He was physically shaking in his seat.

The PM took firm control and what he said was explosive.

'This is potentially very damaging not just to Her Majesty's Government but to the whole reputation of our country in the world.

'So we must find him but without alerting everyone he is missing.

'We must hush it up. I will not yet even tell Her Majesty, the Queen.

'We can't have a police search and a general lookout at all ports and airports as we would for a missing person or escaped prisoner.

'Do you agree?' They all just nodded forlornly.

Turning to the Home Secretary. 'What about his upcoming public appointments?'

'We will obviously cancel all these immediately. Illness maybe!'

'That's just not on. It will alert the press and they'd go wild with speculation and digging,' intervened the PM.

'If I may,' said the Head of British Intelligence.

'We have a plan for this eventuality.

'We could let all his appointments continue as normal.'

They all looked mystified.

'We can use a body double, an impersonator.'

They had all seen several impersonators on TV lampooning the Prince but was he serious?

'How will you find one quickly?' asked the Home Secretary.

'We already have two on the books and they don't just look like him. They have been trained to adopt his mannerisms and his speech. In fact, one of them is a full time member of my organization.'

They all looked on with amazement.

'They have already been used a few times when the Prince was how shall I say it – not himself.'

The PM firmly said, 'Just do it.'

And added, 'And what is the assessment of his mental state you alluded to?'

'Some incidents in the past. And I remember that dreadful pitying interview he gave on TV talking about his estrangement from his mother. What was the quote, "I don't think mummy ever loved me."

'We have a report here from an eminent psy
who has in fact been talking to the Prince, as a pa

'He is regarded as fragile, suffering from depres
low self-esteem and possibly  Post Traumatic Str
Disorder from his army days.'

Several present groaned at this dramatic information.

'So how will this manifest itself? What is he likely to
do? Where would he go? Where has he gone?' the PM
asked rhetorically.

# ..apter 32

King Willem Alexander was at home in Huis ten Bosch, situated in the woods of that name within the city boundaries of The Hague, one of the king's three official residences. His mother, Queen Beatrix lived here for over thirty years. When she abdicated and moved out it was given a massive renovation and five years later the King and his family, Queen Maxima and their three children moved in. It is outwardly an ornate baroque palace and the interior parts used for official functions still reflects its style, but the living quarters are ultra-modern and totally out of character with the original design.

He was sitting in his favourite chair in the huge games room. His growing paunch suggested he was doing this too often. In contrast to the public, official part of the palace, this games room was a teenager's dream and a couch potato's home. It had a pool table, a bar, a bar football table, several dart boards and lots of assorted board games. But it was dominated by the obscenely large screen with full Dolby surround sound system that an Art House cinema would be envious of. It was connected to a state-of-the-art games console as well as a top of the range virtual reality set up. He was watching a replay of the Dutch women's hockey team

Olympic final win against Argentina on this giant screen. He never tired of watching this victory. He, his wife Maxima and their children all dressed in orange fan jerseys and waving scarves, had seen the match live and had cheered on the team as much as any ordinary Dutch fans. This had cemented their popularity with the people even more. King Willem Alexander had a knack of being an ordinary bloke, a man of the people. Who could forget the medal he had worn at his wedding - one commemorating his taking part in the Elfstedentocht ice skating race around 11 towns in northern Holland together with 30,000 other Dutchmen. This was in sharp contrast to the Duke of Devonshire, Prince Arthur's father, a mere guest at the wedding, who had worn a chest full of medals on his military uniform, none of which symbolised any action he had personally been involved in.

King Willem Alexander was vaguely irritated when he   picked up his private vibrating iPhone.

"Willy here."

'It's Prince Arthur,' whispered the speaker.

'Aha! Arthur, how are you my friend? I haven't heard from you for some time.'

'I'm ok, I suppose,' he replied in a not very convincing fashion.

'You don't sound too good. What's up?'

'I'm feeling a bit down and I need to get something done.'

'So what can I do for you?'

'I want to ask you a big favour. I want to see my mother in Argentina. But you know I'm not officially allowed to. She is persona non grata to the UK government. I'm desperate to see her. Can you help with your flying connections and maybe Maxima, being Argentinian, can help too?'

'Can't you fly incognito directly from UK? There's an RAF Airbus A400 Atlas C1 flight from Brize Norton to The Falklands twice a week, I hear. Stops off on Ascension Island for refuelling just as the planes did during the war itself. You can then fly from there into Argentina, by the back door so to speak.'

The king was knowledgeable about aircraft timetables. There was indeed a twice weekly flight on Wednesdays and Sundays to Mount Pleasant airport near Stanley on The Falklands.

'No, that's too risky. Too many Brits on that route.

'I can see KLM fly from Amsterdam to Santiago in Chile and then there is a direct flight from there to Argentina.'

'Yes, I know. But it is not a transit flight, so passengers need a Chilean visa,' added the King revealing his obscure knowledge of airline schedules.

There was a pause and then Willy said, 'Let me think about it. I'll come back to you.'

----------

The Prince pulled up into the car park of the twelfth century Swan Inn in Llantwit Major, a lovely, small village in the Vale of Glamorgan in Wales, in a nondescript second hand Range Rover. They were common in this affluent area just west of Cardiff. He saw Willy just entering the pub and they took a table in a quiet corner near the log fire.

The king was dressed casually, for a bald dutchman, in corduroy trousers and a rusty coloured woollen pullover disguised his paunch effectively. He still looked well, being only six foot tall - medium height for a Dutchman. He had an avuncular, friendly appearance with his reddish face and was generally regarded simply as a nice man, open to all and socially relaxed.

'How are you today?' said the King, trying to hide his shock at the Prince's appearance. His face was pallid and blotched; his frame, never an impressive one, was floppy and sagging and he was stooping and not making much eye contact. He looked furtively around as if he was being chased by some apparition. A real mess.

There was just a hint of a shrug from the Prince and Willy started reminiscing to break the tension.

'My mother used to bring me here often when she visited me when I was a student at Atlantic College. Just her and one bodyguard. She used to fly into Cardiff airport in a private jet. No one ever recognised us. I don't think you expect to see a foreign Queen and Prince having a quiet drink in a Welsh country pub!

'By the way, I didn't tell Maxima a word about all this. I suspect she wouldn't have approved and I always listen to her!' He smiled mischievously.

'But you look nervous. Don't worry it will be fine. Trust me. I have booked two rooms in the college for tonight and we'll fly to Schiphol on the 6.25am flight tomorrow morning. I often stay at the college when I'm in Cardiff. I meet up with my   old tutor. He was a big influence in my life. Pretended to let me do my own thing but was always there to look after me when I was in trouble.'

ıduction helped the Prince relax a bit and
ɔng and emotionally exhausting chat in the
mbibing three pints of Heineken.

drove up to the college, the Prince was given
an amusing history lesson by King Willem Alexander.

'So this is the old entrance gate to the castle dating
back to the 12th century. St Donat's castle was in use by
various noblemen until the 18$^{th}$ century when it fell into
disrepair. Its claim to fame is that it was bought and
renovated totally by Randolph Hearst, the American
newspaper magnate as a place to hide and shag his
mistress, the actress Marion Davies and have lavish
parties with film stars, the Kennedy family and others.
Oh, he also furnished it with lots of antiques and other
valuable paintings he had accrued over the years.

'Now as you know it's a United World College
school of about 350 students doing the International
Baccalaureate Diploma in their final two years. It's had
lots of famous students – such as the Finnish head of
Nokia, a female US astronaut who was also a concert
pianist and me of course. It's a wonderful place with
over two hundred nationalities, roughly two from every
country in the world and it made me who I am today.
Make of that what you want. The college is very liberal.
I had my 18$^{th}$ birthday in the school staff room. I phoned
up Freddy Heineken, the boss of Heineken and   had a
lorry load of beer delivered direct from the brewery in
Amsterdam. What a night that was!

'I better not show you round though for obvious
reasons.'

So they retired to the two guest rooms, one always
kept for Willy for his overnight stays when he flew to
Cardiff.

----------

'This is your co-pilot speaking. On behalf of the captain and crew I would like to welcome you on board this Fokker Friendship F70 from Cardiff to Amsterdam.

As the cabin door was closed due to the latest security, no one saw the speaker, who was a bit of an unusual member of the crew, he only flew about once every two weeks. He had been doing this for over twenty years. His other job was King of the Kingdom of The Netherlands. He had hardly ever been identified although some people now and again thought the voice was familiar. He had revealed his moonlighting to De Telegraaf, a leading newspaper in the Netherlands only recently. He claimed it was a relaxation from his royal duties.

The disguised British Prince sitting in row A1, kept his head in his newspaper for the whole flight. He had known his friend Willy for many years and knew he could count on his help when needed. Earlier he had simply been driven right up to the plane steps by the king himself with no customs formalities whatsoever in tiny Cardiff airport.

King Willem Alexander would treat this as a bit of fun, he had always enjoyed life. He had not been  called the Pilsner Prince for nothing, though people had been surprised at how he had grown into his royal duties, mainly influenced by his wife and consort, Queen Maxima.

Arthur's disguise was a familiar one; the thick ımed spectacles and beard were quite effective. ı used it many times when on non-official royal dutıۍ and it was accepted as being ok by his inner circle, including his official minder, his equerry. He also had an officially produced false passport with professional photo using his wig and spectacles, which he used when required, although he was never quite sure if it was working as a different identity or whether it triggered off orders to let a royal through.

After the plane had parked some way from Schiphol airport terminals, he waited in his seat until all the passengers had gone off on the bus to the regular gate D9; the plane was too small for proper landing stairs. He also saw the crew go off in a small minibus. That left him and the King. As always when the King flew, a small car drove right up to the plane and took them both to the VIP area where a special room was allocated for the use of the Dutch royal family and their guests. There was no customs check. No X ray machine for the King and his friend. One does not question the King. Schiphol was like his own personal airport; he could do whatever he liked there.

The KLM 701 flight to Santiago was leaving from Gate E24 in a couple of hours.

The king said, 'A friend will take you from here to the plane after everyone has boarded and you will get a quiet seat with no neighbours in first class – the flight is not full.'

# Chapter 33

Pieter Van der Valk, the head of the Dutch intelligence service, the General Intelligence and Security Service, the AIVD, was having his evening meal alone in the members dining room of De Nieuwe of Littéraire Sociëteit De Witte. Founded in 1782, this is a private club with exclusive membership, situated in a classical old building in Het Plein, just around the corner from Het Binnenhof, the Dutch Parliament. His private cell phone rang and with great embarrassment, he retreated immediately to the corridor but not for privacy. Use of cell phones is strictly taboo at the club.

'Hello, I'm Ross Morgan, King Willem Alexander's former tutor when he was a student at Atlantic College in Wales. Sorry to call you, I've never used this number you gave me before. I thought my job with you was done when he left the college, but I think you need to know something.'

Van der Valk recalled that they had recruited the tutor, a British science teacher at the school, to help ensure the future king's security and to generally keep an eye on him as he was a bit of a loose cannon who could potentially embarrass the royal family and the Netherlands.

'Go ahead,' said Van der Valk.

'Well there's something fishy going on. The king stayed at the college last night, he does so when he's flying the Amsterdam-Cardiff route. Normally I meet up with him and he tells me everything but last night he came with a male friend and they stayed in their rooms. That is so out of character for him, he always meets up for a drink. The head of catering told me as they had asked for meals to be sent up to his room.'

'Yes. I see. Is there anything else?'

'No but they both left early as the king must have been flying the 6.30 a.m. flight to Amsterdam.'

'Can you ask the Head of Catering or whoever took the meal up to them for a description of this man and ring me back? I'll also send someone out to the college to see if he can find out more.'

Immediately after this call the tutor went to see the head of catering, who it turned out had taken the meals up himself to their important guest and his friend.

He wrote down the description on a piece of paper and immediately rang Van der Valk in The Hague again.

----------

The tutor then rang a number at British Intelligence with the same information about the king's strange behaviour and the description of his mysterious friend.

British Intelligence knew about him being King Willem Alexander's tutor when the king had been a student at Atlantic College. They knew he reported to the Dutch Secret Services at the time. He had been contacted as a source by the British secret services after the king's wedding to the Argentinian woman whose father had been in the military junta during the Falklands War. They felt this father confessor could be a source of information about Argentina and in particular, The Falklands, via King Willem Alexander's wife, Queen Maxima. All possible sources were recruited however unlikely their contribution.

----------

'We've found him, Prime Minister,' gushed the head of British Intelligence in evident relief, before he greeted him formally or been asked to take a seat. He was clearly not his normal unflappable self. But it is not often one has to deal with the disappearance of a Royal prince, the only son of the Duke of Devonshire.

'Just sit down, calm down and tell me the full story.'

It was rare for The Boss to ask for a personal meeting with the PM at very short notice. Luckily, he was able to cancel his immediate appointments to see him.

'Well a few nights ago, GCHQ intercepted a phone call from the Prince to his old friend, King Willem Alexander, the King of Holland.

'The Prince was asking the king's help to go and see his mother in Argentina!'

Even the PM himself dropped his guard with a big look of horror at this news.

Then we had a call from a source about an hour ago saying a stranger had flown with the King from Cardiff to Amsterdam early this morning.

The description we got of the stranger matches the disguise the Prince uses when he travels on unofficial informal business in private.

'So, have you got him? In Amsterdam? Or the Dutch?'

He had now regained full control and told the Prime Minister.

'No, not yet. But we know he's on a plane to Santiago, Chile.'

----------

They had, with some very quick work, located him in the VIP Royal room at Schiphol airport. CCTV there had shown the Prince waiting for his plane to Santiago. With more time they could have got an agent on that flight, but the flight had taken off before this was possible. He had definitely been seen on CCTV boarding the plane.

So they contacted the Santiago, Chile embassy and instructed their resident, the designated attaché, to meet the plane arrivals at VIP in Santiago.

But this time there was panic, as the attaché was caught in traffic going to the airport. The flight had arrived and the VIP Lounge was empty when he got there. Nobody there recalled the man he described arriving.

'The VIP lounge was empty when I got there and what's worse there is no CCTV there.'

The VIPs are well and truly protected.

'We've lost him. I've lost him. I'm so sorry,' the attaché uttered as he contemplated the end of his career. He had been posted as far away from London as possible already and there was nowhere else to go apart from out. He had been a dismal failure before this and the incredibly feeble excuse of "Traffic," even though in this case it was true, would surely be the end of him.

Only The Boss himself seemed to take it all in his stride and did not seem particularly perturbed. Maybe that's why he was boss, because he was able to stand above the battle when everyone and everything was collapsing all around him.

# Chapter 34

Tenson and Gibbard were sitting on the lovely patio of Gibbard's little French cottage in the evening heat on the edge of Lac de Salagou in the province of Herhault, France. This was their annual little tradition and secret get together. Tenson liked to recharge his batteries in this one week of leave that he granted himself, while both reminiscing and plotting with his former boss, a legend in the history of MI6.

Gibbard, now in his eighties and long retired, looked sprightly and fit though extremely weather worn in appearance, prone as he was to be outdoors most days.

As the previous boss of MI6 he was Tenson's one and only mentor and confidante on all matters, not that there were many matters that were not work related. Marriage would have been one if they were married to a person instead of to the job.

They both gazed out at the beautiful ochre colours of the red, iron rich soil on the mountains around the lake. Putting down his nearly empty glass of malt, Gibbard said, 'You were quite handsome when young and I know you were pursued by many a young woman. I sometimes took advantage of that when I made you the runner of some attractive young female agent from the other side during your days in the field.

'Now, you yourself are getting on a bit. Nearing the end of your career.'

'Four years as The Boss can take it out on anyone,' muttered Tenson.

He looked hunched and weary, battle scarred if you like, and this was accentuated by his thick lensed horn-rimmed black spectacles which gave him a wise old owl appearance.

'I know I may look quite old and grumpy but hey, I'm still quite fit you know. I walk everywhere, every day.'

But he knew himself it was only walking. Any short run would have caught him out.

'You've had a tough time, been in an unique position dealing with the merger on top of everything else.'

He was the first boss of the amalgamated services, MI5, responsible for internal security, catching spies and MI6, the external security organization, running spies. All these years there had been antipathy, no enmity between these two organizations which had, if truth be told, led to a lack of cooperation, a deliberate holding back, a lack of sharing of sometimes vital information that had resulted at times in a completely dysfunctional situation. The new organization was called simply, British Intelligence.

Gibbard continued.

'It had been obvious for some time that the distinction between internal and external security was non-existent, especially since the rise of international terrorism. I made sure that you were my successor as the only one of the old guard who could carry this merger off.'

'Well yes it has been difficult, but it did coincide with the retirement of many of the old guard as you call them, on both sides, with me being one of the survivors.

'And many of the younger recruits, the new recruits appointed outside the Oxbridge route and even recruited from newspaper job advertisements, gave me their full support and were just pragmatic and logical and not tied down to some defunct historical traditions and loyalties.'

'We recognised in appointing you, that although you were from the traditional route of entry, you were extremely open minded and progressive in your methods. In particular, you knew and accepted that modern technology and the predominance of information from GCHQ in all your work was essential.'

'But also,' intervened Tenson, 'it wouldn't have worked out if the new young bucks and does were not highly competent in their IT knowledge and appreciated its power and potential to move things forward.'

'You're too modest as always.'

'Well put it like this. As The Boss, I have been office bound but I've never been a bureaucrat and am still in active close charge of events in the field.

'You and I both know that we have been instrumental in many of the successes of the company, but we also know that there can be no widespread public knowledge of these. They will remain secret for ever, known only to the close teams involved in each.'

'Because of your record over many years, they all look up to you and respect you, but I hear that now some are even beginning to like you,' Gibbard chuckled.

'We don't speculate on why we made it. We both know we have our inner reasons driving us,' mused Tenson.

He, in particular, had made it to the top because of his devotion to the company. It meant more to him than anything else, not that there was much else. He did not have a hinterland, any hobbies or pursuits or other interests. There was simply no time.

'For me it's quite simple really. I find that I am always totally absorbed by the problems at hand, that I like to solve more than anything else. The challenge is still there for me.'

He did have one piece of unfinished business that was in progress as they spoke. At the moment it was not even something that he would mention to Gibbard. Perhaps when it was all over maybe. But in this case, he thought, probably not.

Yes, he would like to go out with this one final achievement even though it perhaps would only ever be known to him and a few close others. Or, and this is what intrigued him now in his position as The Boss, maybe something that only he would know about. Sure, some others would have been involved in the field, following his quite close instructions, but only in their own specific area, and none of them would know the full picture, the main achievement, let alone the motives for it, that The Boss would never share. They were too personal to him, maybe even too embarrassing for him to share. Namely his love of his country and its noble achievements. His belief in liberty and freedom above all else.

Others could question quite how far he would go to defend these, how he would interpret them and whether he was in some ways betraying them in his methods. But not many, if any, would be in a position to know this.

Yes, it was a strange old world being The Boss spook, where your greatest achievements would only be known to yourself and that you would be the only one to judge them as great achievements. It was a powerful but lonely situation to be in something that could only be achieved by someone with great self-confidence and inner strength.

'So, what do you plan to do when you retire?'

Tenson just looked at him blankly. This was forbidden territory. There was a melancholy side to it all that he dared not dwell upon. In this role as The Boss, he never thought of his future. Was it because he instinctively believed that there was no future for him beyond his job, no, his calling, and that he would be utterly lost, in a purposeless limbo? With no reason to live.

# Chapter 35

Gonzales Edwards was back packing around the Middle East on his way to work as a volunteer in a wildlife conservation area in Saudi Arabia.

Here he was, in central Doha, the capital of Qatar, amidst all the towering architectural extravaganzas that make up this desert anomaly. Built by the Sheik to flaunt and somehow spend his wealth, Qatar especially, had found novel ways to spend its money, having attracted the Soccer World Cup to a country with only one major football stadium and with temperatures of 40 C plus during the day. Bribery may have played a part but seven more magnificent stadia and an impressive infrastructure were now being constructed on the backs of semi slave labour from Asia.

But some things are sacred. He was in the falcon market amidst all the shopping malls and multinational offices and banks. The premier falcon market in the world. He felt he needed to know more about the ancient tradition of the Middle East of hunting with falcons before starting his work in the conservation area. There he would be involved in the conservation of the Houbara, a magnificent bird in its own right. It is an endangered species precisely because it is the traditional prey for falconry.

He was with a group of western tourists who were taking a break from shopping to discover some local culture.

In the centre of a sandy courtyard was a magnificent falcon, commonly called a saqr, resting on a trainer's hand. The trainer  was also an experienced guide who churned out fact after fact about these amazing creatures.

'My hand is protected from the sharp talons by this cylindrical covered straw cuff known as the Mangalah.

'Here you see the braided cotton about 30cm long that holds the falcon around the ankles - the Al Sabbuq. This as you can see is connected to a longer leash to allow the falcon some freedom to move.

'Saqrs have amazing eyes. They can see a small movement of their prey from a mile away. So their eyes are covered by Al Burgu, a hood of decorated leather. As part of the training process the eyes are gradually uncovered.

'Falconry is an ancient art and has long been established as the sport of royalty in the Middle East. It thrived here two thousand years ago. The first Arabic book on falconry was in the 8th century and we Arabs gave many tips on falconry to the Crusaders, leading to falconry spreading to  Europe.'

'Emperor Frederich II wrote a famous book on falconry in 1247 and this led to the beginnings of ornithology. The many references in Shakespeare to falconry shows it was as well understood then as football is today.

'It died out in many places but here in the Middle East it is still a flourishing sport enjoyed by both poor and rich.

'For the poor in the desert, the falcon was trained to

catch their food. Otherwise it was a diet of dates, milk and bread.

'Hunting with falcons is highly skilled and respected and highly valued in the Bedouin society. There are many highly developed techniques for trapping and training falcons for the hunting season.

'Look at these sharp claws. Razor sharp. It makes it almost impossible for the prey to escape.'

'How much do they cost?' asked one of the tourists?

'The price depends on strength, age, clarity of eyesight and speed of movement.'

'But how much?'

'Hundreds of thousands of dollars for the best ones.'

There were loud gasps at this.

'As I said it is the sport of royalty now.'

'What do they feed on?'

Pigeons and chickens mainly. They only need water once a week as they drink the blood of their prey.

'A female Sakr like this one is best suited to desert hunting.'

----------

It had not been difficult for Maria to get the job as an air hostess for Saudi Arabian Airlines, the national line. She had already trained and worked as a hostess for Aerolíneas Argentinas, the Argentinian national carrier, and her stunning looks had done the rest. The personnel officer at the interview training board had no hesitation in employing her immediately for her first-choice route from London to Riyadh, the common route of the playboy Princes from their luxury pads in London to their Princely duties in their native land. The Princes all wished they could reverse the amount of time spent in each place such was their antipathy to any sense of loyalty to their subjects who they had always treated as slaves. They were far too arrogant to see that this could no longer continue and ignored the growing sense of unease and impending crisis.

Maria stood in the shade, the desert heat was intense at this time, but within view of the exit from the special parking area at the airport reserved for the Royal family, all 250 reserved car places. She was still dressed in her stewardess' uniform and had just arrived on the flight from Heathrow. He had been on the plane and she had served him the regulation tonic water with a large and surreptitious touch of gin. The whole of the first-class area had been cordoned off for him and his three colleagues and several well-connected foreign businessmen had been turfed out to club class despite a valid first-class business ticket. They were experienced travellers to Saudi with several lucrative contracts still running and knew better than to argue when they'd heard who was in their seats.

When she saw the cream coloured Rolls Royce Silver Shadow emerge, she quickly ran down the tarmac and struggled unnecessarily with her quite compact and light suitcase. He was driving himself; this was one of the few ostentatious things they could do openly, and stopped immediately. Although the car was less than six months old it had several scratches on the doors and even one or two dents in the mudguards. She was amazed but had heard that such was their wealth that they did not have much respect for a mere car, however bountifully

230

engineered and constructed. The window rolled down and he asked in an excellent English accent with only a slight trace of foreignness,

"Can I give you a lift into the city?"

She gave one of her blatantly inviting smiles and just opened the back door and climbed in. They both knew she should have been on the regulation staff minibus to the Riyadh Marriott Hotel along King Saud Road, but neither were too concerned. He was too conceited to ask himself why she would be doing this and she was only following in the footsteps of many others who had done exactly the same thing. She had frequently seen white European girls, mainly nurses at the King Fahd Medical City Hospital, being given lifts into town by the rich Saudi men. It was an open secret that many of the Royal Princes and other members of the Saudi ruling class had white mistresses, which they saw openly in Europe, but could only keep under wraps at home. These white girls were showered with what they considered expensive gifts but were mere trinkets to these supremely wealthy men. They were given little respect and were mere playthings, but there were quite a few who succumbed to the lure of unadulterated and corrupt wealth.

Neither said anything on the route along the motorway from the airport through the almost featureless and arid landscape to town. His interest in her was purely sensual and did not require any conversation. There was no pretence at any meaningful relationship. Her look, when she stepped into the car had told him all he would want to know about her. She was quite content to enjoy the luxurious ride in the fabulous Rolls, even though it was probably the tattiest one in existence, from its dented and scratched bodywork to the Macdonald cartons and empty cans and bottles which littered the floor.

He pulled in just in front of her hotel and turning around said, 'Give me your phone number please,' and she knew she was OK. He was a rogue but a polite one. He took out a lovely gold pen and wrote the number down on the leather upholstery of the front seat. Her number joined that of many others though she was pleased that he drew a special circle round hers. He handed her the pen, she stepped out and he drove off.

She was due to fly back in three days' time and was relieved when on returning
from the hotel pool the day before she was due to leave, she had a message at reception.

"Be at the side entrance of the hotel at 3 p.m."

She dressed in her most provocative outfit, risking the wrath of devout Islamists and certainly arousing the desire of males of all beliefs. The Rolls was waiting already and again without a word between them she was driven a few miles to what looked like a dingy small hotel in the rundown Batha area of town. He was certain he would not accidentally come across any embarrassing acquaintances in this location. He led her to a small room on the 3rd floor, where without any preliminaries, except the removal of clothing, they made love in a most basic and unfeeling way. In a couple of hours, she was back at her own hotel. At breakfast the next morning she was handed a small but elaborately wrapped parcel. It contained a ladies Rolex watch which she knew from duty free shops would cost £2,450.

The liaison continued in this sordid way every time she flew in for the next two months. She would get a note to meet him at the regular hotel and the hour-long ordeal was almost identical each time. All her attempts to make it more intimate and bearable for her, with some preliminary flirtation, were totally ignored. Only the gifts provided some variety. She gradually accumulated a range of expensive toiletries and jewellery. But they did nothing to temper her unease; the fact that she had no control at all made her feel very insecure. It was imperative that the affair continue for another five weeks, but she felt that it was out of her hands and she could only hope for the best. She could not afford to fail but was at a loss to know how she could begin to get a hold on this cold-hearted man.

# Chapter 36

The Houbara or Maqueen's bustard is a powerful bird that can weigh up to four kilograms and can be up to 75 cm tall and is known for its great speed in flight. These rare birds have been traditionally the main prey of the falcons in competition. A dedicated conservation area now protected this very rare species. During recent decades the population has declined dramatically and they are regarded as a vulnerable species (one category above endangered) by the IUCN, International Union of Conservation of Nature.

The species has been able to survive a long tradition of falconry in Saudi Arabia but the introduction of four-wheel drive vehicles has led to more desert areas being suitable for hunting.

For these reasons the Saudi National Commission for Wildlife Conservation and Development had set up this protected area at Mahazat As`Said and the entire 22000 square kilometre area is fenced in to ensure complete protection against hunting and grazing.

It is to this conservation area that a large convoy of Mercedes M class 4-wheel drives turned up in the early hours. The gates were opened by two researchers at the NWRC who emerged from a guard post.

They were mortified that several years work of

breeding and releasing the Houbara into the wild to save it was going to be undone  in a day, but they were equally aware that to protest was to risk being executed on the spot.

They had known that the Sheikh, the king's youngest son, and his entourage were coming. The Sheik was going to unleash his new falcon for the first time. Like his two brothers, he was a fanatical falcon hunter.

The Sheikh was one of the foremost experts on falconry having been a trainer since his teenage years and having published a famous book *Hunting with Falcons*.

They had been ordered to reveal the location of the fastest and fittest Houbara in the area and were now herded into the first 4 x 4 in the line in order to lead the way.

The main method of obtaining falcons is through the trade in Qatar, and the UAE. Upwards of 1800 falcons can be traded in Qatar in mid-August. the falcons come from captive bred falcons in the USA , Canada and Europe as well as the Sudan and the Yemen. There are no methods of control and regulation to reduce the number of falcons being taken in the wild.

But the Sheikh had got his new falcon via a circuitous route. He was not averse to obtaining the best falcons illegally.

He had got this one from Indian smugglers in Uttar Pradesh in India.  Each falcon is a Schedule One Bird in the Indian Wildlife Act, on a par with a tiger and can fetch as much  in the international smugglers market.

A few hours later the scene was set. Several large caravans and trucks had been parked and all the facilities for a day's hunting - Sheikh style - had been assembled. A large Bedouin tent had been erected containing all the equipment needed and several large cages put in the shade.

The Houbara had earlier been released, itself a splendid sight. But now all the Sheikh's followers were waiting expectantly for the new falcon to make its first appearance,

The Sheikh himself was patiently stroking one of his saqr (Al Hurr), a female peregrine falcon. She looked magnificent on the flat padded top surface of a round ornately carved wooden mushroom shaped perch called a Al Wakr.

There were gasps as they first set eyes on the new falcon.

'What a beautiful bird.'

'Indeed, a wonderful specimen.'

'They say it cost him over US$300,000.'

'But that's just pocket money for a Sheik.'

'And he still got it cheap.'

'I've heard it's from illegal Indian traders, smuggled to Bahrain and then over the causeway into Saudi Arabia,' whispered one of his entourage conspiratorially.

'Yalla,' shouted the Sheik and the saqr, in a split second, with full power but regal grace had flapped its large wings for a powerful takeoff into the sky. It soared upwards to a commanding height and circled about looking below for its prey.

Suddenly the chase was on. It had spotted the previously released houbara, carefully bred here by the researchers. An exciting chase took place, climaxing more than once, as the houbara itself a very fast bird, escaped by a hair's breadth. But in the end the superior speed of the saqr, which can reach a speed of 250 km an hour, much more than a cheetah on land, prevailed. On its very first flight it performed the famous downwind loop high in the sky and to the gasps and whoops of delight of the watching party, she made a spectacular midair kill.

'Wow!'

'Woo Hoo!'

'Ahahh.'

'Magnificent.'

'Allah Akbar.'

The Sheik's entourage looked at each other in sheer amazement and hugged and clapped in equal measure.

The Sheik beamed with pride and pleasure.

The researchers present, all enforced watchers, looked on with dismay and quiet anger. The Houbara had been one of their main conservation successes.

Amidst at all the excitement, one man, either one of the researchers or a body guard, had pulled out from beneath his cloak a small hand gun which glinted in the sunlight as he raised it for action. Almost simultaneously with the saqr kill, and very close to three o'clock, a shot ran out and the Sheikh himself fell down, shot in the head at almost point-blank range.

Minutes late in all the panic, the saqr was unperturbed and having already drank the blood of her prey, the Houbara, she quietly drank up from a large pool of blood on the ground, the blood of her now dead master. A just reward for a masterful flight. Her desert dessert would be the blood of Gonzalez Edwards, the assassin who had been killed by the Sheik's security guards. He had been unable to plan an escape route and not contemplating dishonour, had made the ultimate sacrifice for the cause.

237

----------

The camel racing course at Taif is a remarkable one. As well as the ten kilometre track for the camels themselves, there are seven outer paved tracks. One is for the media and all are sealed off from the ordinary public. They are beyond the outer track. However, the Princes have a special grandstand, well protected from personal approaches and with the best view of the finish. But otherwise, security was lax, such was their confidence in their own power.

Juan Gomez was here today attending a race for the first and last time and allowed himself some curiosity to look at the races and relax as much as he could before his 3 p.m. job.

He looked in amazement as the camels approached. There were apparently 11 categories of camels though they all looked the same to him. And they all appeared to have no jockeys! But as they got closer, there was a deafening noise as the massed paws pounded on the turf and even through the clouds of sand, he could see that there were very small jockeys. He had heard of the four-year-old boys, bought and sold as slaves to camel owners and semi starved to keep their weight down but thought they had been abolished as one of the relatively minor    liberal reforms brought in to appease global public opinion. But they had gone further and showed the world bizarrely how they were modernizing and using technology. There were jockeys, but they were robots. The early models designed by a Swiss company

238

were too heavy and intimidated the camels. But these weighed only three kilos and had been done up. There was only an upper body strapped securely to the camel, but they had a mannequin human face, caps and sunglasses and wore racing silks. They even had perfume. The camels had adapted very well to their use. The robots were a mass of electronics, radio controlled by their operators driven around in SUVs on the first inner paved track.

He looked at his watch and gradually moved through the standing spectators. He got to a toilet block and without hesitation entered a specific cubicle. He quickly removed his Argentine Mauser '09/73 sniper rifle and silencer from the overhead cistern. It had entered the country in the Argentinian diplomatic bag and he had picked it up surreptitiously in a standard bag exchange. He calmly raised it to the open window and aimed at his target a mere 45 metres away without obstruction.

All this had been prepared and pre planned meticulously. His target was sitting in his designated seat as one of the sons of the king, in fact second in line to the throne, right in the centre front row. He had been trained extensively for such a mission and a few seconds after his phone vibrated at the 3 p.m. alarm, he calmly pulled the trigger. A large red patch appeared and rapidly spread around from the skull of the dead Prince. He immediately put his rifle down, closed the door of the cubicle and swiftly walked out of the toilets, merging silently with the crowds of spectators who were not yet aware that something big had happened.

The mission had been easy to prepare as it was well known that the Prince would be here at this race. He attended all the major races in his capacity as the president of the Saudi Arabian Camel Federation.

The only thing missing was a CNN satellite truck. They only had one in the country and that was in Riyadh.

----------

It was to be Tuesday March 23rd at 3pm. She clearly could not rely on him asking to see her that day even though Tuesdays was one of his days. But she had found out what he did on Tuesdays when she was at work. Borrowing a male steward's rented car and dressed in a chauffeur's uniform, she had followed the Rolls effortlessly as it drove along the Quassim Road. Its destination was the falconry at the purpose-built falconry showgrounds run by the Saudi Falcons club. So she had the location for plan B if he did not invite her to the usual hotel.

On the appointed day she should have been on the flight back to the UK but she had called in sick and her cover had taken over. She had to lie low in the hotel or hide somewhere and as she had no desire to meet him elsewhere, the dingy hotel in Batha was perfect.

Luckily, she had no need to put into action her plan B. She had picked up the message that morning for the regular hotel assignation.

At five minutes to three, just after the sex, she slipped off the bed and went to her handbag on the dressing table. She calmly took out the Heckler and Koch HK P9 pistol with fitted silencer that she had picked up clandestinely from the military attaché at the Argentinian Embassy that morning. She turned towards the Crown Prince,

240

waited until he stood up and shot him in the chest. He fell over on his back and walking towards him she put two further bullets in his head and chest. As the blood dripped from several rivulets on to the floor, she went to the cupboard and took out the suitcase she had hidden there that morning. She took out the sex aids and scattered them on the bed and around the room. She dressed carefully and then made a quick phone call and left quietly, having closed but not locked the door. She went down the stairs and walked past the man at reception and straight out into the afternoon sun. The street was deserted as it always was at siesta time. She walked calmly up the road for about two hundred metres and turned around to look back with a smile on her face just as the pickup truck with satellite dish arrived at the hotel. The CNN camera crew knew exactly where to go and ran inside in great excitement. It is not often that the Crown Prince of the richest kingdom in the world is murdered. While they ran up the stairs the driver positioned the truck and adjusted the S mode portable satellite dish on the back to point directly south at an angle of 24° to the AzerSpace 1 satellite in geostationary orbit above the equator.

----------

Their father, King Fahd al binaj al Hassan, the ruler of the Kingdom of Saudi Arabia, would not be upset at the news of the death of his three sons. He had been in a coma at the King Abdulaziz Medical City of the National Guard Hospital for four months since he had responded negatively to a revolutionary new Argentinian experimental drug he had been administered for his worsening diabetes.

# Chapter 37

Apart from an attempted news blackout by the minister of communications, with martial music being the only thing broadcast on all TV and radio stations, no one knew what to do. The three assassinations had taken place in three different locations almost simultaneously and rumours had quickly spread on social media from those present at these events. But the situation was unprecedented. There was no government emergency plan to carry out in the event of the death of the Crown Prince and his two brothers. Everyone knew about the king being in a coma although even this had not been official. But everyone had assumed that the Crown Prince would take over and if anything happened to him, then one of his brothers would. But this close family had pointedly failed to bring into the succession possibilities anyone from the wider family, however large that was.

There was a vacuum at the very core of power. The family had been too arrogant and overconfident. Although the Crown Prince had been seen as a reformer by the liberal middle classes, his support had dwindled drastically with his apparent involvement in unsavoury murders of opponents at home and abroad. Some were also upset by the apparent lack of concern and attention regarding civilian deaths and the humanitarian crisis created by the Saudi action in the Yemen.

Crucially there had been no mention of who had been responsible for the assassinations. Who was behind it all?

It was in the light of all this that the Ulama convened an emergency meeting when it was clear that the Princes were all dead.

All they knew was that the three Princes had been assassinated. But they were remarkably political considering their avowed religious function and their public piety.

'It is our duty to respond to these events,' began the chair, the Grand Mufti and head of the Ulama, to cries of agreement and the nodding of heads.

And this was indeed something that united them. But how?

The Grand Mufti called their political analyst forward to relate more of what was known.

'Who is responsible? And what do they hope to gain? We have not been involved nor heard anything about any impending action.

'Probably not Western powers, who all depend on oil for their economies to function. Even those that do not buy Saudi oil don't want the supply disrupted and prices to rise.'

'What about the Russians?'

'They would not benefit much from higher oil prices for their own gas and oil as they don't have the capacity to increase production quickly.'

'The Chinese then?'

'They seem to be a force for stability in the world economy these days. They don't want disruptions to their slowing economic growth.

'That leaves terrorists, Islamic fundamentalists like ISIS or others. But we don't have any information about this.'

Despite their ignorance of the cause of the assassinations, some present could hardly contain their glee at what had happened, though it was a big surprise to them. They had been unhappy with the behaviour of the leading figures of the monarchy, the three sons, who seemed to be out of control when their father was no longer able to moderate their behaviour.

Others were more circumspect and aware of their sense of responsibility.

'We need to see who emerges from the monarch's family as their leader and decide, as is our role, whether he is obedient to the Prophet, before confirming him in power.'

There was no obvious support for this and quite a few panicky comments.

'Who knows who will emerge?'

'No one has been prepared.'

'No one has the experience.'

'Yes, confirming the new ruler. This is our role normally, but this is unprecedented.

'We have to be ready to reject potential successors until we find one to our satisfaction and not act as a rubber stamp to whoever comes forward.'

'What will the people want?' said one very naive and young member of the Ulama - he was in his early sixties.

'The people will want the will of the Prophet interpreted by us on their behalf.'

'So we just wait? It could be ages. It could result in bloodshed between competing factions. It could result in chaos.'

'Yes, the Prophet will want his will to be clear. We do not want another split as happened to create Sunnis and Shia.'

'We must ensure that Wahhabism is preserved and indeed elevated in the Royal succession.'

'Why should there be a Royal succession?' piped up the rebellious Muhammad ibn al Wahhab suddenly. 'They - the monarchy - have been poor servants of Islam and have not set a good example. Why should we still maintain this system, this balance of power between Islam and the monarchy.'

'Hear. Hear.'

There was suddenly a growing chorus of support for these ideas gradually forming in their minds.

'Indeed. We can run this state ourselves more wisely. I mentioned recently that although they are our mortal enemies, the Iranian clerics have a system which works. We can learn from that.'

'We take power in all majority spheres and delegate the day to day material and economic affairs to highly trained technocrats, some of whom, by merit, will be from the royal family.'

'Let us do this.' There were loud cries off approval.

For such apparently religious teachers ostensibly concerned only with spiritual matters they had a highly developed understanding of more earthly affairs.

'But we need the military on our side.'

At this point Muhammad ibn al Wahhab, seized the moment and standing up in front of them all began a powerful tirade with a confident rhetorical flourish.

'We need to be confident. And bold. The people will not oppose us. True Muslim believers cannot oppose us if we claim we are ensuring stability and carrying out the will of the Prophet.'

'Let us take over. We can ensure that our enemies, the christians and other non-believers in Allah cannot profit from this. We need to turn away from material things generated by our oil sales and do away with materialism. We ourselves have connived in this alliance between token adherence to Islam and the adoption of the worship of material things.

'We can end this at a stroke if we stop the oil. Keep it in the ground. Let the infidels not get their hands on our oil.'

----------

So, it was decided that they would take over. They sacked the Grand Mufti and appointed Muhammad ibn al Wahhab their leader. He had been the most forceful and powerful in the movement and his confidence had been contagious.

So, it came about that Muhammad ibn al Wahhab made a broadcast to the nation only six hours later having received the support of the three top military leaders. They too had been unhappy with the ruling family and their general air of arrogance. They had no respect for the military. Despite spending millions on armaments, they had failed to ensure that the military leaders were onside and fully supported them. And the military, although displaying loyalty, had been very unhappy about the role they had been asked to play in the Yemen. Like the mullahs, they had seen an alternative working model in neighbouring Iran where the military had a strong and influential role with a system developed to ensure its sustainability. They quickly agreed to the religious takeover after safeguards guaranteeing the role and function of the military had been ironed out and signed up in a formal agreement. It was not that difficult as a draft had already been prepared by the far-sighted military leaders some years before, to cater for just such an eventuality.

There followed four hours of intense action by key military troops, who surrounded all the royal palaces, the key government offices and installations in the capital and set up a rapid plan to surround all the major oil installations in the country.

The martial music broadcasting on all TV and radio channels ceased and the screen showed Muhammad ibn al Wahhab dressed in his normal modest clothing sitting on a simple wooden chair facing the camera. The background was a plain yellow painted wall devoid of any decoration. It was an austere scene in deliberate contrast to the lavish and almost obscene displays of wealth that the monarch displayed in similar circumstances. He began his speech to the people.

'To all the peoples of Saudi Arabia.

'We have relieved the royal family of their responsibility to rule the country. They have shown by their actions that they were not responsible. It is no longer the kingdom of Saudi Arabia. We declare the

248

Islamic Republic of Saudi Arabia is born today. The prophet Muhammad. has decreed to us that this is the way forward. Wahhabism will truly declare to the world of unbelievers that its resources are no longer available. There will be no more oil. This dark, satanic liquid has stained too many people.'

'We will live by the words and gifts of the prophet Muhammad alone.'

In the words of the quran. Surah Al – Humazah, 104:1-9

Waylul-likul-li humazatil-lumazah

1. Woe unto every slanderer, fault-finder!

'Al-lazii jama-'a maalahu wa 'ad-dadah,

2. (Woe unto him) who amasses wealth and counts it a safeguard,

Yahsabu 'an-na maalahuuu 'akhladah!

3. thinking that his wealth will make him live forever!

Kal-laa la -yumba-zan-na fil-Hutamah.

4. Nay, but (in the life to come such as) he shall indeed be abandoned to crushing     torment!

Wa maaa 'adraaka mal-Hu-tamah?

5. And what could make thee conceive what that crushing torment will be?

Naarul-laahil-muuqadah,

6. A fire kindled by God,

'Al-latii tat-tali-'u 'alal-'af'idah:

7. which will rise over the (guilty) hearts:

'In-nahaa 'alayhim-mu'-sadah

8. verily, it will close in upon them

Fii 'amadim-mumad-dada.

9. in endless columns

'Inshalah.'

----------

General Suarez had completed the micro-managing of his military coup but was still busy organising the deployment of the invasion of Las Malvinas when he was interrupted by a very apologetic aide.

'I am so sorry to disturb you, General, 'but there is something happening in the outside world that you should maybe be made aware of.'

He was not quite sure if this interruption was appropriate and timely but he somehow sensed that it was. It was after all a major world event and a quite surprising, exciting, shocking event.

'Go ahead.'

'The monarchy in Saudi Arabia has been deposed. The Crown Prince and his two brothers have all been killed.'

General Suarez merely exhaled. He was always calm and in control, an unusual characteristic for someone with a so-called Latin temperament. But he was probably one of the few people in the world who was not surprised at this. He and maybe a half dozen others were aware that this was going to happen. In fact, they had made it happen. The General's ambition, and the sheer scale of his imagination had led him to come up with this plan. And his own military intelligence branch had provided the three assassins. He remembered also that the inspiration for it had come from the Argentinian working as an analyst for Shell, who had sent him the secret internal report on Saudi Arabia.

His aide continued, 'and the mullahs have just made a broadcast saying they are in power. They have taken over with the support of the military,' he gushed out without a moment's pause.

The intention in the plan to kill the Princes at this exact time had been to cause maximum disruption and distraction to the world community on the day of the coup and invasion and to destabilise the oil supplies from the Middle East to the benefit of the new Argentinian oil finds.

But the news of the fundamentalist takeover was a surprise. He had expected the royal family to somehow survive with maybe some cousins or other family members taking over in some way.

His excited aide continued.

'What is more, they have declared that there will be no more oil sales! They see it as the cause of the materialistic culture encouraged and epitomised by the royal family and its outrageous spending.'

Now this was an unexpected surprise even to the General. No more Saudi oil. This would result in much higher long-term oil prices to the benefit of their own new found oil and to some extent counteract the downside of the Americans getting a big share of it.

This caused him to beam widely and to share smiles all round. No one there could quite explain why the General was so pleased with the news of the Saudi coup.

# Chapter 38

It was a clear moonlit night as the cars drove along the dirt road towards the ground station. Not the sort of weather they wanted, they would much have preferred a cloudy night with perhaps even a bit of rain so that there would be less traffic about. They were now only a few miles away and could clearly see the outline of the two dishes in the distance. These dishes, just outside Kingston in Tasmania, were the satellite ground station links with the Antarctic research stations. Such was the power of the electronic systems available these days that it was no longer necessary to have a large diameter dish even for a commercial link to a geostationary satellite. As the first car approached with a driver and one passenger only, they looked at their watches and slowed down slightly as they still had few minutes before the action. They presumed correctly that this timing was essential in order to coordinate it with another or maybe several actions in other places. If only they knew what was planned altogether, they may have been a bit more nervous about the importance of their particular part in the whole picture. But being true professionals, they had not spent any time surmising about the total plan. They were loyal to their bosses and trusted that there were good reasons for what was coming. Besides such an audacious act was not common even in their line of work and they were excited at the prospect.

'Right, in we go!' were the only words spoken. They drove up the short drive into the fenced compound. It was not a security fence, more one to mark a boundary. There was one single storey building of yellow painted brickwork, the size of two double garages consisting of one large comms room and two smaller rooms for storage, a small poorly equipped kitchen and a toilet. After all it was a small civilian commercial site in an isolated area and there were no reasons to suspect any criminal or terrorist activity. All had been rehearsed carefully. They knew there were only three men present on the night shift and they would be all in the main, dimly lit central room quietly observing the continuous telemetry being transmitted down from the satellite to the dish outside and then into their monitors. Their work was termed housekeeping and indeed it did really amount to just checking that everything was ok on board the bird 36,000 km away at 140° East above the equator. Rarely did they have to intervene physically as these systems were well established and extremely reliable as any good communication system had to be.

The three men dressed casually in T shirts and jeans and sitting quietly in front of their monitors were very surprised to hear the door knock. Nobody visited them at night, but they were not alarmed. They had no reason to expect anything suspicious.

'Who on earth could that be?' said the youngest and recently arrived recruit doing only his second stint of night work.

'Well there's only one way for you to find out,' piped the other two, who had quickly let him know that any chores were to be his responsibility.

As soon as he had opened the door a hand was over his mouth in a firm but not painful grip. He also felt a small indent in his back as he was pushed into the room. As in all such cases, he correctly surmised that the man was poking a gun into him. He led the way involuntarily into the main room followed by his assailant and one more man. They both wore dark clothing and balaclavas. The second man moved past them and stood about 3 metres behind the two staffers. They could see his gun pointing menacingly towards them. Not much chance of attacking him as he was just out of their range and no chance of him missing them from that distance.

'Quick both of you stand up and move towards the wall. You, you first,' he gestured to the short, thickset middle-aged man who he'd identified correctly as the man in charge. They were both made to face the wall well apart with their hands in the air and palms touching the wall above their heads.

While he stood there the youngest and most vulnerable of the staffers was made to sit down in the middle of the three chairs. He was clearly terrified and he felt limp with a palpitating heart and very sweaty limbs. Clearly his training as a satellite telemetry officer had not mentioned anything about armed assault and his many hours on very realistic virtually reality computer battle games had turned out to be not very realistic at all.

'Now switch off transponder number 9!'

'But there's no backup for that one. It will cut off all contact with every Antarctic Research Station.'

'Exactly! Do it!' He did not look at the others and quickly typed in a few instructions on his keyboard. After a short wait the screen turned blue with a warning in red. DO YOU WANT TO SHUT OFF T9?

Without even waiting for a prompt from them he nervously typed in "YSE" then "YES."

T9 IS NOW OFF AIR

By now the third man had entered carrying a small case. From this he took out three pairs of hand and leg cuffs. He quickly got to work putting these on all three as they were made to lie well apart on the floor.

Then he took out a roll of tape and expertly taped over their mouths so they could not talk to each other. There was no way they could have called for help as the station was along a quiet road 15 km from the nearest village. They now carried one to the kitchen, one to the toilet and one to one of the storerooms. They left quickly, carefully closing the doors. Their colleague who had been on guard standing in the shadows outside joined them and the two cars quickly drove off in opposite directions.

They were never contacted during a night shift so the three men, bound and gagged securely, would only be found when the first of the next shift arrived the next morning at 8 a.m.

The whole operation had taken 18 minutes and had gone exactly as they had planned and practiced many times on a full-sized mockup. The details of the station had been precisely as drawn, described and explained by an agent trained as a comms worker who had got a job there three months before. There was no doubt that T9 was out of action and would be for long enough for the other actions of the night to be carried out safely.

----------

Antarctica, the final wilderness, the seventh continent and easily the most mysterious, is vast in extent - it is bigger in area than the US and Mexico combined. But even this vast land area doubles in size in winter as the sea freezes. Large slabs of ice frequently break away, the largest to date being the size of Belgium. Most of the continent is covered in a thick layer of ice, 2000 m deep on average and 4,776 m at its deepest recorded point. The ice is 90% of the earth's glacial ice and two thirds of the theoretical fresh water resources. Amazingly, the greater part of the continent is technically a desert, with less than five cm of snow a year.

Its late discovery in 1820 is disputed - the Briton, Edward Bramfield and the Russian, van Bellinghausen both laying claims in that year.

As seal hunting and whaling grew in importance, the British Empire and Norway, the two main whaling countries, claimed most of Antarctica. In 1942 Argentina laid claims to parts of British Antarctica.

Scientists first started up various bases in the nineteen sixties - the British Antarctic Survey, the US , Russia and a few other countries. There are about forty permanent research stations, most scattered along the coast with only two deep inland. One of these is the US base at the South Pole itself, with about eighty people and the other is the Russian Vostok base on the central plateau.

Some bases are very small, a solitary hut, while others such as Esperenza, the Argentinian semi military base has a supermarket, a church, post office and accommodation for hundreds of personnel, and their families. The largest scientific base is the US one at

Mcmurdo Sound with 800 personnel.

Britain's four bases have been leading researchers. It was the British Antarctic Survey at these stations that discovered the ozone hole, the ozone depletion layer above the Antarctic. Crucial research on global warming, involving drilling of the ice cores could only be done here. Much of the scientific work undertaken is in the form of collaborative projects involving many countries.

----------

The visits had been arranged two weeks before as required for inspection visits under the Antarctic Treaty. The Argentinians had requested to visit the UK Rothera Research Station, the largest British Antarctic facility situated on Adelaide Island to the west of the Antarctic Peninsula to be undertaken on Tuesday March 23rd. There had been previous inspections but not on a regular basis and there had been no problem in obtaining authorizations. There was nothing to hide at this research station with all personnel being civilians, about a third being scientists and the remaining two thirds being support staff. This was unlike the Argentinian station where the so-called scientific research was just a front and it was populated mainly by military people. They were there to make a claim for ownership and had even brought in some women and children to live in highly difficult environment to promote their claims. The wife of a station chief had even had a baby boy, the first native born Antarctican. In mitigation, it could be argued in a court of law however, that the British could be establishing ownership and jurisdiction more subtly, as their research workers were taxed a "British Antarctic Territory" tax raised by the British government appointed commissioner.

Ten minutes before the arrival of the Argentinian helicopter for the inspection at Rothera, the station had totally lost its communication links with the outside world. The satellite link was down but this had not been discovered as everyone was too busy preparing for the arrival of the inspection team. If anyone had attempted to use a portable mobile phone link to the outside world, which was also now possible since the launching of the full constellation of satellites in the Iridium private network system, they would also have failed to make contact. Any such call from the ground would have been disabled by an Argentinian plane containing jamming equipment, their own home-grown primitive AWACS circling the peninsula.

Now the Chinook CH47 helicopter rotors were coming to a halt, the Station Head, Dr. Colin Mcintosh, bearded and beer gutted but surprisingly smart looking walked towards it to be met by the tall and proud looking Colonel Alvira Ramirez Sanchez wearing his full military parade uniform complete with medals. Mcintosh had not expected the Head of the neighbouring Argentinian station himself to be leading the inspection and he was even more surprised, nay shocked, by the sight of armed soldiers disembarking from the helicopter. He was now becoming aware of a loud drone and quickly turning around he saw that three Bell UH-1H helicopters were coming in to land at three different locations around the station. The troops from the colonel's helicopter had all run very quickly to specific buildings and clearly knew exactly where to go as if this was a preplanned assault.

'What the fuck .........?Jesus we're being invaded,' he shouted in his broad Cowdenbeath accent.

Two armed soldiers came up to him and stood on either side. Clearly it would be pointless to try and do anything foolish.

They were of course entirely defenceless. There were no troops stationed at the British base, not even any security guards. What would they do, refuse permission to the Friday night folk concerts to visiting penguins?

Still it would have been impossible to defend against any attack on this scale without having become a full military base oneself. By now the roar of the landing choppers had died down and the sound of troops shouting orders was clearly heard as his men were being herded quickly into the various buildings in a highly efficient and professional operation. There was no opposition, there was not a lot they could have done except shout. Most were too dazed and bewildered by what had happened in the last 10 minutes to do anything except meekly allow themselves to be shepherded into the various buildings.

When this had been done and there was no obvious sign of any dissent, Colonel Sanchez stepped in front of the now abject looking Mcintosh and took out from his pocket a sheet of paper. He solemnly opened it and began to read in English.

'As chief representative of the Government of Argentina, I do hereby declare that this is Argentinian national territory and has been since 1903 when the first base was opened on Orcadas island. The temporary occupation of part of our territory by a foreign nation is now at an end. Long live Argentina.'

At this Mcintosh noticed that one of the troops had climbed to the roof of the "town hall" and having ripped down the Union Jack was now carefully unfurling the blue and white flag of Argentina.

Fifteen minutes later the same proclamation was loudly heard on the intercom and Tannoy system throughout the base followed by a military version of the Argentinian national anthem and any Brits who had not been able to work out what had happened were now left in no doubt.

They now began to seriously worry about what would happen to them. They couldn't keep them all prisoners here for any length of time. Surely, they wouldn't all be taken to Argentina. Yet what else could they do?

Colonel Sanchez had already spoken to the AWACS command and control centre and was now reflecting on how well they had done. There would be promotion for this. The rough plans of the UK base had been known from previous visits and inspections; more accurate pictures had been taken by passing Argentinian flights but the detailed plans that he had been sent were clearly obtained from satellite spy photos. With help from some intelligence officers, the plan for the assault and takeover had been mainly his work.

By now Colonel Sanchez and his two subordinates were sitting in Colin Mcintosh's office drinking their third toast of his best Laphroaig Single Malt whisky. Mcintosh himself, bound and gagged, was sitting on the seat of his own locked toilet. He would be there for some time.

# Chapter 39

As soon as Jake Diamopoulos, the US Secretary of State came into the office, he was talking to a top analyst from the NRO, the National Reconnaissance Office, responsible for all satellite intelligence.

'Here are the images from the NROL - 74 of the Southern Ocean at 0800 this morning local time.' This was the latest US optical sensing spy satellite with a resolution of 6 cm in black and white imagery.

He was handed two black and white printouts which did not seem very dramatic to him.

'They are both taken on the same southerly pass of the satellite. The first shows activity at Puerto Belgrano Naval Base. It is the main Argentinean naval base at Punta Alta about 700 km south of Buenos Aires.' Looking closely, he could now see the harbour with lots of ships, all seeming to be going in one direction.

'Basically it shows the deployment of almost all their ships based here. They are all at full steam and headed in a south easterly direction.

'This second image shows a smaller number of ships heading out from the smaller naval base further south at Rio Gallegos. These are heading almost due east also at full steam.'

'Are they exercises?'

'No emphatically not, sir. Such a large-scale exercise has never taken place and it would be very costly. No one does such large scale exercises these days.'

'So it is a naval task force and headed to the British held Falkland Islands, judging by the directional headings.'

Jake was jumping the gun and had anticipated what his now disappointed looking image analyst had been eager to tell him.

'Absolutely sir, the two headings do point to only one place.'

'Thanks very much,' he said brusquely. He needed to move on and was soon in the Oval office. It was just him and The President - no aides and no other cabinet members.

'Yes Mr. President, they are advancing to The Falklands with a mission to reconquer the Islands for sure.'

'And you said the military coup to take over the country is scheduled for Monday? Today is Friday.'

'Yes, I had a phone call from General Suarez, confirming that date as part of our agreement on backing the coup in return for some of their oil.'

'But no mention of an invasion?'

'Nothing. But it is two days by sea to the islands so the invasion could take place the same day as the coup.'

'Wow. If that is the case then it's a very clever move. The coup will be welcomed if it coincides with the return of the islands to Argentina,' said the president.

'It certainly is. I can't help admiring the audacity and ambition of Suarez,' replied Jake.

'So we keep quiet about the invasion just like we're keeping quiet about the coup?' asked the president.

He felt a tinge of regret about this.

'We're dropping the UK in the shit?'

Last time, during the Falklands War, the US satellite photos had been shared with the Brits and the UK counter invasion task force were fully supported. They had the use of the US Ascension Island in the North Atlantic as a stopover and refuelling base for British ships and aircraft. But the biggest help had been telling the Brits the location of the Argentinian Navy, in particular "The Belgrano" troop carrier from satellite images.

The Belgrano had been sunk by the British submarine "HMS Conqueror" as it was steaming away from the British imposed exclusion zone, resulting in the end of the war.

Satellites had played a key role on both sides. The Russians had used their Kosmos 1365 spy satellite to help the Argentinian Sky Hawk A4 fighters sink the British ship
HMS Coventry. And they had also located the Atlantic Conveyor troop carrier for the Argentinians to use two AM39 Exocet missiles launched from the French built Super Etandard fighters to sink it with the loss of 12 sailors and 10 helicopters.

'So Jake what do you say?'

'The Brits are no longer a strong ally.

'They would not develop the oil so our best interest is to back the Argentinians all along the line.'

'Wait a minute. We agreed to support the coup for the oil. But they didn't even tell us about this invasion. So, we can leverage them for more oil to back the invasion.'

'That's a possibility,' replied Jake unconvincingly.

'Go for it,' said the President aggressively.

----------

Two days before the coup and Suarez was monitoring the departures of the Argentinian navy from the two naval bases, Puerto Belgrano and Rio Gallegos. Destination. The Islas Malvinas. The invasion and reconquering of the Malvinas.

He had no time for dealing in detail with all the correspondence from his own personal inbox, but he was intrigued by one letter which was simply headed "For your attention only." It had been despatched from the US Embassy in Buenos Aires but not through any official channels. They had the means to deliver it clandestinely to the inbox of the head of the Argentinian army, General Ricardo Suarez.

He opened it carefully.

It was devastating.

It was a personal two page note from Jake Diamopoulos, the US Secretary of State.

But it was quite impersonal. It wasn't even formal; it was bordering on bullying and blackmail. It was blackmail.

"We thank you for your previous signed agreement to deliver 40% of all the oil you will develop with Royal Dutch Shell in return for our support for your military coup.

However, we also wish to support you in your just claim and your plan to take over the Malvinas Islands."

How did they know about this? They didn't even use the word Falklands.

"For this additional support for your invasion and our recognition of Las Malvinas to be part of Argentina, we wish a further 20% of the oil in perpetuity."

It was blackmail alright. But it was all or nothing. Without US support it was not certain that the coup and invasion would be sustainable. They went together.

But it was his life ambition to lead his nation to glory and all the work and planning had been done and it was all in progress. He simply had no choice. He felt it was his duty.

He would have to deal with the internal consequences with his fellow collaborators later.

He looked at the second sheet of paper and saw the dotted line.

"I, General Ricardo Suarez, President of Argentina do solemnly declare, on behalf of my Government and the citizens of the sovereign nation of Argentina that we will deliver an additional 20% of our oil development from the Southern Ocean Field, in addition to the 40% already agreed, to the government of President Sanders of The United States of America.

In return the government of the United States will recognise Los Islas Malvinas to be a sovereign part of the Republic of Argentina according to the dictates of international law.

Signed. ......................

Date ...............

Please return the signed document to the Ambassador of The United States in the Republic of Argentina by a secure channel of your own choice."

He signed it slowly, as he tried to overcome his anger but his hand was shaking and his signature looked weak and frail.

----------

'So Monsieur President, we have incontrovertible evidence from our CSO1 optical imaging satellite that the Argentinians have launched a fleet of naval ships from their main naval base in Puerto Belgrano and the naval port of Rio Gallegos.'

The head of the French intelligence services, Direction Générale de la Sécurité Extérieure, the DGSE, was talking directly to the President of the Republic of France. He had a very good relationship with him. You could say they were friends rather than colleagues.

'Well. Well. So they are going for The Falklands again. Or should I say Las Malvinas. After all Madame Thatcher is long dead. How interesting.

'So keep me informed of their progress.'

'But aren't we going to tell the British. They don't have our satellite sophistication.' He was referring to the 20 cm resolution of their three CSO1 optical spy satellites.

'No, since the debacle of Brexit, they are reaping what they sowed. This is what happens when you leave an alliance after forty years of cooperation and a spirit of collaboration. And not amicably. No, not at all. Basically, they said we were *merde*.

'So they have to live with the consequences. Maybe this will even be good for them. They still have not learnt the full lesson of their decline as a world power.

'Besides, do you know about the conflicting claims to these islands?'

'No. I don't. Who's are they really? The Argentinians or the British?'

'They're actually ours. They are French.'

'Come, come. I know that you are something of a historian in your spare time but...'

'No. No. Let me tell you a bit about this. I know a lot about this.

'They are our islands! They are French!

'It is true that they were first named The Falkland Islands. A Brit called Viscount Falkland named the sea area between east and west Falklands "The Falklands Sound" but he was only on an expedition and did not settle or claim anything. This was in 1690.

'The first habitation was much later in 1764 by a French explorer, Louis Antoine de Bougainville. The islands were given the French name Isles Maloiunes that the Spanish translated later as Islas Malvinas.

'Two years later Bougainville was gone and the British came back. Then the Spanish invaded from South America with 5 ships and 1400 men and forced the Brits to leave.'

He was struggling with all this unnecessary detail, but he couldn't very well tell his boss to shut up, even though he could be a pompous old pedant at times. So he kept on listening patiently as his boss continued incessantly.

'Eight years later the Brits left again, and the Spanish left in 1806/11.

'So it was empty apart from passing fishing ships sometimes stopping over, until Buenos Aires, it was not yet Argentina, claimed the Spanish territory in 1820. They put a garrison of soldiers there. In 1832 the Brits were back. They declared it a Crown colony in 1840 and Stanley became the seat of government in 1845.

'So, you see, we the French, specifically de Bougainville, made the first habitation, an occupation, in 1784.

'And something that's not general knowledge. It seems that early on in government, Margaret Thatcher considered giving it to the Argentinians.

'But the junta didn't know this and invaded anyway. We all know that led to the Brits launching a massive reaction with American help.

'What did the islanders get? One hundred and seventeen minefields and twenty thousand mines, a big military airport and not much else.

'Now it looks as if it's going to be Argentinian again. Who would want such a God forsaken place?

'Good job we gave it away.'

Even the prospect of oil would not change this view. The French are unique in having 70% nuclear power for their electricity generation needs.

And he turned to look out of the window at the fluttering Tricolour with a satisfied grin on his face.

# Chapter 40

The coup was not taking place in isolation. It was a four-pronged plan. The invasion of the islands had to be synchronised with the coup, although it began two days earlier, the sailing time  from the two naval ports, Rio Gallegos and Puerto Belgrano Naval Base at Punta Alta. Also, the third element, the actions in the Antarctic had to take place at the same time  as did the fourth element, the action in Saudi Arabia.

As for the coup itself the latest PRINCE project management software had been used for the invasion and General Suarez was monitoring the coup and the invasion from a spreadsheet on his iPad.

He was prowling around like a cat on springs inside the bunker at the main Argentinian army base just north of Buenos Aires. There were banks of TV monitors all around, but the big picture was on the small tablet in his hands.

He glanced at the main tasks for the invasion that had to take place more or less at the same time.

Disruption of communications
Arrival of air support
Arrival of ground-based invasion force from ships
Support from other naval deployments.

He turned to his aide and said, 'Let me know when each of these is finalised. I don't want  progress reports unless there is a delay at the outer acceptable limits.'

He exuded confidence despite the fact he could not stand still, such was his charisma and charm.

'Yes, sir, I am getting reports in all the time. I will let you know the when each task is completed.'

As part of the plan for a complete communications blackout on the islands some high-tech state of the art actions had been prepared.

A top military communications expert glanced at his target on a screen.

The computer simulation showed the positions of all satellites in geostationary orbit above the equator. These were all in a parking orbit; they were all completing one orbit in the same time as the Earth - 24 hours - so appeared to be stationary at a fixed point above the earth. This was essential for broadcasting and communications as fixed antenna dishes could be used on the ground to receive the signals. This had been the brainwave idea of Arthur C. Clarke, the science fiction writer in a magazine article he wrote in 1948. It was now the reason why there were over 400 geostationary satellites orbiting at a height of 39,856 km above the equator. Physics, in fact, good old Isaac Newton's Laws, dictate they have to be at that height above the earth to take 24 hours for one orbit.

The target was the Intelsat satellite Epic IS 29, broadcasting TV signals and internet to the Falkland Islands using microwaves at a frequency of 4 to 8 Gigahertz. Ascension Island, Diego Garcia and St. Helena also used this satellite for their TV and internet. All the Falklands TV stations and internet were picked up from this satellite by a ground-based receiver satellite dish just East of the car park at the offices of "Sure South Atlantic," formerly "Cable and Wireless," the communications provider for the Falkland Islands. TV reception was fine as it could cope with the 500 milliseconds round travel delay in the signal; up to the satellite, about 40,000 km and down again the same distance at the speed of light. But it was a real pain for two way internet browsing, Skype and so on. The bandwidth was small and a major bottleneck. Videos had to be downloaded at night and online courses were impossible. People still resorted to ordering and using CDs and DVDs and memory sticks, such was the slow speed. But it was their only means of communication with the outside world.

Blocking of this communication by jamming could be done in two ways. You could block the receivers on the ground - all the TVs and smart phones, computers and tablets on the Falkland Islands, by using a local jammer. A mobile jammer could fit easily in a car and would cost about US$6,000 from "Shoghi" an Indian company or "Wonderland Technology - WLT," a Chinese company sponsored by the Chinese government. But this jammer would have to be local, it would have to be on the islands and getting it there and driving it about would have been problematical. So, they used a much more dramatic method by jamming the broadcasting satellite Intelsat itself, 39,000 km above the equator.

This is what the operator in Argentina was doing. From a ground station dish antenna at the military base he was sending up a powerful signal of the right frequency directly up to the satellite. This noise would drown out the correct signals from the satellite. It showed how sophisticated the Argentinians had become. It was believed this method had only been used once before, by the Iranians, to block off unwanted external TV channels.

The engineer flicked a switch and directed a powerful beam at the antenna of the Intelsat Epic IS29 positioned at 310° East above the equator. And that was it. No TV or internet anywhere in the Falkland Islands. But also, no TV and internet to their users from other countries who were also under the very large footprint of the satellite broadcasting signal. A sledge hammer to crack a nut. But the nut was well and truly cracked.

'We have successfully disabled the Intelsat satellite, General Suarez.'

Outwardly calm he was inwardly in turmoil. This was exciting and daring stuff. Invisible action at a distance can be very intoxicating.

'Thank you. That is good.'

He ticked it off his iPad spreadsheet list.

'What about the airport radar?'

He was referring to the AS 9 airport radar at the Mount Pleasant airport on East Falklands. The airport was  built after the last gallant war by the British at a cost of £215 million. This radar, the typical red and white half-moon shaped antennas one sees rotating at all airports sends out microwave signals at 2.7 to 2.9 Gigahertz frequency. These signals reflect off any incoming aircraft up to 60 miles away and up to 25,000 feet altitude. These reflections are picked up by the airport radar. Every  plane is being tracked and its changing location known.

At that very moment a powerful jammer transmitting from a  Russian Beriev A50 AWACS plane, flying just over 60 miles from Mount Pleasant airport was beaming its jamming signal and completely disabling the main radar at the airport. The oldish plane had been bought on the second hand market but the jammer was Russia's state
of the art Krasukha-2 EW system that detects the frequency and signal type being emitted and then jams that specifically. Suarez' s weapons buyers had managed to get one by corrupt dealings with ex Russian air force pilots now running private companies through their contacts in the Russian military. Money had talked as usual.

A secondary radar at the airport picks up signals from transponders on any aircraft that reveal its GOS coordinates, altitude and its identification. This too was disabled by the Russian jammer.

'Just in General. Both radars at the airport completely disabled.'

'Excellent.'

He knew that immediately behind this aircraft with the jamming equipment were all the other planes to be used in the invasion.

And at several locations around the Falklands, naval ships were being deployed and positioned for a variety of purposes.

----------

'Reflexes slowing down?' Mike laughed. He had just beaten his mate Colin, in a high-speed shooter game on their console in the day room of their accommodation block at the base.

'Hmm. That's the first time you've beaten me.'

There were the only two pilots there. The six others were either training or on R and R, but still within the base itself, which was basically self-contained.

They were dressed in their state-of-the-art flame-retardant material flying suits for one of their 24 hour shifts. For a shift they even slept in these and did not shower. They had to be ready for a scramble exercise and never knew if it was a practice or live. Live here meant there was a threat from Argentinian forces!

There were only two Typhoon Euro fighters here now at Mount Pleasant air force base on East Falkland's charged with defending the islands. There had been four initially, three called Faith, Hope, Charity after the World War II defence of Malta by three Gloster Gladiator aircraft from the same squadron, 1435. The fourth was called Desperation for some reason.

The two pilots were on 24-hour shifts on one day in four. In the main Typhoon base back at Coningsby in the UK, they still had the luxury of being on one day in every seven. There, their main duties would be to scramble and investigate any unusual planes or flight patterns, usually Russian fighters but also possible terrorist highjacks. They were all prepared for the instruction they may have to give.

"I am instructed by her Majesty's government of the United Kingdom to warn you that if you do not respond immediately to my orders, you will be shot down."

The shift pattern on The Falklands meant there were 8 pilots in total for the two planes. To be a Royal Air Force pilot in the UK takes four years at a cost of £400,000 per pilot. But then only the crème de la crème of those are selected for the additional training of three years and £4 million cost to become Typhoon Euro fighter pilots. There is a huge dropout rate such is the difficulty of their training. They have to be amazingly skilled and have the right temperament for flying what may be the best fighter aircraft in the world. Each one cost £90 million pounds.

These eight pilots had their own accommodation block which was the closest to the runway and the hangar that contained the two aircraft. The block had eight single en suite rooms, a day room and the pilots' flying clothes changing room. All close together and close to the planes.

Suddenly, seconds after the end of their computer game, the intercom alarm sounded. This was what they lived for. The scramble. They had practised it many times and this was almost certainly another training scramble but each time, they could not help feeling exhilarated, with their hearts pounding and accompanied by a generous flow of Adrenalin.

They dropped their play station consoles and ran out and down the corridor to the changing room. They went into their own clothing bay where their additional clothing, on top of the flying suits they were wearing, was hanging from coat hangers. They started putting them on, first the g suit - this protects them from the intense g forces encountered in flight - then the harness for possible ejection, with the survival vest, the oxygen supplies, the gloves and soft skull cap. Although some of these were clumsy to put on, they had practised so much they were ready in a couple of minutes.

At this point, the flight equipment technician, who had also scrambled, came running in with a terrified look on his face.

'The helmets! The helmets!'

'Yes?'

'They're not there. They're missing. Gone.'

These were kept in a locked cupboard of their own. Securely. Each one cost £250,000 pounds.

'What about the other crews' helmets?'

'All gone, all eight gone.'

But this did not actually matter anyway as each one was customised for each individual pilot.

Yes, they were designed for protecting the pilots as do all helmets. During an ejection from the plane the head of a pilot would suddenly be subjected to a 600 miles an hour wind force.

But these helmets were much more than that. They were in effect the pilot of the plane, enhancing in various ways the powers and senses of the human pilot. In other words, the plane could not be flown to anywhere near its full potential and capability without the Augmented Reality provided by the electronics and software embedded in the helmet. They were easily the most superior AR tools in existence. Amazingly, the pilot only has to turn his head to look at a target aircraft and the electronics in the helmet know the change in his directional coordinates, sends commands to the plane to change direction to aim at the target and then launch the weapon to destroy it.

'So what do we do?' asked Colin blankly. This was by far the most major problem they had encountered in all their training. There simply was no plan B.

'Mission aborted,' said Mike who was the most senior of the two.

The loss of the helmets, effectively disabling the planes, was a disaster to him. He was not aware that disasters on a slightly larger scale were taking place, the Argentinian invasion and the abject surrender without a fight.

Neither was he to know that what had happened was the ultimate cockup. Alone and isolated on the base, the Typhoon pilot block had not had the normal scramble signal disabled for the stand down announcement that had been broadcast to all the others.

# Chapter 41

General Suarez addressed his troops in a pre-recorded message that was broadcast a few hours after the mobilisation began.

Some listened from their quarters on the ships out at sea on their way to The Falklands. Some were in their briefing rooms in full kit before flying out. All were listening intently as they knew something big was going on.

"My dear honourable soldiers, sailors and airmen of the Fatherland.

You have been charged to perform a glorious action on behalf of your countrymen. You are ready. You know you are ready.

Many years ago, your fellow men were not ready. They had been badly trained, they had poor equipment, poor provisions and were badly led and badly treated by their superior officers. You all know this from the Rattenbach report that we commissioned.

Now look at you. You have new equipment, new weapons, plentiful resources and you are the best trained ever. And most important we, your leaders respect you and trained you well, as we can only succeed together. We have prepared well. Everything that needed to be planned has been done. All the circumstances and conditions are in place. But in the end, it is still up to you. To liberate the Malvinas Islands will not be just a military action. It will turn out to be the most glorious achievement of your life. Your grandchildren will look up to you and the whole nation will be proud of you.

I salute you."

There were cheers all round. They all believed him and much of what he had said was probably true. It was a masterly performance. How could they fail? Morale was never higher.

----------

The first few Argentinian transport planes had landed at Mount Pleasant Air Force base and were surprised to encounter no opposition at all. Suarez had known there would probably be none as the contents of the hard disc obtained by his intelligence agency had shown but he could not be sure. Everything had been planned with military action in mind, though he did know that the Typhoon jet fighters were not going to be in action. Thank God for the advanced technology in those helmets. The helmets were more intelligent and indispensable than the pilots who wore them. This would be a good talking point in years to come.

The rear doors of the transport planes opened and three armoured carriers quickly disembarked.

'Action stations.'

'The helicopters are in the expected positions. Armoured car A to go the Sikorsky, armoured car B to the Westland.'

'All clear sir. We're in our way.'

'Armoured cars C and D to go to the transport planes, you know where they are.'

They could be clearly seen at the other end of the runway.

They immediately drove the few hundred metres to the helicopters and some men surrounded and secured them. They encountered no opposition.

They did the same with the two transport planes that were unoccupied at the end of the runway.

The armoured car moved on and a small group of soldiers ensured the Rapier air defence system was out of action. They finally made way to the two hardened hangars containing the Typhoons. They had not moved an inch and there were no pilots in the cockpits.

The place was deserted.

'Where are they all?'

'It's clear the troops have all been confined to barracks. They had no intention of fighting us. They have been told to surrender,' was the confident opinion of one colonel.

'What! All that training for nothing?'

There was a clear sense of disappointment amongst some of the more unthinking Argentinian troops. They were well equipped and well trained and the whole operation had been meticulously planned but some of them could still have ended up dead.

'It's because of our training and strength that they know it's not worth fighting.'

Others realised that it was a classic example of overwhelming force forcing a surrender to avoid unnecessary bloodshed on both sides.

Seeing there was no opposition, Suarez was able to safely order his two troopships to come into Mare Harbour, the harbour that served the base about 15 miles away and for two support frigates to anchor nearby. Other ships could all proceed to safely enter Port Stanley docks and some troops to be disembarked to secure the second and smaller, Port Stanley airfield. It was all almost symbolic as there was no military presence at the airfield. The runway was too short for any modern aircraft. It was now just used for inter-island flights and to the science research bases in Antarctica.

The British troops confined to barracks were merely bemused. They had been told a few hours before that an invasion was expected and that the orders were not to oppose it. They stood idly by, some watching TV and some on their play stations. They must have known that although they were busy training here, that it was not the sort of training for an all-out military battle against an invasion. But they had not given it any serious thought as an invasion had not been contemplated. There was no anger. There was no call for action. If they were really honest, none of them wanted to be there. It was not as bad as being in Afghanistan, but it was not a posting anyone looked forward to either. It was a sad ending to a sad state of affairs.

# Chapter 42

The commanding officer's Batman burst into his room without knocking with a desperate look on his face.

Brigadier Thomkins looked up from his desk wearily and said, 'Calm down and tell me what's going on.'

'We've lost all communications.'

'The island mobile provider network is down. The civilian satellite link for internet and international calls is gone.'

The military communications satellites Skynet, used by the British military, did not cover the Falklands.

'We have nothing. We are totally cut off. This is clearly beyond a coincidence.'

'Well of course it fucking is. Can't you see what's coming?' said the hitherto unflappable Brigadier.

'Yes, I suppose so. The Argies?'

'Yes, of course, the Argies. Who did you think the Martians?' But he realised he was totally rattled and began to calm himself down.

'So what do we do? What are our orders?'

'There aren't any. You know we have not been put here to defend this place. We would have been practising our response regularly if that was the case.

'Can you please let me have a moment?'

'What do you mean?'

'Just close the door and get out,' he said very quietly.

He went to the strong room and looked at this small safe never before opened and using the one-off code from his onetime pad, he opened it.

It was empty apart from a small sealed envelope. He was taking out the actions required for this situation. Yes, it had been thought about and anticipated.

Opening it carefully he read the short paragraph the one-page note contained.

"TOP SECRET

To the commanding officer of the British garrison stationed in The Falkland Islands.

In the case of a complete breakdown of communications with the outside world, in particular to your senior command in UK, you are to act as follows.

Any external threat is to be met with no military response. You are to politely receive any visitors and treat them civilly and note what they have to say. If there is an ultimatum demanding the surrender of our sovereignty of the islands, you are to accept it.

We, the British Government, realise this will put you in a situation beyond your control but military and political reality requires this response at this time."

He let the paper drop gently and it spiralled to the floor.

He had not been surprised at the content. From the time he was appointed he could see what was happening. He had been reading between the lines for years all the missives from high command. Yet to see it so plainly in black and white made him feel an intense and immense shock. He had never really thought this day would come. He looked outwardly calm, but he was a broken man.

And so it was that a  mere two hours after landing, General Lopez was able to obtain the surrender of Mount Pleasant air force base with his counterpart. Not strictly true, he a general, was dealing with a mere brigadier.

----------

Down at Port Stanley another man was also preparing to do his duty. He was ready to do the right thing, even though it was a pathetic right thing to do.

He was the UK Governor of the Falklands islands; the most famous one as he was going to be the last one. He was the boss of the islands with no qualifications at all to be one apart from a confident manner and soft people skills. He was smooth, silky smooth, a BS in less polite company. Nominally he had the ultimate power but his only role was to appoint the chief executive who actually ran the island, helped by the rubber stamping of the fifteen elected councillors. Now he knew what he should do.

He turned to his assistant and said, 'Can you get the chief executive and all the councillors to assemble here as soon as possible. We are expecting to have some visitors and we have to give them a proper official welcome.'

'But the phone system is down.'

'I know the phone system is down. Just go out in your car and round them up. You know where they all live.'

This was the case in this tiny little town, this God-forsaken little place as far away from anywhere civilised as it is possible to be.

No one knew that he, the Governor, hated the place; he was such a good team man. The UK team that was so good on style and so lacking in substance. Yes, he was secretly glad the Argies were coming, so he could go home at last.

He had had very little to do with the British forces 35 miles up the road at the Mount Pleasant airfield base over the years. It showed they cared little for him and the local inhabitants. But today there had been contact. A brief phone call from Brigadier Thomkins. It politely informed him of the imminent arrival of some unwelcome visitors. The orders were to surrender.

So much for the hundreds of millions of pounds spent to defend their way of life. It had involved the construction of a large Military Base and airfield and the presence of thousands of squaddies. This had of course, totally changed their way of life.

----------

There was a hushed silence as the general entered. General Alvarez was one of the new breed that Suarez had trained up.

The general and the governor shook hands in a very civilised manner and there was no Argentinian gloating or triumphalism this time around unlike the uncouth previous lot who just did not know how to behave. After signing the formal surrender note the general went around shaking the hands of all the councillors and lo and behold it was time for a warm cup of tea and some cream cakes.

And that was it.

# Chapter 43

General Suarez was meeting his senior intelligence team tasked with planning the invasion.

'So last time we sorted out all the plans to disable the communications set up on the islands. Today we need consider the Mount Pleasant Air Force base.

'What is your current assessment?' He turned to his intelligence chief.

'Well they have been running down the defences and have not upgraded at all.

'On the ground, unbelievably, they still have the Rapier surface to air missile they had during the previous invasion. It's launched from a vehicle or trailer, has a 5 km range and has a manual optical guidance system that sends info by radio link to the missile as it travels. It is claimed to be very accurate so direct hits are possible, meaning a light payload explosive is sufficient. They say 1.4 kg. But we know from the UK's own assessment of its use during the previous invasion that the high-count rate of targets downed they initially claimed was grossly exaggerated and that it is not that good. But they still use it until they upgrade it to something called Sky Sabre. This is similar to Israel's Irin Dome air defence system that has been very successful in shooting down missiles launched from the Gaza Strip.'

'So what is your conclusion?' asked Suarez impatiently.

'My assessment is that the Rapier is not a major threat to a large number of incoming aircraft.'

'Ok. So what about the aircraft they have?'

At Mount Pleasant at the moment they have one Chinook helicopter, one Hercules transport aircraft, and one refuelling tanker aircraft. The other helicopters they used to have, another Chinook and Sea King, have been replaced by civilian ones, two Sikorsky S61s and two Westland AM89s that just do rescue work at sea. The only major threat to us are the two Typhoon Euro fighter aircraft, down from four but still formidable fighting units. Apart from the new US stealth F22 Raptor, maybe the best fighter in the world.

'So we have to disable those two Typhoons,' interrupted General Suarez.

'Not necessarily,' said one of the intelligence officers. 'We could take out the pilots. Maybe easier. The planes are so sophisticated with all their electronics that only a handful of pilots are capable of flying them. If they have two Typhoons they probably only have six to eight pilots for them altogether.'

'But we won't get a chance to eliminate those easily. They won't be together in a group at any time. It will be two on duty, two on standby and the others off duty and on leave, said another colleague.

'But they do all live in one block, we know that. So they may all be there some nights.'

'Ok,' said Suarez. 'Let's look into disabling the planes on the ground or taking out the pilots. Or anything else you can come up with by the next meeting.'

----------

Paul Thompson has set his alarm for two a.m. and on hearing it had quietly left his bunk. He hadn't undressed that night and quietly walked out into the cloudy night.

He had checked the piece of paper with the date on it every day that week. And tonight, was the night. It was always cloudy on the Falkland's; the moon was a rare sight. He could have travelled along the underground corridor, called the Death Star Corridor from the Star Wars film, linking the barracks, the messes, the recreation and welfare areas but that was what everyone wnormally did, so he was likely to meet someone even at that hour.

He took less than five minutes to get to the changing block. He had the key to this and to the cupboard that held the eight helmets. It was very quiet and there was no one about at this end of the base. It was an isolated spot on the very edge of the base. He quickly put the helmets in the  large bin bag he had taken along as suggested. He was soon walking back past some skips that held rubble from a temporarily abandoned building project. He had decided on this hiding place after a fair bit of looking around in the previous weeks. He looked around and slipped the bin bag under a pile of loose rubble. No one would see it and he didn't think the builders would be back anytime soon. He had thought of the rubbish bins, but they were collected regularly and he had ruled that out. Everyone would think the helmets had been stolen and taken off base immediately. Why would anyone just hide them? But it was what he had been told to do and that made the job much, much easier. He was ecstatic when he crawled into bed about 40 minutes later to the sounds of snoring from his mates. Just that very simple little job had made him a rich man.

----------

Pablo Garcia, a retired member of the Argentinian intelligence services had been charged directly by General Suarez to pursue this special mission. Even the existing intelligence services were kept in ignorance of this.

Garcia was trying to contact one of the Mount Pleasant garrison who was involved in some close way with the Typhoon fighters based there.

Squadron 1435, the Typhoons, is based in The Falkland's and personnel serve six months there with short breaks back in the UK with their families.

The identity of those coming back on leave to the UK can be found from the flight list on the incoming RAF flight to Brize Norton in Oxfordshire. He had obtained this by looking at the bookings website for service personnel. He was then able to look up their function from the Squadron 1435 website and pick out a possible contact who fitted the bill. After several months of regular checking he was able to find a target. This was Leading Aircraftman, Paul Thompson, who was an equipment technician for the Typhoons. Perfect.

This was why he was now sitting at a quiet table at the White Bull pub in Coningsby, a fifteen minute walk from the Coningsby air force base in Lincolnshire, where Paul lived in the married quarters whilst on leave with his wife and three-year-old daughter. He had observed that on Thursday nights Paul was a regular at this pub as a break from the Mess on the base itself.

Garcia, although Argentinian, had lived in The States both in college and after for over ten years and had a strong American accent. He saw Paul alone at the bar and went up and stood next to him.

He had no extended time to cultivate and build up a relationship, which would be the ideal way to approach this task, so it would all have to be very direct.

Paul had only had a couple of pints so he would be quite sober by his standards.

Garcia turned to him and said, 'So are you one of the guys who work on the air force base down the road?'

'Yes, but not really. I just live there while I'm on leave from a tour of duty in the Falkland Islands.'

'But you're going back, right?'

'Yes, I've got a few weeks leave left.'

'Wow. I've always been into planes. They have those Typhoons there don't they?'

Paul suddenly pricked up. He guessed this guy was a visitor, a stranger, with his American accent.

'How do you know that? And who the hell are you anyway?'

'Sorry, I should have introduced myself. I'm John Carsdale from Boulder, Colorado. I work there for an aerospace firm. In fact, I'm here at the base on business, dealing with navigation software.

He was quite forthcoming in setting up his cover. And he had attended college and worked in Boulder, so he was quite familiar with the place.

'And like I said I've always been into planes. I'm a total nerd for them, especially the latest fighter planes. Are you into the Typhoons?'

'Yes, I work on them,' said Paul unable to stop himself.

And straight out, a provocative starter question to grab Paul's interest.

'How do you rate the Typhoon compared to our stealth fighter, the Lockheed Martin F22 Raptor?'

'Aha! That's a good question.' Paul was now engrossed, he always loved to talk about his beloved Typhoon, his baby. Although only a clothing technician for the pilots, he was very lucky to be so involved in its daily care.

'I bet the Typhoon can't detect ours early enough in a dogfight and will clearly lose out. Our Raptor has the latest stealth technology. Almost zero radar profile,' continued Garcia, alias John Carsdale.

'Well I wouldn't be so sure. They say the No. 9 Squadron Italian Typhoon pilots training at Nellis Airforce Base, Nevada - the same base as your Raptor - has had some interesting training exercises against them. They didn't go so well for you and your guys didn't want to play ball after that.'

'Yes, that will be the Augmented Reality, AR helmets the Typhoon pilots have that make the difference. They are clearly superior to ours, especially in targeting. Most people have no idea how clever those helmets are. When the pilot just looks at and locks on to a target, his helmet location coordinates are known very accurately and this feeds in automatically to turn the plane's weapons on to the target and it's a gonner.'

'Yes, that's how it works. But how the fuck do you know all this?' asked Paul in his usual blunt manner.

'It's not a secret for us nerds. Our Internet forums have people who worked on these planes, even former pilots, who just love to talk about it all.'

'Oh. I had no idea it was so well known,' replied Paul, who thought all this was a big secret.

'But also, I have to confess. I do work for a US company that is a rival to  British Aerospace -  that developed the helmets.

'My bosses would love to have a close look at those helmets.'

'What do you mean? What the fuck do you mean?' Paul was now not just puzzled but alarmed.

'Look it's not the Chinese or the Russians were talking about here. It's just rival companies who are both on the same side. You could argue they should be cooperating and sharing info anyway.'

'So?'

'So could you get hold of some helmets?'

'Well I do have access to them,  the keys to where they're kept but no. Fuck no. No way. I would be court martialled  and thrown out of the airforce in disgrace.'

'Look, all you have to do is to move them and hide them. We'll do the rest.'

'You're crazy.'

'And you get paid.'

Paul laughed out loud. 'You would have to pay me a fortune to do that.'

'What about £250,000?'

This was a bargain for the Argentinians if it resulted in putting the two Typhoons out of action.

Paul was struck dumb. He couldn't believe what he was hearing. To him that was a  fortune. More than he could imagine.

He had another four years left on his air force contract and he was only a clothing equipment technician. No qualifications and no skills. He hadn't had the motivation or the ability to use the forces to prepare for a job in civvy street.

He hadn't thought about his future much but now he had a family and responsibilities. He was literally thinking about this for the first time. He did have a wild dream to start a small business and this money could help him there. And they could have a nice holiday somewhere. More than one nice holiday. And a car. He had never owned a car.

Garcia let the silence continue. He could see he had Paul thinking and that could only be a good thing.

'What if I do it? And get caught?'

'You'll only get caught if they find the helmets. And all we want you to do is to hide them somewhere safe straightaway.  It can be inside the base. You don't have to risk taking them out. It's really quite an easy job.'

'So, one helmet?'

'No, no all of them. There can't be many.'

'Well there's eight.'

'Well that's not a lot for 250 grand. They'll all fit into a large bin bag or two. You could even hide them in the bins.'

He didn't think to ask why they needed them all.

'How can I trust you? When will I get the money?'

'Just to prove we're serious, you get £50,000 in advance, in cash, provided you don't draw attention to yourself by banking it. Then we'll transfer the rest into a new bank account you can set up anywhere in the world.

'We trust you with our advance payment to do the job. You trust us to pay you the rest later. It's a win, win situation.'

Paul was quiet. This was too much. He couldn't think clearly. He had never been a clear thinker.

'Can I think about it?'

At this Garcia gambled. He thought he had the measure of his man.

'No. It's now or never. You say yes now, or I ask someone else. This is your chance.'

There was a long silence.

'Right I'll do it.'

And they shook hands.

'So meet me here tomorrow night and you'll have your first instalment.'

Garcia left leaving Paul to finish off his pint and contemplate his fortune. The amount had been a key factor in the Argentinian calculations.

Garcia was glad he hadn't had to use any crude threats. He knew where Paul's wife and young daughter lived. He had this info in reserve.

The following night was a very short visit but quite significant for both.

Garcia handed Paul a small plastic shopping bag containing £50,000 in the toilet.

He had driven up to the Argentinian embassy in London to collect the cash that day.

And making sure they were alone, he whispered, 'So, it must be done on the night of July 25th at 1a.m. That's all you must remember.'

He handed him a piece of paper with that date and time on it. It was crucial that the helmets went missing just before the invasion but not too early for a possible practice scramble to uncover their disappearance.

# Chapter 44

General Suarez paced nervously back and fore in front of the large screens in the command centre of the military base, Compo de Mayo, about 30 kilometres north of Buenos Aires, the largest military base in Argentina. It is infamous for its detention centre, La Casita, where it is said, new born babies were taken from pregnant women detained by the military and given to military families. He was overdressed, in all his finery but he needed to be ready for his TV appearance later on that day.

Today was indeed the day. The previous night, "The 5th April Group" had met for the very last time. Everything had been planned to the finest detail and a run-through of today's action had taken place, point by point, with each person present knowing their full role and responsibility.

But he was still very tense as success depended on timing and coordination. It was not possible to actually rehearse all that was required. They had done everything possible. Computer modelling and simulations had been undertaken on several occasions and the plan fine-tuned accordingly.

It was 4 a.m. on the Wednesday morning. This was psychologically the best time to take action according to research. This is when people are least alert and unprepared. A cabinet meeting was due to take place at 11a.m. that morning in the Casa Rosada and a final check had taken place of the whereabouts of all cabinet members. As expected, they were all at home in bed in their various villas or apartments in and around Buenos Aires.

At exactly 4 a.m. two armoured cars arrived outside each of the twelve locations, nine villas and three apartments.

Each location had a member of the security forces as a guard but they politely stepped to one side when confronted. Those who tried to use their cell phones found they were disabled. For security and secrecy, the coup organisers had decided not to put their own men in as security guards, although it could have been done. This would have been an unusual action, was too risky and would have caused suspicion.

Three armed soldiers entered each location and meeting with no resistance, were able to confront and confine each surprised cabinet minister and their wives or mistresses, dressed as they were in their chosen night attire.

'Here General. The checklist of all cabinet members.'

He could see a list of twelve names all ticked off.

'They have all been successfully put under house arrest.'

'No problems? Excellent.

'But what about the president?'

'No define news yet, but the action has begun.'

This was a more elaborate action as there was clearly more security around the President.

The Casa Rosada, the presidential palace in Playa de Mayo, was only an office for the President. He lived in another palace, Quinta de Olivos, in the affluent suburb of Olivos, in the north of the capitol. This large estate on a bluff overlooking the Rio de la Plata, the River Plate, is surrounded by a red brick wall about three metres high. Its main but somewhat underwhelming entrance, along the Avenida Maipu, is a sealed wooden door about five metres wide flanked by two smaller doorways for pedestrians only.

The estate has swimming pools, a golf course and tennis courts as conventional trappings of a large mansion but also some eccentric, notorious additions. One of its previous occupants, Peron, after the death of his second wife, Isabella, in 1952, converted the polo stables into a "Union of Secondary School Students." This school for teenage girls was linked by underground tunnel to his residence.

Troops could have stormed over the wall but would still have had some distance to go to the main residence along a straight, open and exposed, cobbled road. This could have raised the alarm and given the president a chance to escape in his private helicopter. So, much simpler was to land by military helicopter at the large concrete square which served as a helipad and ensure the president could not use his own to escape. Previous presidents had escaped by helicopter but from the roof of the Casa Rosada.

A US built Bell 412 military combat helicopter landed at 4.02 a.m. Some troops guarded the president's own helicopter and others entered the house promptly. The guards, although armed, immediately gave way to superior force and simply stepped to one side. No violence was necessary although it would certainly have been used. They found the president looking dazed on a sofa in his large TV room. He may have fallen asleep there watching some late-night movie.

He didn't say a word and was led, almost gently, to the helicopter and soon found himself in a cell in the military base not far away. No comfortable house arrest for him. General Suarez and his wife, the Princess, would be moving in soon to make Quinta de Olivos their new home.

'General we have it,' the attending colonel gushed, smiling broadly.

'The president, no former president, the deposed president, is safely held in his new cell here in the detention centre at Compo de Mayo.'

Again the General barely reacted as his brain moved on to the next thing.

And a few minutes later.

'Here is a list of all the major trade union leaders put under house arrest. We have 17 but two more are still free. We'll soon have them, we know where they've gone to.'

'Have you got Alfonso, the boss of the CGT?

'Yes, yes we do.'

'That's good.'

The CGT, the Confederacion General del Trabajo, was the largest union. Trade unions have played a big role in Argentinian politics. Colonel Juan Domingo Peron, as he was then known, had built up his support amongst the unions until they were able to threaten the government and sweep him to power. Forty per cent of labour in Argentina were still unionised. So it was important that the current leaders were neutralised.

Soon, further ticked off lists of possible rivals apprehended were presented to him. But it was not a huge number. Only the very top level was involved. There was no mass and indiscriminate round up of all possible opposition. This would be a very modern and efficient coup, that would not alarm foreign governments and even some of the more naïve and wishy-washy human rights groups.

'General have a look at the screens. The top right is the Playa de Mayo. The tanks are arriving.'

And a few minutes later. 'They are all in place in front of the Casa Rosada.'

Again, a limited number, about ten; this was a symbolic act as the Casa Rosada was almost empty overnight and only housed civil servants during the day.

'And tanks are surrounding the parliament building, the home of Congress, the Senate and the Chamber of Deputies, the Palace of the Argentinian National Congress on the other side of Plaza de Mayo from the Casa Rosada.

'General, if I may have your attention.

'The other screens show all major public buildings guarded by tanks or armoured plated vehicles. Screen 4 is the Ministry of Justice, Screen 3 is the Banco Nacion Casa Central, the Bank of the Argentina Nation just next to the Casa Rosada. Then the Post Office and the City Hall and the …..'

'Good, good,' interrupted the general a trifle impatiently.

'What about the newspapers?'

'Editors of Clarin, La Nacion, Cronica and Diario Popular all under house arrest and their offices sealed off. These are the top five. We're dealing with the other minor ones.'

'What about the TV and radio stations?'

'Nothing yet. I'll go and check.'

'Yes do, they are the most important.'

A few minutes later, he hurried back.

'We have secured the broadcasting facilities of the four major TV stations. The buildings are secure, but we are also inside.'

'What about the internet and social media, cell phones?'

'All telephone service providers networks have been closed and jammed. All cell towers are down.'

'Great. And internet?'

'Same again. The Mobile ground based EWs – electronic warfare systems are in place close to transmitters. We are jamming with high frequency microwaves of the same frequency and modulation as the receivers. You can see one of those mobile units on Screen 9.'

The Argentinian military had secretly bought the Russian Borisoglebsk 2 system used so effectively by the Russians in Ukraine.

'Remember we switch off all jamming as soon as we can physically stop broadcasts. This has to be done as soon as possible.' He had been briefed that the jamming signals were cancer causing.

'Yes, General. We are aware of the importance of this,' he said, although he and most people involved in the coup did not know about the cancer aspect.

'And any news of a reaction to what's happening?'

'Yes, General. No one is opposing. There has been no reported opposition at all.'

This was excellent news reinforcing their belief that their action was necessary and would be supported in general.

'OK General I have an important message.

'It is time to go to the TPA.'

This is the Television Publica Argentina, the government owned and run TV station, the smallest of the big 5.

'For your public broadcast to the Nation.'

'Wait, I need full reports from the rest of the country.'

One third of the population of Argentina, about 15 million, live in Greater Buenos Aires, which dominated the country in all respects but there are important regional centres such as Córdoba and Rosario. Between them they have 1.3 million people.

'The latest info. There is no open opposition. The military in all 23 provinces are ready to ensure we have control. They are confined to barracks but at full military alert ready for any development.'

'So it's only in Córdoba and Rosario that we have troops and tanks and armoured cars on the streets, in front of all public buildings?' asked Suarez.

'Yes, that's all as planned and is under control.'

'Right. Let's go.'

A few minutes later they were driving in an unmarked BMW 5 series past the massive and world famous Recoleta cemetery. He could see the hundreds of large

ornate and over the top family tombs above the cemetery walls. They soon arrived at the HQ of the TPA, the Television Publica Argentina, broadcasting on Canal 7, channel 7.

# Chapter 45

The makeup lady splashed a bit more powder on his face. He was calm and composed. Everything was under control after years of meticulous planning.

He glanced at the teleprompter. His whole speech had been transposed onto it and he had played it all through before the public broadcast. Everything was planned down to the finest detail.

It was now coming up to 8 a.m. and most people would be getting ready for work. They would all know something big was up as their favourite radio and TV channels would be off the air and their phones and computers would be down too. Not many normally watched TPF; it was the least watched of the big 5 TV stations but today it would have 100% of the market share. Everyone in Argentina would know it was the only one that was broadcasting. Martial music had been playing on it up till 8 a.m.

There he was. Everyone knew the dashing young soldier and former top polo player who had married into foreign royalty. Not just any royalty but a Princess who captivated anyone who met her. Most knew that he was now a general in the army. But none knew that he was a leader, their new leader.

'Good morning, fellow Argentinians.

'I am your new leader.'

They did now.

'Today as your new president I take over the function of commander in chief of the Argentinian Armed Forces.

'Everything is under control. There has been very little opposition. This is because I know that you, the people, have grown tired of yet another corrupt and inefficient government.

'We have detained temporarily, the former president and his cabinet. They are on gardening leave but if they pledge allegiance to the new government they will be released and back at work in some capacity in a few days. We have also confined temporarily, the top level only, in several sectors of public life.

'But only the top level. We recognise that violence is not the way forward and no one will disappear. We aim to unite the nation.'

His tone had been a breath of fresh air as far as military coup announcements go. It had been relaxed and not pompous. It was underplayed and almost avuncular in its tone. It was a masterly performance. He had been well coached by his secret media team headed by Steve Wagner, the US media mogul.

But up until now, it was essentially nothing new. Yet another military coup, despite the apparent low key tone, after the failure yet again of civilian government. It was almost a cyclical process in Argentina.

But suddenly, the bombshell. No. The bombshells.

'But I want to tell you more.

'We have been busy.

'We have conquered and regained Las Malvinas.'

305

Remarkable. No one had an inkling of this. The realisation of a dream and it had happened without anyone knowing.

'Our noble troops are in Port Stanley and the Argentinean flag is flying there, in our land. We welcome their return to the fold. We will develop the islands so the Argentinian inhabitants there can benefit economically and be proud of their country. They will become equal first-class citizens of the fatherland.'

This was big, over the top and mysterious. What did he mean?

'Let me explain.

'As you know we have territory in Antarctica. But it is also claimed by The British and Chile. Our case in international law is strong and we have taken that into account by physically exerting our sovereignty. The Argentinian flag is flying proudly there too. And only the Argentinian flag. It is now indisputably ours. We can now develop our resources there. A substantial oil field has been discovered and working with a multinational oil company with experience and expertise in deep sea oil production, we will bring the oil ashore in Las Malvinas and the whole of Argentina will benefit as we export it globally.

'So, my fellow countrymen, the future is bright. We have rid ourselves of an incompetent government that has failed to develop our country. We have rightfully restored las Malvinas to the Fatherland. And we have secured immense natural resources that we will develop for the benefit of all Argentinians.

'I think you will agree we have made a good start,' he said with massive understatement.

'I hope you will support us as we begin to work with you and for you. My wife and I and all our military colleagues pledge to serve this nation till our dying breath. We love you all.'

Corny! But Steve had insisted on this last sentence. His media empire was built on such sentiment. He knew it worked.

'Long live Las Malvinas. Long live Argentina.'

Finally, with his last two sentences, he had succumbed to the normal way that dictators talk about their country.

But it was the right way to end. An amazing speech not just full of words and patriotic fervour. It was full of substance too. Three dramatic and totally unexpected announcements about territory and resources.

The martial music resumed.

The first reaction of almost everyone was silence, stunned silence.

Had they been dreaming? Had they really heard all that? If so, it was the most dramatic development in their country's history for a hundred years.

Gradually the silence turned into smiles, then cheers, then tears. Then all three. First families hugged each other at home. Then people hugged their neighbours and fellow travellers on the buses and trains and bikes as they made their way to work. Cars tooted, buses tooted, trains tooted. The barrage of sound was loud and constant, for hours. Such a great outpouring of national joy as to be beyond reason and all comprehension.

----------

Henry Irvine had been a left winger all his life, promoting and advancing all sorts of international causes and freedom movements. Now in his seventies, he had against all expectations won a general election and was Prime Minister of the United Kingdom. Yes, the circumstances had conspired to elevate him and his party to a position of responsibility. The people had chosen. They could hardly have had a worse choice and as often happens in such circumstances they had voted for change.

He was perspiring freely as the makeup lady stepped forward once more to wipe his face just seconds before his TV broadcast to the nation.

He and his government were powerless to stop what had happened but a long chain of events had led to this well before he had somehow reached the top of the greasy pole.

'Good evening,

'You will all have heard the news that the new Argentinian military government have made an incursion to the British Scientific base in Antarctica and have claimed sovereignty. Our men there were in no position to object. As the force was a military one, the Argentinian Government has effectively broken the terms of The Antarctic Treaty which says the Antarctic up to 60° latitude is a scientific and civilian territory. We will be taking this matter up with the United Nations in due course. But we will wait to see first what action the Argentinean Government will take. We fully support the Antarctic treaty which bans any military use of Antarctica and any mineral exploration and development.

'You will also know that the Argentine Military Government has landed some forces on the Falkland Islands which are in name a British overseas territory. So far there has been no resistance and no casualties. We hope that this will remain the case. It is not clear how the islanders view this incursion. We know that they have become closer to Argentina in recent years. We will wait and see what they say and fully respect their views.

'We must be aware of the geographical location of the islands vis a vis Argentina with all that entails logistically and economically.

'We will go to the United Nations fully committed to a peaceful resolution to this event and negotiate in good faith a sensible solution.

'Our belief in peaceful resolution of conflict is paramount both at home and abroad and we are proud that our foreign policy is ethically based.

'Good night.'

With that he waited until the TV lights went out and stood up with a sense of pride that politics was a worthy calling.

He could feel a trembling sensation though. Some of the older pros in the studio present may have felt it was the high-speed rotation of Margaret Thatcher in her grave.

----------

As for the rest of the world, it was the main news item on all the airwaves. And this was a good news not a bad news story.

The Times Square New York banner headlines read,

"President sends his congratulations and support to General Suarez and his wife. "

The world would not yet know, if ever, about the way US support had been obtained. It seemed to be all about Suarez and his wife and their charismatic hold on the media and the public.

"World greets new Argentina with great enthusiasm."

The world here was of course, the Western world media with its "down-market, gossipy sales are everything" approach.

But even if canvassed, world support was generally positive, although other oil producers wouldn't like the news about the oil find if substantiated. Many were sceptical about this.

This scepticism didn't last long.

"Royal Dutch Shell announce major new oil find in Southern Ocean."

Their statement, released on the very same day as the invasion was very short with no indication of its exact location or other details. No mention of Antarctica by name, so no one thought of such technicalities as The Antarctic Treaty.

But the markets were buoyant.

"World markets soar after Argentinean feelgood fairy tale."

Always fickle, they were now totally irrational. No high-flying math whizz kids working round the clock in investment banks could write an algorithm to predict how today's markets would behave. That holy grail remained elusive.

Contrary to Suarez' belief, the Argentinian fairy tale had totally eclipsed the news of the fall of the House of Saud. The full global repercussions of that had yet to be developed and discussed. And no one had any idea of Argentina's role in it. Maria and Juan Gomez had escaped and Gonzales Edwards had been shot dead in the Saudi desert, his fake passport would not reveal anything to do with Argentina.

One pitiful side issue received some coverage.

"Poor UK eclipsed once more. Country in terminal decline."

The Brits didn't even bring up the invasion of The Falklands to the UN Security Council. Besides it was The Malvinas Islands to everyone else now. Only the Brits called it The Falklands. Likewise, their claim to part of Antarctica, BAT, the so-called British Antarctic Territory would receive short shrift in any international forum now.

And it was pointless to bring it to the General Assembly as they had never supported the position of Britain as a still decaying colonial power desperately trying to hold on to its last remaining territory. Gibraltar had gone soon after the Brexit debacle.

# Chapter 46

The Casa Rosada, the pink palace, was all lit up with an array of powerful searchlights which revealed this unique arena in all its glory. At its very top is the clocktower bedecked with a single flagpole from which the Argentinian flag was proudly erect in the evening breeze. The palace's large central archway is caressed on either side by two open balconies. Above the archway are three larger covered balconies, the central one being the gravitational centre of the whole magnificent edifice.

All eyes were on this one balcony awaiting their arrival.

Was the Casa Rosada painted using cows' blood instead of paint that always pealed in the humidity? Or was it painted pink in an attempt to diffuse the tension between two rival parties in the late nineteenth century - the Federalists, the Reds and the Unitarians, the Whites? It hardly matters as it has always symbolically represented much of Argentina's history. The fact it was designed by an English architect ironically reinforces this.

It is remembered for the fiery speeches of General Peron and his wife, Evita, from its famous balcony in the 40s and 50s of the twentieth century. A more recent memory of the Casa balcony was Madonna's majestic song from the heart "Don't cry for me Argentina" while filming "Evita." Its hold on the masses is undeniable. This intoxicating mixture of myth and reality that it embodies makes it the very soul of Argentina.

So it was tonight also.

Once it had become clear that the coup had been a success, millions had congregated in the huge square, Playa de Mayo, in front of the Casa Rosada, with flags waving, much cheering and celebration, firecrackers letting off explosion after explosion accompanied by huge pink plumes of smoke.

In contrast to the previous coup this was one that was heartily welcomed by the masses.

There was much to celebrate.

The searchlights all went off apart from one. It focussed in on the famous balcony from which every new chapter in the country's dramatic history was first revealed.

From the shadows of the alcove they emerged, as if spontaneously generated. General Roberto Suarez, looking the epitome of power and success wearing his full military uniform in all its finery, strode out and waved to the crowds. Massive waves of cheers swept around the square. But this reception was nothing compared to the total pandemonium and chaos that greeted his wife, the Princess. She was as beautiful and charismatic as ever in her revealing pink dress, that somehow seemed to be saying that she belonged here, was at home here. That she was part of the very fabric of the Nation. Evita 2.0 stepped imperiously forward, in front of her husband and holding his arm aloft shouted impetuously,

'Here is the saviour of your country. Yes, your country. Long Live Argentina.

'And your country is whole again.'

They all knew what she meant and the huge roars of approval drowned out the rest of her attempt at speaking.

After over ten minutes of waving and cheering, cheering and waving, the General stepped towards the microphone and suddenly, there was a hush of expectation, although everyone knew what he was announcing.

'My fellow countrymen, the people of our noble fatherland, Argentina, I want to tell you….'

He paused.

'The country is whole again.'

The wall of noise started once more and many in the massive crowd could not hear him.

'Las Malvinas has returned to its rightful place. It is ours again. It was never going to be anything else.

'We have waited long for this dream to come true. Now it is a reality. Tomorrow my wife and I will go there, go to Las Malvinas, yes, yes ….. and kiss its soil, …….to welcome it back to its rightful place as a province of Argentina.'

Normally self-controlled and not that emotional for an Argentinian, a Latin, he was now revealing an immense and deep passion as his voice soared and shook with the immensity of his declaration. There were tears in the eyes of this strong and powerful man.

'Long Live Las Malvinas. Long Live Argentina.'

The crowds were once more ecstatic in their joy and the cheering interrupted his speech for some time. He began again.

'And our Antarctic territory, historically our possession is once more truly ours. It is a sovereign part of our country and always will be.

'All its rich resource of new found oil is rightly ours. We will develop it for the benefit of all Argentinians and the Argentinians of Las Malvinas will be an important part of that process. They will benefit equally from it. This is their right and their future is secure.

'Long live our Antarctic region. Long live Las Malvinas, Long live Argentina.'

He bowed low and remained in that position for some time as the crowds chanted again and again the three magical phrases he had uttered.

The General and the Princess were there for another hour basking in the adulation of the crowd.

But it was another eight hours before the last of the exhausted revellers slowly drifted out of the square and made their way home, tired but exalted, and full of hope and enthusiasm for their new future.

# Chapter 47

The following morning President Suarez entered the Hall of Busts, a magnificent hall containing marble statues of previous Argentinian Presidents, in the Casa Rosada, to cheers and clapping from his co-conspirators.

He stood and waved a few times, waiting for the acclaim to end. But he then prepared to address them and he knew he had to tell them the true costs of the coup now rather than later, when they were all still elated and before the dust had settled.

'My fellow officers, my compatriots, my friends. You know that the response to my TV announcement and my speech at the Casa Rosada has been overwhelming support. Better than we could have hoped for.

'But it is all due to our resolve, our patience, our discipline and maybe most of all our careful planning over all these years. The whole world admires our dramatic and highly professional actions. We have shown that we can organize and run things as well as anyone.

'Yes, we have done it. We have taken over from the corrupt politicians.'

More cheers and foot stamping.

'And we have restored our beloved Las Malvinas.'

Even wilder cheers after this.

'So we now have a responsibility to our country to see this through. To wipe out corruption, to restore economic stability and produce sustainable economic growth.

'And we have pledged to do this without undue violence and retribution. We need the people, all the people on our side. It will not be all plain sailing. Not everything has gone our way. We will have some problems.'

What's this? He was becoming gloomy when the moment should be one of pure unalloyed optimism.

'The coup and invasion have not come without costs. Yes, we will benefit from the oil that Shell is sharing with us but we had to make deals with others to get their support.'

'What's this? This was the first time we have heard of this,' shouted out a brave conspirator.

'Is this why the Americans were on our side this time,' asked the Navy commander presciently.

'Yes,' admitted Suarez. 'They demanded some oil in return.'

This emboldened some others to ask for details.

'How much?'

'And what is our deal with Shell? They are the ones who can deliver the oil. Our own oil industry is backward and useless.'

Suarez seemed hesitant in his answers. He had planned to explain this proactively in his own way, but he seemed to be responding to outside pressure now.

'Well, the deal with Shell is 50:50.'

There were quite audible murmurs all around.

'They extract the oil from deep under the sea and we provide Las Malvinas for the main oil extraction bases and Ushuaia will also be developed by us as a new Aberdeen to build all the infrastructure for many years to come.

'It is a fair deal.'

But the murmurs were louder now.

He continued. 'Neither we nor Shell can do this on our own. It is a joint venture from start to finish.'

But now the real trouble began, as there was a hard core of anti-capitalist, anti-Americans amongst them. They didn't want to be part of America's back yard.

'So what did the Americans get?'

'If Shell get 50%, how much of our 50% left are the Americans getting?'

'Well, it is complicated,' said Suarez. He wanted to dominate, he wanted to defend his actions strongly, but he knew he was on weak ground. Very weak ground.

'How much? How much?'

'Well it's in two parts. Unfortunately.

'They found out about the coup and the oil and wanted 40% of our share of the oil for their support in that.'

'Yes, but what is the second part. What are you saying?'

'Well, they didn't know about the invasion plans. Until their satellites saw our ships beginning to sail.

'So we had to get their support for the invasion too. They could have stopped it in its tracks and without the invasion, we may not have got the wholehearted support of the people. It is the restoration of Las Malvinas that is the most popular act we have taken.'

He was defending his actions bravely.

318

But there were groans as the significance of this sank in.

Before they could ask, he shouted out, 'They demanded another 20% of our share for their support for the invasion.'

They were all very bright and after a few seconds several shouted out, 'So we have only 20% of the oil to ourselves.'

He just stood there. That bare number was devastating.

'20% of our own oil. It is on our territory.'

'Shame.'

Some boos began.

But he held up his hand and they were quiet. They still felt their leader deserved a hearing.

'It was necessary to do this,' he declaimed strongly. 'And to do it on my own but on your behalf to maintain secrecy. I take full responsibility.'

A brave statement indeed. The words of a leader?

'A week ago, corrupt politicians ruled over an economy in ruins and  Union Jacks flew over the Falkland Islands.' He had dared to use the British name.

'And we had no oil of our own at all.

'Now we have a new beginning. We have a new government that all of you will be part of in various important capacities. We have some significant new natural resources that we didn't have before and we have Las Malvinas.

'We must celebrate our achievements and stay united. This cannot all be in vain.'

Some clapping began again, it got louder and the foot stamping began. Then it was cheers once more. But not overwhelming. You could feel the provisional nature of this support.

They were not entirely happy, but he had turned the tide his way. He had survived. For now.

----------

The Princess and the General were alone in the president's office in the Casa Rosada. They were exhausted from their night on the Casa Rosada balcony. But they were euphoric too. The welcome had been much better than expected.

'My husband. I am so proud of you. And the people love you now.'

'They love you more, my darling. Without you I am not so sure it would have gone down so well.'

'Well we are a team.' She kissed him gently.

'What did help was the invasion and conquest of Las Malvinas. That could have been the clinching factor, I believe,' said Suarez.

He hadn't said a word to her about the troubled meeting he'd just had with the junta members.

But he was concerned about his own position after he had revealed to his fellow conspirators the true cost of their actions in terms of the oil give away. That had not gone down well. He did not have their full support. He knew he had to rely totally on his popularity with the people to survive.

The popular response to his TV appearance and their joint one at the Casa Rosada had been overwhelming and that support was for him and the Princess almost exclusively.

But he was aware that people in general could be fickle and things could easily go wrong.

'Yes. The invasion got us the support of our fellow countrymen, but we know deep down that the islanders will not be  happy though they gave no resistance at all to the invasion.

'That is why we are going to see them and say that they have a good future as new Argentinians.

'What I said in my speech last night was genuine. They will benefit enormously from the oil development. But we need to tell them that.'

----------

The two-hour twenty minutes flight from Ezeiza airport in Buenos Aires to Port Stanley was uneventful and Suarez spent some of his time rehearsing his speech and then some thoughts as to his cabinet appointments. The Princess also had her notes in front of her.

The crowd gathered in front of the quaint Town Hall was tiny, a few thousand, compared to The Plaza de Mayo millions the previous night but it was pretty certain that all the islanders were there. None had been killed or injured or even arrested. That was a strict order and totally unlike the previous coup. No, all the action had been against the British troops, short as it was. And rather than holding the Battalion as Prisoners of War it had been quickly negotiated that they would fly out and back to the UK. Some were in the air now on their way to Ascension Island for refuelling and then the UK. They were all packed into the four transport planes available on the island.

The General and the Princess stood together on a small wooden platform erected hastily and were flanked by security personnel who had come with them from Buenos Aires.

Apart from a small number for crowd control, the Argentinian troops who had made up the invasion force were now in the British barracks at Mount Pleasant air force base. They would meet up with them later to thank them for liberating the island. But now the islanders themselves were the priority. They were affectionally called "kelpers" after the thick seaweed that surrounded the shore; collecting that was a major industry. There was a more unattractive, unkinder nickname too, from some of the British troops - "Bennies" after a character called Benny from a British TV soap, who was not very bright.

The crowd waved quite enthusiastically though there was no flag waving but a chant of "Princess, Princess" could be heard. They had not just turned up out of curiosity.

The Princess clearly was the attraction such was her charisma and charm and an apparent common touch. She seemed to be popular wherever she went and had the magic something that could turn enemies into supporters, even strong friends.

It had been planned for the General, the new President, to speak first but that clearly had to be reversed.

The Princess went up to the lone microphone.

'Thank you. Thank you for your welcome. You are all good people. We mean you no harm. You can see that already. No one has been hurt or arrested. In fact, we will make sure that you benefit from.......'

Some shots rang out from somewhere near the front of the crowd and no, it couldn't be. The Princess was hit. She fell forward, her head already a bloody mess and her stunning white dress was also turning crimson.

Security was amateurish and no one dragged the General away. He had immediately moved towards his dying wife as further shots rang out and he too fell to the ground. He died immediately and the Princess soon followed.

There was utter chaos and confusion, with screams ringing out all over as some of the security guards seemed to be firing into the crowd that was desperately trying to move away in all directions.

They had in fact identified accurately the source of the shots and were all aiming at the same target.

Soon after, with the square almost deserted they went down towards the assailant who was lying in a pool of his own blood. His spectacles were broken in his fall and were in pieces on the ground. They turned him over and he was clearly dead. For some unknown reason one pulled at his beard which maybe looked fake as it seemed to be now at an unnatural angle on his face. With his beard and specs removed he looked familiar to the attending security.

'Oh no. It is Prince Arthur, the Princess's son,' one of them shouted.

Yes, it was Prince Arthur. Not a political assassination at all arising from the invasion and the coup. But a family affair. A family tragedy. His estranged mother and his new imposter step father that she clearly preferred to him.

That is the tabloid explanation, but it rang true.

The chaotic circumstances and the general incompetence of the authorities meant there was no analysis, forensic or otherwise of the three bodies, victims and assailant alike.

If there had been, they could have established from the bullets that there were two assassins, one each for the Princess and the General.

No one had noticed as the bullets were flying from the security guards that one of them had clearly shot at the General from close range.

----------

The kite surfers were having a ball. Atlantis beach was a fifteen-minute drive from Kralendijk, the capital of Bonaire, part of The Netherlands just off the coast of Venezuela. It is a kite surfers paradise with twenty knot side offshore winds for 300 days a year and blue green water at 28°C.

The colourful array of kites made a splendid sight and the expert kite surfers were showing off with their massive aerial gymnastics. Jumps of 50 feet with backwards somersaults were common.

One kite surfer was slowly coming in on to the beach, obviously exhausted but also exhilarated. Kite surfing has a short learning time compared to surfing or windsurfing and the Prince had mastered the basics before as his privileged life allowed him to indulge any

wish. Although not quite up to any stunts yet, he
more than able to cope with today's wind and waves.

He looked well. He didn't have the body of Adonis
but it wasn't bad. Nothing like the pale and timid soul
he had been when he had landed off the plane.

Leaving his kite surf spread out on the beach, he took
off his helmet and slowly walked up to an umbrella near
the dunes at the back of the beach.

The lovely tanned lady wearing only a G string ran
towards him and gave him a long hug and a kiss.

She had met him soon after he arrived and had been
charmed by his shy but friendly demeanour. He seemed
to be rejuvenated and enervated by his surroundings and
by her presence too, she thought. It looked like he was
putting some dark shadows behind him. He was also
rich, with plenty of money flowing freely, so this was
another reason to be with him.

The Prince smiled. He had started a new life in a new
place with a new identity. He was beginning to feel like
a new person altogether. He already had a new passport,
care of King Willem Alexander, who was more
enterprising and cleverer than people gave him credit
for. The King had also arranged for him to get plastic
surgery soon, in a medical tourism hospital in Cancun,
Mexico.

Then he really would be almost new. At least in
appearance. And was he not living on a wonderful
paradise island with his own beautiful woman? He had
never wanted to be a Prince, with all it entailed. Was the
tangled and confused relationship with his mother no
over. Surely, he didn't have to hate her anymore.

# Chapter 48

The Speaker of the British House of Commons stood up and announced, 'The Prime Minister wishes to make a statement to the House.'

The Prime Minister rose and there was hushed silence from the 600 plus Members of Parliament present. It was a full house with many standing in the aisles and behind the Speaker's chair.

It was an unenviable task for the PM. Who could strike the right note in such circumstances? What was the right tone?

It was a mess, a disaster of huge proportions and deeply embarrassing to the Royal family, the government and the people of the United Kingdom.

Put simply, a mad Prince had murdered his mother, the Princess and his father in law, the ruler of another country.

'Members of the House.

'It is with the very deepest regret that I have to announce that Prince Arthur has been responsible for the death of his mother, Princess Alexia and her husband on the Falkland Islands. We believe, although it's is not confirmed, that the Prince was suffering with severe mental health issues that have led to this tragedy. The Government and Parliament pass on our heartfelt condolences to the Queen and the Royal Family at this most testing of times.

'We ask the Argentinian Government of ex President Suarez to return the body for a private burial as requested by her Majesty the Queen.'

At that the PM walked out of the House.

The normal PMQs, Prime Minister's Question time had been suspended.

There was no mention of the Argentinian military coup that had led to the invasion of the islands, an act that had been met by quiet resignation by the British Government. As a result, there was no official declaration that justice had been done with the removal of General Suarez, the coup leader and his wife and cheerleader.

Indeed, there was not much point in feeling this as the military was still in power with a new leader and new president, Admiral Oscar Gonzales.

And the Falkland Islands mentioned in the PMs statement were still Las Malvinas and under Argentinian control.

There was clearly a sense of justice amongst the general public at the outcome of this act despite the identity of its unfortunate perpetrator. They were buoyed up by a sense of patriotism that did not seem to be shared by their supine government.

Only one or two people in the world knew the truth of what had happened and the chances were that it would remain that way.

----------

There was no appearance on the balcony of the Casa Rosada from the new, hastily sworn in president, Admiral Oscar Gonzales, the former Head of the Navy, Suarez' nominal deputy in the coup and his main rival.

He had to somehow put on a brave face and restate what had been achieved and sympathise wholeheartedly with a whole nation in mourning.

He began his TV broadcast with a faltering voice and tears in his eyes.

'My fellow Argentinians. Our beloved General Suarez and his wife, Princess Alexia, are no longer with us - physically.

'Their cowardly killer is himself dead and buried in an unmarked hole in the ground. This is where he will remain. The impudence and arrogance of the UK government in asking for the return of the body has been met with the utmost contempt that it deserves.

'But they, President Suarez and Princess Alexia will be forever remembered as heroes of our fatherland for uniting our country with the return of Islas Malvinas and securing strong economic governance after the mismanagement and corruption of the past.

'I, as the new president and my government, will do everything in our power to honour and live up to their memories as the founders of a new and glorious period in our history.'

His voice was shaky and his body was trembling dramatically. This drama demanded such acting. Such duplicity had to be disguised.

'Long live President Suarez. Long live Princess Alexia, Long live Argentina.'

No one was more deserving of an Oscar for that performance than the new President of Argentina, Oscar Gonzales.

There was no mention of the newfound oil. If it was still going to be developed the country would only get 20% of it. This was what had prompted him and his newly found  supporters to depose Suarez so hastily and conveniently on a distant island. But they would still have to explain this to the people one day. No doubt they would be economic with the truth.

----------

The response of the rest of the world to this most dramatic of assassinations was not a partisan one. There seemed to be sympathy on both sides, to a sad and deranged Prince and to his two victims.

But one country more than most and as was often the case, had a greater interest in what was happening.

The US President was in one of his most glorious ranting and raving episodes.

'What the fuck has happened? Who allowed this to happen? We back up these guys to take over a country and invade the UK Falklands in return for an oil concession and they collapse in a few days.  Do they have any security, any protection?

'And can't the Brits control their Royal family anymore? It seems to be time for them to chuck them out as we did a long time ago.

'And worst of all. Why didn't we know about this? Why didn't we stop it? Don't our diplomats and spies learn about anything before it happens?'

He turned to Jake, his Secretary of State.

'What have you got to say for yourself after this almighty cock up?'

But before Jake could respond he resumed his ranting.

'What's going to happen? We still need all that fucking oil. More than ever now those Saudis have also been killed. I guess they had it coming. But for Christ's sake why didn't we stop this? Those Muslim ayatollahs are laughing at us.'

He stopped. He was panting with rage.

'Jake. Please tell me something good.'

Jake drew a breath and began somewhat nervously. This impossible man was a challenge to anyone.

'Well Mr President. We are talking to the new Argentinian president. It is still the military in power. But we have a problem. Our deal was with General Suarez personally. The new lot are very unhappy about it. And we don't know if Shell will carry on developing the oil. The Brits will try and stop them. But the Dutch will not. We'll have to see what happens after Shell and the new Argentinian government get together.'

'And that's good news?'

'It's all we have at the moment. I do have strong links with the boss of Shell.'

'Well. Tell him to get that oil out.'

# Chapter 49

Willy looked around as the pub was gradually filling up. After he and the Prince had broken the ice with his story about his mother, the Queen, bringing him here when he was in school, he became more serious and began to probe into the Prince's obvious problems.

'So, you're looking awful if I may say so. What's up?'

The Prince looked down into his pint and was unforthcoming.

'Come on. You know you can rely on me. Tell me what's bothering you.'

'Well, it's hard to explain. I don't know where to start. It's all getting on top of me,' he answered in a quivering voice, still not making eye contact.

The King passed him a packet of crisps and just looked at him sympathetically.

'I found it hard after coming back from Afghanistan and leaving the army. Life seemed so empty and unimportant. My royal appointments are trivial and boring. It's a non-job for a non-person. I do not want to be a fucking Prince. I know that sounds like a spoilt brat with all my privilege and wealth, but I didn't choose the job. I'm not free.'

'What about your time out there?'

'Well I was protected a bit and didn't do as many front-line tours as my mates, but I did do a few.' He looked forlorn.

'I saw some nasty things. Some horrific things.' He paused. 'I still have flashbacks and nightmares and I can't sleep easily.'

'It looks worse than that if you ask me.' He could see the Prince trembling and sweating even now.

'Have you seen anyone?'

The Prince looked up.

'Yes, I have been seeing a private shrink.'

'Does your family know?'

'No, that's the worst of it. It's all about stiff upper lip. We royals are supposed to be stronger and braver than anyone else. No emotion to be revealed and everything is hunky dory.'

'So, has it helped seeing him?'

'Not really. He has basically diagnosed that I have mild Post Traumatic Stress Disorder. But if you ask me, I had those symptoms before I went away. I had them in prep school when I was sent away to a private boarding school at the age of six. To make me a man. To strengthen my character and to prepare me for life.

'But what sort of life? A life where you can't be emotional, where you can't share your fears and worries, can't .....'

He was really almost in tears and he was clearly very embarrassed at showing this.

Willy was a good listener and just nodded now and again to encourage him to talk, to encourage it to all come out.

'But what about your mother and father. Can't you talk to them at all?'

332

'No, that's the worst of it all. And I have no brothers or sisters to maybe confide in.

'Father? Father is father, brought up to be the way he is and he seems to have accepted it all. I don't think he thinks much about things - just carries on day after day, waiting and waiting for the job of king - which he may never get.'

'But your mother is different surely?'

'No. No. No.' He was almost crying.

'She is not from that background, so you'd expect her to be different. But she is self-centred and only cares about herself and her image. She was quite happy not to have to take care of me with nurses and maids and helpers doing everything. She barely noticed me unless there was a camera about. And when I was away at school, she never wrote to me or phoned me or came to visit. She was so busy buying new clothes and going to parties and ….. seeing people.'

'What do you mean - seeing people?'

'Seeing men. She was protected and it was all hushed up. But she's a whore. My mother is a whore. And nobody knows it. She loves them all more than me. She's never loved me. I have no one who is close to me.'

And finally, 'I'm so afraid.'

Willy touched him gently on the shoulder. He was stunned and shocked by these revelations. His own upbringing and family life had been almost normal, apart from the wealth and privilege of course. But he was well grounded and shaped his sons in his own image, unlike the Prince who was clearly having a prolonged breakdown of sorts.

The Prince seemed to pull himself together and pronounced, 'That why I want you to help me. I want to go to see her in Argentina and stand up to her for the first time. I want to tell her what I feel about her and her new polo playing general, my so-called father in law.

'I hate her. I hate her. And I need her to know that. To her face. I need to do that, I need to ...'

Willy said, 'I don't think that's a good idea. Nothing good can become of it.'

'But I can't carry on like this.'

'No. No, I can see that. And I don't think you can carry on being a Prince. The situation is too far gone for that.'

Willy was surprisingly open, confident and decisive in his startling advice.

'But what can I do?'

'Do you have any close friends that you would miss if you went away somewhere?'

'No, no I don't. I meet my army mates now and again for a giant piss up. They are all as crazy as I am in their daily lives.'

'And is there anything you would miss that you do now?'

The Prince looked blankly when he realised that the answer to this was also no.

He shook his head. 'No nothing. It's all empty. So, so empty.'

'So, you are free to start a new life.'

'But what do you mean? How can I? Everyone will know me. I'm a royal. We're all trapped in that life.'

'No. I really mean a new life. With a new identity. A new beginning somewhere else.'

'How can that be?'

'Just like you see on TV when witnesses are given a new life after testifying in a murder case. Or something where their lives afterwards may be in danger.

'So, what do you like?

'Do you like lying on beaches with the sun shining down on you and a beautiful girl lying next to you?'

Willy was teasing him with a big smile on his face, but he was also serious. Thinking about the Prince's plan to fly to South America had reminded him of just such a place. He had been there incognito several times himself and it was paradise. No one knew or recognised him. It was such an isolated little place with lovely friendly people, unencumbered with daily cares as they enjoyed their laid-back easy-going existence. It was possible to enjoy such a place without getting bored.

'Here's my plan. I can get you to a very isolated, very out of the way place, Totally off the beaten track. And it is going to stay that way for quite a while I believe.

'I've been there myself. I know.'

'So where is it?'

'It's a small island of 20,000 people. Off the coast of Venezuela. It's called Bonaire and is still actually a part of Holland. The Antilles Islands broke up into several parts and Bonaire opted to be part of Holland instead of independent.

'The best snorkelling, scuba diving, wind and kite surfing place in the world but only a few people know that, and they're all keeping it secret.'

'So how do you know about it?' The Prince was beginning to show interest.

'Well, after a row with the Curaçao government about airport taxes, KLM built their own runway at Bonaire for refuelling on the South America route to

Santiago, Chile. They don't use it anymore as the planes have more range.'

But, with a glint in his eye, 'I, as King have the power to ask a fellow KLM pilot to land in Bonaire for a fuel stop, if necessary, on the way to Santiago. And that's where you get off.' He laughed. 'There is a small shed for customs attended by a very friendly man, I'm sure.'

Even the Prince smiled at this. It was outrageous and probably true.

'But what about money and so on?'

The Prince seemed to be catching on to the idea.

'You tell me your private account numbers and I'll get your money there. I've done exactly that myself.

'And for a new identity you need a new face. A temporary beard and long hair for a few weeks there while I fix up a plastic surgery appointment for you.'

'You're joking of course.'

'No. No I'm not,' said Willy, looking straight at the Prince for some time without blinking.

And at this point they paused. The Prince needed some time to digest all this. But Willy was convincing. There was much more to this man than most realised.

'Think about it tonight and let me know at breakfast time if it's on.'

Willy was willing him to accept. He genuinely felt this was a realistic way out for the troubled Prince.

They finished off their pints in silence.

# Chapter 50

The Boss was seated in his club with his regulation brandy in his hand, the trusted Remy Martin VSOP. He was in his favourite leather armchair in front of a bay window. There were no other chairs around him and the room was empty. It was after all 2 a.m. but this particular foible was a regular habit for him.

He was not reading anything. Apart from his attaché case that he had taken out of his private locker earlier he had nothing with him except his thoughts.

This is when and where he did his best thinking. Everyone has a system to stimulate their creative brain.

This was his system.

He was intensely rational and logical. He had a way to dispense with emotion and treat everything as if it were a problem to be solved, a puzzle to figure out, maybe almost like a crossword. But his puzzles were almost all life and death ones with national security the priority.

What did they know, or in particular what did he know? He was the only one with all the facts gathered separately by others. They were the jigsaw piece collectors. They didn't even know that. He's the one who put it all together. Some jigsaw puzzles are too important for anyone else to be allowed anywhere near them. The first problem was to decide which jigsaw any particular piece belonged to, if any. He was usually working on two or three separate jigsaws at a time. But maybe there was another jigsaw to begin also.

The puzzle tonight was the whereabouts of the missing Prince. An important puzzle to solve. It is not often that the second in line the throne of the Kingdom of Great Britain and Northern Ireland goes missing.

He knew that the Prince had gone missing and he had three or four jigsaw pieces to put together.

He knew he was on the plane from Schiphol. Airport in The Netherlands to Santiago in Chile. They had CCTV to prove that. That identification was not conclusive. But he had to assume it was, to proceed further with this first line of thought, the first few tentative steps in moving the pieces.

He knew that his man, or fool in the Santiago Embassy had missed the plane's arrival at Santiago Airport. Traffic. The lamest excuse in the world, but often true. The trail hadn't been picked up since then. That is where they had lost him. But wait. That is assuming he was still on the plane that landed at Santiago. They did not have CCTV at the VIP lounge there or any witness to his arriving in Santiago. And checking the manifest, the names of passengers, did not lead to anything. The Prince would have used a false name.

Why assume the Prince was still on the plane when it landed in Santiago? Because he had very strong reasons to believe that the Prince was headed to Argentina to confront his mother. A telephone conversation between the Prince and King Willem Alexander of the Netherlands had been eavesdropped by

GCHQ in which the Prince was heard to say that he wanted to go to South America to see his mother. That was the sole reason for his flight was it not? And there was no other explanation. It was a direct flight from Amsterdam to Santiago was it not? A range of 12,000 kilometres.

That's a long flight without refuelling he thought. But it was obviously possible with the new long-haul aircraft used on that route. He looked through the KLM website and saw that the plane for that flight had been a Boeing 777-300 with a range of 10-13,000 kilometres.

But that big plane had only started on that route a few years before. So, what happened when the planes used had a smaller range?

He typed in "KLM forums/South America" into Google and spent some time reading from disgruntled staff about their treatment by the company. But there were also some questions and answers from aircraft nerds about how things were done? And nerds love detail. After much patience and perseverance and quite a few dead ends he hit something of possible significance.

"Q. Where did the 747s (range 10,000 kilometres) refuel on their flight to Santiago?

A. Hi! As a KLM employee who was based in the Dutch Caribbean (AUA, BON, CUR and SXM), I have worked the KLM flights from Amsterdam to Santiago many times. They used to refuel at the commercial airport in Curacao, in the Dutch Antilles but when the government of the former Dutch colony dared to impose airport fees on KLM, they switched the refuelling from Curacao to Bonaire, a neighbouring island that could not impose taxes.

They even lengthened the runway specifically to accommodate MD11 and 747 aircraft. Bonaire, being a quiet backwater was happy for this to happen as it might help it develop as a tourist destination.

This tiny island protectorate of The Netherlands is basically KLM's own private airfield. One could hardly call it an airport as it has one runway and one small corrugated iron roofed shed as a terminal building. I know all this as I've been there in that shed myself."

Aha! Tenson thought. What if for some reason the Prince's plane had stopped off at Bonaire?

Logically the Prince could have left the plane at Bonaire. There was no reason for him to do so. Why would he stop there on his way to Argentina via Chile? No there was no reason he could think of, but it was a logical possibility.

Was this the other jigsaw piece? Did it belong to this jigsaw?

He kept that new and surprising thought in his head as he moved on further.

It was still more likely, more probable that he had reached Santiago and that is really where they had lost him. That is where their efforts were concentrated and he had sent two more men down there to continue the search. How would you get from Santiago to Buenos Aire or some other Argentinian destination? He began looking up the KLM and Aerolineas  Argentinas websites as the  main and obvious routes were by air. Santiago to Buenos Aires direct. Santiago to Buenos Aires via Ushuaia. Or to other Argentinian cities. Santiago to Rosario, Bariloche, Cordoba, Mendoza and so on. By road was possible, but highly unlikely. A long

trip across the Andes over many perilous mountain passes. Possible yes, likely no. Likewise for
a boat trip around the Cape of Good Hope. A bizarre way to get to Argentina but still possible.

All just as possible and as unlikely as the Prince being able to stop off in Bonaire on his way by some other route to Argentina.

But all possibilities should be investigated however unlikely. But the best resources had to be allocated to the most probable possibilities.

This led him to think of sending his worse resource to Bonaire to see what might have happened there. Yes, his man delayed by traffic in Santiago would have a final chance to save his job by going off to Bonaire on a wild goose chase. But wild geese are sometimes captured.

----------

He opened his attaché case and took out a plastic bag. In it were half a dozen very old mobile phones just about capable of international phone calls.

He took one out and dialled a number from his contact list on his own private day to day smart phone.

Derrick picked up his private cell phone from his desk and said, 'Derrick Markham, Military Attaché at the British Embassy, Santiago.'

'Hello Derrick, How's the traffic today? Busy?'

Derrick knew what he was referring to straight away. A bizarre reference to the traffic situation could only mean one thing.

'This is your boss speaking from London.' He gave no name.

'Right, OK,' said Derrick tentatively.

'Look, I want you to do a special job for me in your work for us.'

He paused for Derrick to prepare for this sudden request.

'I want you to go to Bonaire, an island just off the coast of Venezuela, and see if you can find out if there is any possibility our missing friend is there or got off the plane there? Ask about refuelling stops by KLM.

'If you find him, ring me up on our special number at any time of the day or night.

'Go there as a private citizen and use your own money from your monthly pay for all this and I'll make sure you're recompensed later.

'See if our missing friend is there.

'I will send you a photo of him wearing a disguise that he uses. He may still be using this. But you cannot show anyone a picture of the real man at all. We don't want anyone to know he's missing.

'Is that clear, Derrick?'

'Yes, yes sir,' murmured Derrick.

The Boss put the phone in his pocket. He would dispose of it in a nearby street dustbin in the morning.

The Boss, to keep his work totally secret, was acting like a field officer of old, agent running, a job he had enjoyed as much as anything.

# Chapter 51

The island of Bonaire, about 50 miles off the coast of Venezuela is tiny, about 24 miles long and 4 miles wide with a population of 19,000. It is so isolated that it took Derrick 18 hours to get there from Santiago via Panama City and Curacao. He was looking quite dishevelled when he got off the French built ATR 42 twin turbo prop after the final 30-minute leg from Curacao. He was feeling even worse.

But he knew he would have to be on his toes to keep his job. He knew this was his one and only reprieve.

The plane's complement of forty passengers disembarked. Most looked like locals who had come from Curacao itself. One or two of them may have been tourists.

Flamingo International Airport, Bonaire was not exactly busy. He decided to stay at the end of the queue through customs. It consisted of a ramshackle shed with a corrugated iron roof and was manned by two customs officers who looked very amateurish and laid back in their demeanour.

After a quick look at his passport he was free to go.

Dutch is the official language as Bonaire is a part of the Netherlands and 90% of the population also speak the local creole language of the west Antilles islands, Papiamento. But English is the lingua franca of flying.

'Can I ask you guys a couple of questions?' he asked in English.

And as in most places, these customs men spoke reasonable English.

'Are they ten dollar or fifty-dollar questions?' smiled one of them and his friend laughed.

'What happened when KLM from Holland lands here for refuelling? Do the passengers stay on the plane?' Derrick ploughed on regardless.

They looked at each other. Both knew that legally the passengers are supposed to disembark for refuelling for safety reasons, but they also knew that they always stayed on. It was hot in the plane but hotter still if they came off as there was no place for the almost 400 passengers of a Boeing 777-300 to shelter from the searing heat of the sun.

'That's a ten-dollar question,' said his mate feigning disappointment.

Derrick fished in his wallet and handed the note over.

'They all come off,' said one but at the same the other said, 'They all stay on.'

They laughed again.

'Did anyone stay here last time it happened, or did they all go on to Santiago?'

Now they looked serious, concerned. There had been no refuelling stops for years until a one-off event recently. They both remembered that last time very well.

Derrick handed over a 50 dollar note.

'Yes man, maybe one guy did come off and maybe he stayed off.'

344

That man, they both recalled, had handed over five $100 notes and although looking nervous and tense had just smiled at them and walked straight on.

How could they forget that? They had shared two hundred each and immediately left their work to spend the rest on a glorious evening at a waterside bar with their mates.

'Was this him?' asked Derick, showing them a picture of the Prince in his disguise.

They both sheepishly nodded. Forgetting to charge for this third question. They felt a bit mean to do so.

Derrick now also smiled broadly and walked on. It had been so easy; he too had forgotten to ask one or two more questions from these very knowledgeable men.

He took a rundown, dust covered taxi, the only one probably, into Kralendijk, the capital city with its three thousand inhabitants. It just made it before the last bit of exhaust fell off. The town was less run down than the taxi. It had a cheerful laid-back look to it with its single-story houses painted in a variety of primary colours.

Feeling suddenly very tired but elated he had only asked the driver to take him to a cheap, hotel. He had signally failed to continue questioning in his search for the Prince.

After a wonderful cold shower, he laid down and slept deeply despite the noise from a creaking spinning roof fan, waking up in the early evening to the even louder street noise of conga drums blaring out the local tumba music.

He walked out hungry but didn't risk the street food that he came across on the short walk to the sea front.

He had a quick but delicious Galina Stoba Chicken Stew at a small Krioyo restaurant but did not dwell there. He felt he had to keep up the momentum of his search and the pressure of his task kept him focussed.

The waitress in this busy and noisy restaurant didn't seem someone he could question so he left and walked along to the bars on the other side of the marina.

It was still relatively quiet so he ordered a bottle of Heineken, what else, and stayed standing at the bar.

'Just arrived?' asked the bar man, trying to size up every newcomer for possible income. Are they rich or not was the only worthwhile question as trade was not that good.

'Yes,' said |Derrick. 'Just come in from Curacao.'

'On a holiday or business?'

'Just a break. I have a friend who is already here. Been here a few months but has moved on from the address he gave me.'

Derek thought this a good line and continued.

'Have you seen him?' he asked, showing the photo.

The barman looked closely but eventually shook his head. His main question having been answered in the negative, Derrick did not pursue any other line of inquiry and simply sipped on his drink.

But the barman was quite talkative. 'You could just ask around I guess; someone might know him. We don't have many normal tourists but the ones who do come usually end up staying quite a while. So, there's quite a lot of surfing dudes here. It's a nice place to be. I was born here and have never left. The sun, the sea and the surf, man.'

Derrick ended up showing the photo at another couple of bars without success.

Most laughed and said there were hundreds of gringo dudes looking like that on the beaches.

346

His tiredness returned and he retired early, now feeling the strain of those long and boring flights and stopovers.

He spent the next morning along the beach. There did seem to be hundreds of hippy type dossers about. He didn't fancy asking them anything. Some looked drugged up and others just looked aggressive. But the majority in reality, looked well-tanned and rippled.

He was beginning to get despondent despite his early promising start. He showed the photo in a desultory way to a few stallholders and other tradesmen but they all just shook their heads. He couldn't keep on simply doing this.

He would have to think of a better plan. Asking at hotels and boarding houses.

He regretted not asking the taxi driver. He hadn't seen him since. There must be some more taxi drivers and bus drivers around he thought.

He decided to have an afternoon siesta before venturing out at night one more time.

He tried some more bars across the other side of the harbour.

All negative but then …..

At a lively seafront bar called the Hang Out Beachbar, at the far end of Kaminda Sorobon, a young barman laughed and said in a very light hearted way.

'You need to talk to Imelda. She likes to survey the new arrivals to see how rich they are. Amazingly, she then falls in love with the richest ones.

'Are you rich?

'She's quite a chick. Very pretty.'

Although Derrick didn't like the tone, he had nothing to lose and asked, 'Where can I find her?'

'I haven't seen her for some time. It probably means she is busy with her new beau. But I know she always visits her mother on Tuesday nights.'

'Can you tell me where?'

'Well my information is special. It's valuable.'

Derrick semi reluctantly took out his wallet and handed over a twenty dollar note. He had quickly cottoned on to the system but was still feeling his way about the going rate for certain types of info.

This seemed to work as the barman wrote down an address on a bar mat and handed it over.

'Good luck.'

Today was Sunday so he had the whole of Monday just waiting but this was his best and only lead. Just asking at random was unlikely to be fruitful. He didn't know if this would lead anywhere. He felt he should probably begin the hotels and boarding house route. Boring but essential for his long-term survival.

He spent all of Monday and most of Tuesday traipsing from one hostel to the next with no success whatsoever.

He was now very down and wondering how long he could keep it up, how long it was worthwhile keeping it up. The Prince, although he had turned up here may well have left some time ago. Would the customs guys have told him that? No. Probably not. The value of their information to him would have dropped considerably and he might have caused trouble.

----------

He turned up at the address in the early evening. It was quite a rundown looking, single storey clapper board house in a very poor area of town. The road was gravel and covered in potholes and the tiny shack had a rusty corrugated zinc roof. It's only redeeming feature was that it was painted bright yellow. Most of the houses on the island were very brightly coloured. He hung around nearby for about half an hour but there was no sign of a visitor. Maybe she was there already.

He wasn't quite sure how he would approach this inquiry. Was it better to meet her alone afterwards? Maybe she stayed overnight.

He decided to be direct and knocked on the door.

A stunningly beautiful girl answered, dressed in denim shorts and a halter top.

He had not prepared an entry line into the house and was almost lost for words or an idea of attack. He resorted to what had worked so far.

'Hello. I am looking for Imelda Driel.'

'That's me,' she answered putting on an innocent and fetching blushing look that she was a master of.

'I need to meet you tonight for a few short questions in an inquiry I am conducting.'

'Are you police?'

'No, no. It is all friendly. Here's 50 and another 50 later,' he sort of pleaded.

Although this was not big money for her anymore, she never refused it and now being quite confident, simply said, 'See you at the Blue Garter at ten o' clock.'

And closed the door. She was curious to know what this stranger really wanted. He looked a bit older than most of her visiting friends but maybe he was her new sugar daddy even though his direct approach was curious.

He slipped away but not before he heard an altercation ending with her shouting, 'I am not a whore.'

She was standing at the bar with an expensive looking cocktail in her hand. She was still dressed as before. She could hardly look better in anything. The Blue Garter was a lively pub with lots of dancing, so he immediately asked her outside to a quiet garden section.

'I have just arrived on the island and will not stay here long. I was given your name by someone who thought you might be able to help.

'Sorry to bother you at all. I have no ulterior designs or motives, I am simply looking for a friend of mine.'

She simply looked at him curiously.

He pulled out a photo of the Prince in disguise.

'Have you met this man? Do you know this man?'

She immediately recognised him as the man she was now with. He looked very different now though. Bigger and stronger and more confident. Was it her influence she wondered?

But she was careful and said, 'No, no I don't.'

She may have been a good actress, but she was not good enough. He could see that she reacted strongly to his request and obviously knew him.

'Are you sure?' he persisted. 'He may have changed his appearance since then.'

She looked worried. What was this all about? She didn't want to get her man into trouble. Although she knew nothing about his background, she instinctively felt that there was some big mystery, some secret thing about him. And she didn't want to lose him.

He may even be the one for her she thought romantically. They had been together more than most of her men.

'No, I don't know him,' she said more firmly.

This is where I cease to be nice thought Derrick. This is what it's all about. This is what spies must do. He didn't feel comfortable; he wasn't a natural spy. He wasn't a good one at all.

'I am actually investigating him as a suspect in a serious crime.'

She was now scared.

'He is a fugitive from justice.'

'Oh. no. I knew there was something. I knew it.'

'He's a suspected killer.'

That was enough to push her over the side.

'What do you want from me?'

She knew this was the end. But she could start all over again easily. She began to think of a new future.

'Tell me about him.'

'Well he turned up here in a disguise. He had a false beard and spectacles. That was weird. He soon stopped wearing it when we got to know each other but he grew a beard and long hair.'

'Go on.'

'He's rich and we live in the Hotel Islander for the moment, but we were thinking of moving into an apartment.'

'What does he do?'

'We just spend our time on the beach. He's a keen kite surfer; we just eat and drink and well, you know what.'

'Does he have any plans? What's he like?' Derrick had no idea what his bosses wanted from him after he found the Prince. He simply had to find him first. But maybe he had to arrest him or kidnap him or something, so he needed to know a bit about the Prince now.

'Well he is a bit weird sometimes.'

'What do you mean?'

'Small but weird things. Once, on the sand dunes we saw a cute little rabbit and he screamed and just ran away. It took ages for him to calm down.

'And he's just started saying….. well he says he's going to Mexico to get a new face.'

'A new face?'

'Yes, plastic surgery. He says he doesn't like his own face.'

Apart from her saying she recognised the photo of him in disguise there was no other evidence it was him, but this seemed to be a clincher.

It must be him.

She once more asked. 'What do you want me to do?'

'Right. I just want you to point him out to me from a distance, so I can identify him too.

'If you do it carefully, he won't even know you've done it.'

She felt OK with that. She really didn't want to think of any consequences to her actions, her betrayal from his point of view. Just a sensible approach to this new problem from her point of view.

'Ok. We go to Atlantis beach most days. That is where the kitesurfing is. I will be there sunbathing while he's surfing. We have a spot at the back of the sand dunes right by the yellow bus that gives kite surfing lessons.

Derick interrupted. 'So, tomorrow afternoon, when he comes back from the water to you, I want you to stand up and hug and kiss him as a signal.'

'Then that's it? What will you do when you know its him?'

'I don't know yet. But I will let you know so you can make plans.'

'OK.' And she burst out crying. She was sobbing. He gave her a brief hug and just said, 'I will be there tomorrow afternoon.'

He just walked away. They had both forgotten about the second $50. Not so important anymore to either.

# Chapter 52

Life at the Cannes villas was still continuing. Jan Willem and Hendrik were definitely getting older. They were slower out of bed in the morning. They often missed their morning swim and breakfast took much longer. It wasn't just the passing of the years and bodily decline. It was the world outside, the damn outside world. It was changing and quickly too.

Bloomberg news was on and they were both glued to the screens.

The news anchor began dramatically.

'The fall in the share price of all the oil majors continues. This is the third successive year of fall and there is no sign of recovery.'

He turned to their leading analyst and said, 'Is this the tipping point for them? Are they beginning to lose significant value in the markets? Is this happening a long time before resources are depleted? After all, The Stone Age didn't end because we ran out of stones.'

'Yes, transitions occur much quicker than we expect. Horses to cars, sails to steam, land lines to cell phones. And to take a particular example recently. "Peabodies" - the world largest private coal mining company went from Fortune magazine's list of most admired companies to bankruptcy in only eight years.

'It seems the key is when a new technology is responsible for all the growth in a particular sector. And this is happening with renewables. We're seeing price drops for production of wind and solar of 50% in one year.'

'But it's only the coal industry that is affected is it not?'

'No. No. We moved from coal fired power stations to gas ones but even gas is now under threat. Some renewables are now cheaper than gas. "General Electric" was the world's largest producer of turbines for coal and gas power stations. Its share price is down 70% in a market that's up 50%.'

'But why is the oil industry under threat. Even though oil fired power stations are on their way out it is still totally dominant for transport on land, sea and air and can't easily be replaced for that surely?'

'Well, all the car companies have committed to make electric cars with 90 billion dollars investment. The growth in electric cars is topping 20% a year globally. Tesla is worth more than GM or Ford and the Chinese are churning out five times more electric cars than Tesla.'

'So, what do you see happening?'

'The transition is here and now. Investors are seeing that new technologies are accounting for all the growth in the energy sector and are moving their money accordingly. The oil giants share prices will continue to fall and there is no recovery this time. They will soon be pigmies.'

Jan turned the sound down with a sigh. They were definitely older but were they wiser?

'Bollocks. We will still need oil for increased demand for air transport and plastics.'

'Yes, but those two are very popular targets for the activists. And all the public is with them on plastics, especially since that Attenborough guy and his TV programmes showing all the fish eating the plastic bags made from oil. The trouble is they will find sustainable replacements for plastics.'

'The fall in the oil share price is artificially stoked by activists who have no idea of the risks we are taking. The development of our new Falklands oil find is costing three billion dollars, the same as getting a man to the moon.'

'Your son and his mates in the green parties all round the world have been successful in persuading investors to move away from fossil fuel investments. They started with the churches and universities and now they are being successful with mainstream insurance companies and wealth funds. Tens of trillions of dollars have been divested.'

'People are asking why we didn't become renewable energy companies and some think we are doing that, but you and I know our investments in renewable energy companies are tiny.'

'Yes. They are for show and my son rightly calls it greenwashing. Our main R and D money is for carbon capture and storage from fossil fuel power stations so we can keep up the use of fossil fuels.

'We know the return from becoming a renewables company are small compared to fossil fuels. You need to fill your car with petrol every week. That's what's made us great. Providing just that. But you only buy a solar panel once every twenty years. Not a good business model.'

The news item had changed so he turned up the sound again.

The analyst who would normally defend the oil giants and the status quo had been replaced by one of the new trendy economists who no longer accepted the perceived wisdom of the founders of economics.

'So, tell us, what are positives from the decline in fossil fuels?'

'The global fossil fuel industry is run by a small number of companies and countries and all the wealth flows to them. The end of this will mean countries like India saving huge amounts of money in importing most of their coal, oil and gas. And creating lots of local jobs through wind and solar development. For other countries they can miss out the development of a national electricity distribution grid and fixed fossil fuel investments and go straight to local mini grids and wind and solar off grid altogether. We've seen this sort of thing happen when countries avoided the development of extensive copper wire telephone networks and went straight to mobile phones.

'And it will be good for global politics too. Just think of certain countries  no longer having any power arising from  their oil resources. The Middle East in particular.

But the biggest reason to support the change away from fossil fuels is of course climate change. The power and size of the fossil fuel industry is the biggest barrier by far to achieving the aims of the Paris Accord to reduce global warming to 1.5 C by 2050.'

'So it's not all doom and gloom. We see there is a positive side in all this.'

'Thanks Ben.'

Jan Willem and Hendrik looked at each other. No words were exchanged. The world was becoming incomprehensible to them. Shell, 107 years old, once the ninth largest company in the world and the largest energy company outside the US and China, was collapsing in front of their eyes. For much of their life they had devoted themselves to what they regarded as almost a noble cause. Now it seemed it was all coming to an end.

Not many months later it was.

They sacked Jonathan Jones as CEO, mainly for his human rights meddling in the Falkland oil deal with the Argentinians. But also, as a scapegoat for the collapse of the whole enterprise due to the actions of the new Argentinian government and the investors putting an end to it at the Shell AGM. Their machinations to appoint him as their man at Shell had backfired badly. Their behind the scenes influence had come to an ignominious end.

# Chapter 53

The memorial was a very simple one. It had been erected in a clearing in the woods just outside Trelew in Patagonia. It stood about two meters high and was made of Welsh slate imported from North Wales. A simple rectangle about a meter wide, it listed the names of all those who had been abducted by the secret police followed by the words in Welsh and Spanish.

*"May this memorial bring peace and justice to those named and help comfort their family after all these years."*

*"Boed i'r gofeb hon ddod â heddwch a chyfiawnder i'r rhai a enwir a helpu i gysuro eu teulu ar ôl yr holl flynyddoedd hyn."*

On the list were the names Catrin Prys-Jones and Eluned Prys-Jones - Catrin and her mother.

He walked a short distance away in the clearing in the woods to a new looking set of graves.

One was the new resting place of Catrin and her mother and her brother. The remains of all three had been found and brought back here by the commission that had been set up to carry out this exercise in commemoration and reconciliation. It was the exact same spot where they had reburied their brother for the first time.

He slowly took out a small metal box, opened it and scattered the ashes of his own brother on the grave. He hadn't known where to put them after all this time.

----------

So, here was Maria in the dock in one of the minor courts situated in The Palace of Justice of the Argentine Nation in Buenos Aires.

The use of juries in Argentina is there in black and white since 1853 in section 24; section 75 subsection 12 and section 118 of the Constitution. Despite this it has still not been enacted nationally in all cases. Opponents have even argued that it would be unjust that defendants could not see or hear the arguments which had led to their guilt or innocence in a secret jury discussion.

But today there was a jury that would listen to both Maria and Jonathan.

Maria was dressed elegantly and was defiant in her stance and demeanour. She would call it pride.

She looked directly at Jonathan Jones until he turned his gaze away from her.

Jonathan had got what he wanted. He didn't quite believe it was happening. The new government was carrying out what he had agreed in of all things, an oil company agreement with the deceased General Suarez, the leader of the military coup. It was a trial of an Argentinian secret service agent for human rights abuses.

Specifically, there were two charges.

That she identified and passed on names and addresses of Catrin Prys-Jones and Eluned Prys-Jones to her superiors leading to their disappearance and death by person or persons unknown. This was clearly a human rights issue.

The other charge related to her being an Argentinian secret service agent who had obtained information of crucial national interest for the UK from the chief of staff of the UK Armed Forces, in the form of a computer data theft. This wasn't even a human rights issue at all. But it certainly drew the world's attention to the real purpose for the Chief of Staff's humiliation and embarrassed the British government once more.

Clearly in her long career in the Argentinian secret service both at home and abroad she had carried out many other acts relating to abuses of human rights, but she had not been charged on any of these.

These two charges had been selected because they were the ones that Jonathan Jones had specifically asked for and known about. No inquiries had been made by the authorities into any other matters, no attempt to widen the case to cover other possible offences.

So yes, the promise to Jonathan Jones had been kept but only in so far as it related to his knowledge specifically.

Indeed, he was the sole witness sitting in his witness seat facing the jury and Judge. The trial was causing quite a stir as it is not often that a CEO of a multinational company is a witness in a human rights trial.

The prosecuting lawyer stated.

'It is our contention that the defendant Maria followed Jonathan Jones and saw him meet Catrin Prys-

Jones and Eluned Prys-Jones in their house and that she later followed Jonathan and Catrin only to a clearing in the woods outside Trelew.

'Jonathan Jones, did you see Maria Buck follow you that night?'

'No, I did not see her following me and Catrin but when we left the woods, we saw her drive away up the road on her moped.'

Later in the cross examination the defence lawyer asked,

'Did you physically see her and identify her considering that the distance from the clearing in the forest to the road is about 30 metres?'

'Well yes. She had long black hair and she was on her moped.'

'Fine. That is a fair assumption to make as she does have a moped, a Honda Wave 110S.'

'But how do you know it was her on the moped? The Honda Wave 110S is the most common type in all Argentina.'

'Well, it ….'

'And can you be sure it was her? Again, there are many Argentinian women with sweeping long black hair. There must be quite few in Trelew itself.'

'I believe it was her.'

'Turning to the supposed disappearance of Catrin and Eluned Prys-Jones, how do you know they disappeared?'

'Well, I visited their home later and there was no trace of it, literally.'

'Well they may have simply moved away. Did you see a car taking them away?'

'No. That is what the neighbour told me. She said two men came in an unmarked car in the night and took them both away.'

'So, we have the word of a neighbour that one night they went out on a car journey.'

The judge asked, 'Do we have this neighbour as witness, prosecutor?

'Unfortunately, she was elderly and she has since died.'

'Carry on with your cross examining.'

'Thank you, no more questions.'

Judge. 'Very well. Prosecutor. You may continue with your case.'

The Prosecutor stood up once more.

I now turn to the actions of Maria Buck in London specifically at the Corinthia Hotel in London on January 17th and 24th.

'Jonathan Jones. Can you tell us what you found out?'

'Well it was all in the newspapers. Maria Buck and the Chief of Staff of the British Armed Forces, Richard Cobbold, were at the hotel for many assignations not just on those dates.'

'But what did she do?'

'I have the telephone logs from the hotel. On those two days she made a long phone call to a certain number in Buenos Aires.'

'And what were they about?'

'I contend the first was a practice and in the second she sent computer data down the phone line to this Buenos Aires phone number.'

'And what is this phone number?'

'It is the phone number of her brother, who is a computer expert working for the Argentinan secret service.'

'How do you know that?'

'I actually visited the house with this phone number later and saw his room containing his state-of-the-art computer setup.'

Now it was the turn of the Defence lawyer to cross examine.

'Can you tell me who else lives at this house?

'Well, it is the family home of the Bucks.'

'So, who else lived there and who else did you meet there?'

'Maria's mother.'

'So how do you know Maria was not just having a friendly phone chat with her mother?'

'Well her brother was there on both occasions in his room with all his computer equipment.'

'And how do you know he is not just playing computer game on the nights in question?'

'Well, he works for the Argentinian secret service.'

'Maybe he was just relaxing at home. How do you know otherwise?

'And have the British government ever said anything about the missing data?'

'No. But why would they? It would be too embar…..'

'No more questions.'

So, in a fair trial it turned out to be that this was simply circumstantial evidence and on its own - there was no other corroborative evidence - it was insufficient proof of Maria's identity and presence in Trelew. There was no proof of the disappearance of Catrin and Eluned

Prys-Jones or proof that Maria had transmitted top secret data down the phone line.

So, after a jury discussion of only four hours she was acquitted on both counts.

Jonathan was devastated but even his prosecuting lawyer had said that they were on weak ground and it was a fair trial as far as the evidence available and the procedures were concerned. They had no cause for complaint. Their case had been weak in a fair court of law with independent jurors.

The prosecuting lawyer shook Jonathan's hand and he walked away on his own, a forlorn figure.

----------

But this can't be it. This is not the end of this. So, he found himself surreptitiously following Maria and her friends as they went away to have some celebratory drinks at a nearby hotel.

He stood outside the hotel for some time until he saw her friends all gradually leave. But not Maria. She must be staying at the hotel.

So, he found himself slipping some notes to the receptionist in exchange for her room number in the same way a she had done in London many, many years ago.

She opened the door to see him standing there facing her. She was not fazed by this. She was extremely resourceful and could cope with most situations. Had she not assassinated her Arabic Prince in the most calculating way?

He pushed his way in and slammed the door shut.

'So, what do you want? Do you want a drink maybe?'

'How dare you. You dare to party away after what you did? You had them killed. He was beginning to raise his voice and felt himself becoming a bit wild, not his normal self, not his normal behaviour at all,

This woman could arouse in him a huge rage.

'Come on little Welshman. You lost. It's fair game. It was what you Brits call a fair trial too. So, you must be satisfied with that.'

He was totally lost and bewildered by this. She was taunting and humiliating him in the most brazen way.

'But you had them killed. You had them both killed. How could you? How could you do it?'

'They were traitors. They knew what they were doing. They stole the body of a soldier who died in Las Malvinas War from an Argentinian military cemetery.'

'Yes. But ….'

'They were disloyal. You can't be Argentinian and Welsh. They were all spreading their own language not Spanish and they even had Welsh flags hanging up inside their houses. All of them.'

'But you gave their names in to be killed.'

'Yes, yes I did. It was what they deserved.'

He jumped forward and she stepped back but only slightly.

'So, my brave little Welshman, what are you going to do?'

He was completely lost in his anger at this tormenting by this horrific woman.

He had come without a thought, without a plan, just to confront her, he supposed. He had no plan of action, no weapon, no real purpose.

'Are you going to kill me?' she screamed. 'Go on then do it. Do it.'

Consumed by self-righteous rage, he grabbed her by the neck and began squeezing, but not really that hard. They fell on the floor. She was struggling now. He still held her round the neck and began to squeeze even more, but nothing was happening. She was not screaming; she wasn't dying. How do you do it? I can't do it. He felt his hands going limp and slowly slipping away from her throat.

He could not kill her. He was a coward. He wasn't manly. He couldn't get his revenge and justice for Catrin and her mother.

He got upon and slowly walked out. And she shouted. 'You're weak, you're weak, you're a pathetic little man.'

Or was he just a good man?

# Chapter 54

The Prince and Imelda were lying down to sunbathe again in this unknown paradise and did not notice a fellow kite surfer armed with a knife cut halfway through three of the four cords on the supports for his kite.

These would soon fail in the strong winds and without a kite, he would not survive long a mile offshore in large waves with only a small kite board for buoyancy.

----------

Back in London, the Prince's lookalike body double was now unemployed. There had been two of them and he had been chosen to double up as the Prince on three or four public engagements recently. He hadn't been told the reason but now, after the killings on the Falklands, he and the whole world knew why.

He wondered what had become of his friend and rival, the Prince's other double? He had not seen or heard from him for some time.

It turned out The Boss had given him another more challenging job. In case the Prince himself didn't turn up to do the deed, he had been flown out to The Falklands via Ascension Island on the last UK plane before the invasion. From there he could have gone on to the Argentinian mainland but it had turned out not to be necessary.

----------

The Boss held the letter in his hand and began to read it again. The wild and untidy handwriting seemed to be appropriate for this mad missive.

He had read it many times but had not once shown it to anyone or mention its existence to anyone.

The consequence of that inaction was quite dramatic and something that he felt was required for the good of his country.

"My dear mother,

I hate you. I have always hated you. You were never a mother to me. You ignored me. Your dogs meant more to you. I was farmed out to a stranger. My dear, dear nanny - nanny Constance. She is my mother. She raised me, she fed me and clothed me and hugged me. She LOVED me. You saw all that and cruelly got rid of her. Ceased her employment in our household. Sacked her. For no reason except maybe jealousy. But you never intended to become a mother to me again. You simply could not stand I guess seeing me happy for once.

Mama, Maam. Were you happy to bring all those temporary uncles into our house? And cavorting brazenly in front of them over breakfast with all your body in view. You disgust me. And finally getting off with that Argentinian bastard. Could you not see he was using you? No, you only think of yourself and getting the outside world to love you while ignoring the love you could have in your own family. Why didn't you love me, your own son? Why don't you love me? Who are you? How can you behave like this? What is missing with you? Why are you not a normal mother? Why? Why? Did you not think of me at all? I tried to attract your attention. I shot you for Christ's sake with the rabbit gun. Did that not mean anything to you?

You have scarred me. I am weak, scared, unable to live normally. I have no friends. I have never had a girl. I don't know what it's like to have someone love me. Maybe I'm unlovable. Why did you do it? Why do you just disown me and ignore my existence? How could you do it?

Mother, I hate you with all my being. I'm coming to see you. I'm coming to South America. This is it. Final showdown. I need to sort this out. I need to see you depart from this earth so I can live again. I will ensure your departure myself. See you soon.
Arthur."

The Princess and the Prince had both become much more than an embarrassment but liabilities, loose cannons that could cause enormous damage to the country he loved. What better way to end that but engineer they destroyed each other? He smiled at his own cleverness and subtlety. He was a psychologist as much as a spook. A close student and expert on human nature. It hadn't quite worked out as he had intended but the final solution was more than satisfactory. The body double had done his job but had been killed in the process. A very honourable man. And no one would ever trace it to him. The whole world thought the prince had killed his own mother.

The only surviving casualty as far as he was concerned was the man who had sent him the letter, his own brother Gavin, Personal Assistant to the Princess. He had now lost his job and seemed to have disappeared. Gavin had not talked to him or other family since the Princess' death.

He took the letter to the open fireplace. Yes, the security services were essentially old fashioned in their cosy choice of surroundings.

He lit it with a match and watched slowly as the flames spread, the blackened paper breaking apart and drifting in tiny pieces into the embers. His actions were complete. It was a powerful feeling to know what power he had exerted but even more exhilarating was the fact that no one would ever know about it. Only a true spook could keep a secret entirely to himself for his whole life.

----------

The 6 berth 34 foot long Grandezza motor cruiser, Finnish built with Med style open cockpit was luxurious in style with a 200 mile cruising range. It moved at a cracking pace along the corniche, through the clear emerald green waters. Gavin was its sole occupant and was at the helm in shorts and shirt, revelling in the performance of his new toy.

It wasn't a big and expensive one by the standards of these parts, only just over £250,000 pounds, but it was a nice one, nonetheless.

He was content to cruise along the coast between St Tropez and Genoa stopping off at quiet coves for swimming and seaside restaurants. He didn't frequent the high rolling resorts and marinas for fear of being identified. But he still led a life of pure luxury.

All this was not something that he could afford in his enforced retirement merely on the proceeds of his work as PA to the Princess. But his other income, suddenly obtained, was more than enough for the boat and the rental of his new villa just along the coast. And for the beautiful escorts he hired for a week or so at a time, until he grew tired of them. He was feeling young again after all the trials and tribulations of looking after the Princess. He did not wish anyone to die but he felt no guilt at what had happened. He had sent the warning letter to his brother at the very top and had no idea why they had failed to stop the killings.

This solitary lifestyle was one he loved but it was also one he temporarily required. He could not advertise or share his newfound wealth with old family and friends as they would inevitably deduce its source. Later he would write his memoirs under his own name for even greater financial rewards. He already had a huge advance from a publisher to do so.

He looked again at the cover of the English tabloid lying on the table.

"Tormented Prince's final act was inevitable."

The headline was not one he would have chosen but it summed up nicely what had happened and probably why. He read on.

372

"It is now known that the Prince had suffered for years from severe mental health issues arising from his toxic relationship with his mother. Members of a small inner circle were aware of these but were powerless to prevent his premeditated plan to kill his mother. Insiders say that her public image contrasted remarkably with her private behaviour, her tantrums, her selfishness, her self-love and complete lack of interest in her son. Also rumours of her sexual exploits now appear to be true. She had a penchant for short and purely physical relationships with many undesirable characters. The fact that she lost her own father at the age of twelve left her searching all her life for a father figure, but her choices were always doomed to failure. Her final partner, General Roberto Suarez, President of Argentina for one day, seemed to have been the one that would at last bring that quest to an end, but the Prince hated him as much as his own mother and his redemption seemed to require killing them both.

We know this from the horrific contents of a letter he had sent to her while she was in South America.

Showing clear signs of a deranged mind, it warned in very graphic language that he was going to travel out to Argentina, to confront her and kill her. His final words were:

*Mother, I hate you with all my being. I need to see you depart from this earth so I can live again. I will ensure your departure myself.*

The full letter will be published in tomorrow's edition of the paper.

It is not clear why the warning in the letter was clearly ignored by her or whoever else may have had access to it."

# Chapter 55

Imelda and Derrick were closing up their very own bar after another busy night. She had bought it with the money the prince had left her. No-one had seen him after he failed to return to the beach from his damaged kite surfer.

But the short note he had left her gave her access to his money and simply had the cryptic words:

"Sorry but I have to leave to finish off the job."

----------

The Boss was sitting quietly in his own apartment when he heard the doorbell ring. He got up and walked across to the intercom screen. It was a very clear image. But …. What?

With a beaming smile on his face, it was the return back from the dead of the Prince's body double.

'I was almost ready with my rifle on the tripod hidden behind a wall about 200 metres from the stage when I heard the shots and clearly saw her fall. So I just packed up  calmly and walked back to my B&B in Port Stanley.'

----------

Jonathan Jones was the keynote speaker at a human rights conference in London and was in a confessional mode with all his defences stripped bare, revealing his inner vulnerability and newfound purpose.

"I took a long time to realise it, but I've been a drifter all my life. A clever drifter, a hardworking drifter, a high achieving drifter, a secret drifter. Just drifting along with the outside world deciding everything for me. I never took the initiative, but my cleverness, maybe deviousness, kept on leading me, usually by invitation, to higher and greater things. It was so effortless in a way, not having to decide and shape my life, my future. It all just sort of happened to me. And I was happy enough to go along with it.

But my  decision, at the age of 56, unconscious or not, to get justice for the Argentinian born Welsh and peace for my brother was the first time I had lived fully and become free.  Because I had chosen to act and to act in a way that was not in my own self-interest. I did it because it was the right thing to do. It sounds so simple, but it was something that had not occurred to me as I had never been troubled by a conscience, by an inner voice leading me to adopt a certain way of living, a path to follow, a calling.

Now it is exhilarating to be helping others get justice against wrongdoing of any sort. I am driven now by defending human rights, against any oppression. We all deserve dignity and respect and I can help there. Yes, I can help there."

His wife looked on with a look of understanding that owed a lot to her drama school training but was totally unconvincing.

# OTHER BOOKS BY DAVID JONES

If you liked this book, why not try *Justice,* David Jones' previous book, also available on Amazon as  a paperback and ebook.

*https://amzn.to/3jXt3S0*

"This was a fantastic, often heart-wrenching, read, and made me deeply curious to learn more about such a pivotal chapter in the European story. Raises some intriguingly complex questions of morality that still have me and my friends discussing."

"The story draws you in. The fictional plot element is exciting and credibly interwoven with the true story of the Bosnian tragedy. Clever plot twists as it reaches its climax concluding in a powerful and thought-provoking ending."

*"Justice*  is an exciting and informative political thriller. The story begins with the Bosnian – Serbian conflict in 1992 and provides relevant background information. The compelling Serb and Muslim characters that Jones creates draw the reader in and provides an understanding of how the war affects individuals and families. The novel continues in the Netherlands where the International Criminal Tribunal for the former Yugoslavia is trying war criminals. There is a daring rescue of one of the prisoner and the story moves to Brazil for a dramatic finish.

*Justice* is a good read, both for the fascinating insight it provides and the action-packed story. I recommend this novel highly."

Printed in Great Britain
by Amazon